So I Am Glad

by the same author

NIGHT GEOMETRY AND THE GARSCADDEN TRAINS
LOOKING FOR THE POSSIBLE DANCE
NOW THAT YOU'RE BACK

A.L. KENNEDY

So I Am Glad

JONATHAN CAPE
LONDON

First published 1995

1 3 5 7 9 10 8 6 4 2

© A. L. Kennedy 1995

A. L. Kennedy has asserted her right
under the Copyright, Designs and Patents Act 1988
to be identified as the author of this work

First published in the United Kingdom in 1995 by Jonathan Cape
Random House, 20 Vauxhall Bridge Road, London SWIV 2SA

Random House Australia (Pty) Limited
20 Alfred Street, Milsons Point, Sydney,
New South Wales 2061, Australia

Random House New Zealand Limited
18 Poland Road, Glenfield,
Auckland 10, New Zealand

Random House South Africa (Pty) Limited
PO Box 337, Bergvlei, 2012 South Africa

Random House UK Limited Reg. No. 954009

A CIP catalogue record for this book
is available from the British Library

Papers used by Random House UK Limited are natural,
recyclable products made from wood grown in sustainable forests.
The manufacturing processes conform to the environmental
regulations of the country of origin.

ISBN 0-224-03974-1

Printed and bound in Great Britain by
Mackays of Chatham PLC

For E. M. Kennedy, M. Price, J. H. Price
my family and friends who rarely fail,
and with — as ever — thanks to Bob Kingdom.

I DON'T UNDERSTAND things sometimes. Quite easily, I can become confused by a word or a look or a tiny event and then I just can't help but wonder why my life should happen in one particular way and not another. I always end up asking for answers I can't have.

A small part of this discontent started when I used to go to bed at night. Possibly not every night, but most nights, very many of my nights, would turn into something quite incomprehensible.

You can imagine me, I'm sure, tucked up in the customary way with my eyes closed and my body comfortably slipped between two familiar, peaceful sheets in a quiet and sensible atmosphere of repose. Think of that undistracting time before morning where there are no dogs, no engines, no voices, only an infinite extension of the still and dark and gentle air now dozing above my face. And here I am, ready to drop snug asleep in exactly the perfect place to cash in my day. Only then I don't sleep.

Instead I find I take strange exercise. I am tired and unathletic and I am weary back in to my blood and bone, but I willingly waste the priceless hours next to daybreak in an activity which is neither rest nor sleep.

Not surprised, just disappointed, I discover I am having sex again.

I am a partner, I am one half of a larger, insane thing that flails and twists and flops itself together in ways far too ridiculous for daylight. But these are ways that I recognise, ways that I can't help following once I start. So the bed I spent five minutes making this morning – with hospital corners because they appeal to me somehow, and are neat – that bed disassembles in moments, builds ridges up under my spine while my pillows fall off and the lights go on.

My head is singing with lack of air and sickening exhaustion is setting up little explosions of white at the backs of both my eyes. And I am still having sex. Like an inadvertent Irish dancer tied up in a hot canvas sack, like a mad traffic policeman tangoing through ink, like a killer whale fighting to open an envelope, I persevere in having sex.

And it really makes no sense to me.

Sex.

I would lie, flattened out at the end of all the necessary minutes, feeling slightly wild but also useless, and I would be sticky and anxious and far too awake and yet all I had ever intended was to be asleep and I would not know what it meant.

Sex. I don't know what it means. I haven't approached it in quite a while, but I'm afraid my lack of understanding has to stay in the present tense. I can only remain bemused when I consider that on a depressingly regular basis I would render myself, and perhaps my companion, insensible with fatigue for no reason I could ever ascertain. Gathering my breath after the onslaught I would long for a bath and a disprin, insulin, oxygen, a pint or two of evening primrose oil, a sandwich, a small cup of tea, just a nice lie down. I would then be utterly disheartened by the knowledge that all of this longing was happening almost precisely at the point where I would have to get up and start another day, filled with the promise of another night of probably more of the same again.

Not that I object to the activity itself. I can think of countless situations where nothing in particular goes on and ideal opportunities are presented for a quick burst of sex. While waiting for dubiously available medical care, dubiously available public transport, or the results of dubious enquiries into miscarriages of public probity and justice – there are so many opportunities, each one panting with erotically vacant time and space. How actively we could thrash out our hours together, if we all of us only knew. We'd have no more need for chewing gum, waiting-room fishtanks, cigarettes, crosswords, public service charters, patience or even draughts. Not when we've all got sex.

Which would in many cases constitute the removal of a great weight from my mind. I would much rather know that my local MP was rolling along the Pet Food and Condiment aisle in a fellow shopper's moist embrace than imagine him or her juggling with breakable ceasefires, exorcising childhood crime and indulging in lighthearted TV panel games. And as sex with other people is now undeniably dangerous, I should welcome the thought that we might all prefer to spend entirely solitary nights in, not leaving ourselves alone.

My mind is open. We all have it in us to be an opium for every conceivable mass.

So in principle, I can honestly see that sex has many uses. In my own case, I'm sad to say that I have found it to be of one use only – when I'm having sex, I'm not also expected to speak. This is the one major social transaction I conduct where conversation would be a sign of positive discourtesy.

Oh, a few words now and then are unavoidable, of course. I can remember.

THERE
NOW
LATER
and NOT (THERE, NOW, LATER)
YES and NO
DID and YOU
and
HAPPY?
YET?

But that isn't speaking. And I should know because I

really didn't like to speak. It made me uneasy to lock up my door at night and know there was someone else home who was supposed to be special for me. They would wash in my bath and sit in my armchair, they would want me to ask things about them and try to find out about me, they would want to see in through my eyes and let me do the same. Although this was very usual, something I heard about all the time, I couldn't bring myself to accept it, couldn't face it repeating the in-house, involuntary third degree for the whole of the rest of my life. So I became an expert in diversion. I quickly discovered how easy it could be to stay intimately active instead of intimate. Sometimes for many months, I could make almost anyone sure I was like them simply by making myself sure I knew what they would like.

Naturally, my position was not ideal. Months and then years burned away without changing what I came to see more and more clearly as an invincible lack of involvement on my part. Like manholes and poison bottles I was made to be self-locking and I could no longer be bothered pretending I might have a key. I sought out relationships less and less, rented a room and shared facilities in a square, grey house with three complete strangers for whom I had only the smallest responsibility. I stopped trying to be normal and began to enjoy a small, still life that fitted very snugly around nobody but me. I no longer felt inadequate. And when I went to bed I slept.

I once believed I had an overly practical nature and that my lack of romantic enthusiasm stemmed from that, but now I know I have simply been unable to share in the emotional payoff, to feel the benefits of close company and sex. I am not good at emotional payoffs. I am not emotional.

You should know that about me. You should be aware of my principle characteristic which I choose to call my calmness. Other people have called it coldness, lack of commitment, over-control, a fishy disposition. I say that

I'm calm, a calm person, and usually leave it at that, but I feel you should be better informed.

A few things have happened to alter my condition, but it would still be broadly true to say that I am calm. It is assumed that this stems from some kind of self control or confidence, perhaps a type of faith. I am given credit for the massive exertions I must surely perform to sustain my tranquillity.

But I am quite happy to tell you that what appears to be peace and calmness is, in fact, empty space – or, to be more exact, a pause. I am not calm, I am unspontaneous. When something happens to me, I don't know how to feel.

Naturally, I have now lived more than long enough to guess at an appropriate emotion for almost all occasions that arise. Those around me have spent years being furious and chipper, nostalgic, nauseous, glum and all the rest. I know what these things look like and can reproduce them adequately at will. But where someone else will romp immediately off into a chuckle or a gasp, I have to generate a thought, an effort, and any kind of very minor irregularity in my situation may elongate the preparatory pause I need to gather a feeling together until whatever I was going to do becomes irrelevant. I have missed my chance.

This has been less of a problem than you might suppose – most people are too bound up with their own emotions to notice any failings in mine. I have, however, given the matter some thought.

Seemingly, most people have whole hordes of feelings, all barrelling round inside them like tireless moles. As little tiny children they release these emotional moles at the slightest excuse. They will pack a room to the ceiling with riotous, tunnelling mammals for no special reason at all. They have moles and they will exercise them, simply because they are there. Children will be gratuitously expressive just because they can.

Then, I have read, these innocent mole containers go

out in the world and learn to conserve their moles. They are taught that other people's livestock may be unpleasant and do their little charges harm. A room full of moles can be messy and troublesome, even painful. The world is full of sharp little edges and nasty corners and such factors must encourage a level of reasonable restraint to protect both the moles and their minders.

This means that adults can behave quite calmly and safely with barely a trace of their animal insides showing from day to day. Equally, it only takes a first morning of perfect snow, a rapid descent into love or divorce, an especially manipulative film and the moles are out and rolling all over the carpet. So even if we can't see them, we take it for granted that everyone has moles.

Now I'm a calm person, you'll remember that. I am safer than safe. This might imply that my moles are perpetually oh so sleepy and far underground. Or perhaps they used to canter about in the usual way, but then they were scared into hiding by some kind of psychological Rentokil.

Not so.

Almost the first thing I noticed about me when I was very, very young – apart from how my hands worked and what tasted nice, that kind of detail – almost the first thing I noticed was that I had a certain moley something missing. I will tell you soon about my parents and the original ways they could have, but when I do, you'll already know they played no part in making me how I am. I won't say it wasn't useful to have no particular feelings for them to get hold of. I won't deny I made myself as slippery as I could, but you should know that for most of the years I spent near them, I was faking it. I was ringing up every reaction they might conceivably expect me to be attempting to suppress. In other words, I was pretending that I had anything to hide.

As I write this, I can see extremely clearly that nothing terribly bad has ever happened to me. I can't recall a single moment of damage that could have turned me out to be who I am today. I can dig down as deep as there is to dig inside me and there truly is nothing there, not a squeak. For no good reason, no reason at all, I am empty. I don't have any moles.

A LITTLE MORE about me. Just a bit.

My name is M. Jennifer Wilson. The M. stands for Mercy, I've no idea why.

Now I want to show you someone else. His hands, which are square and quick, have just slapped down on to a table top. I can see his tidy nails and solid fingers as they spring up to wrestle and fuss with each other for the length of another sentence. These are hands as an accompaniment to speech.

The knuckles pat together in a temporary halt.

'You truly have an interest in this? Think carefully before you reply.'

It's my voice that answers and I clear my throat before I do – that's a habit I have, a way of buying time for a response.

'Hhrrrhf. I think I'm interested, yes. But if you don't want to say . . .'

'No. So you will understand, this is something about which you must think "I want to know this." If you truly don't wish to know then I would advise you to retire from the field. I have a so great regard for your friendship that in my position currently I would wish to keep it safe by discourteously ignoring your enquiry.

'I, for myself, would much rather speak about these vegetables here – these are very remarkable things. And a person will always know where they are with a vegetable. They are an excellent comfort to me in times of distress. Do you see?'

Needless to say, I don't see. Not at all.

'Martin, I only asked you how you got here. It was

small talk. I didn't mean it metaphysically – not anything like it.'

He presses the heel of one hand between his eyes and smiles, rather tired, as it seems to me. The kitchen makes its small noises round us, the flutter of the ventilator, rain on the window, the pit-pat electrical ticks of the clock. Martin scuffs his feet under the table and raises his head.

'Eh, well. Now I am going to sleep upstairs. Please don't be afraid of making noise, I dream very deeply and will not be disturbed. Tonight, we might speak, hnn?'

He gives a little formal nod and gets to his feet.

Standing, he generally seems slightly shorter than expected, less imposing. I remember thinking that. His height is in his body, not his legs.

If, at this point, I had taken Martin's picture and then showed it to you we could have looked at it together and seen:

a) the corner of a failed Welsh Dresser.

b) part of a doorframe painted in magnolia gloss because it surrounds a door in a shared house and, although all of us hate magnolia, it is the least offensive possible shade of compromise.

c) a small man with the air of a prize fighter turned poetic, or a dancing butcher – all we can actually see of him are his hands which are fading olive and too large for their arms and his head which is supplied with longish, coarse-ish, thinningish, apathetically curly hair and very striking bones. His profile has a remarkable, even predatory, focus that weakens down into a neat, soft mouth and an oddly tiny chin. A ghost of bristle shadows his upper lip. Because he has a habit of frowning with his mouth and not his forehead, he can seem either prissily savage or savagely prissy – like Red Riding Hood's granny, mixed in with her wolf.

d) a pullover with a laddered hole in the sleeve, traces of a collarless shirt and a portion of Oxfam trousers which finally crumple over soft, long slippers – this assembly covers the rest of the small man.

e) nothing of me, except maybe a smudged twirl of steam from my tea. I've never liked being seen – my job involves being completely invisible and suits me no end. If we took the picture today, I'd even have cut out the smoke, so I wouldn't leave a trace. Of course, that wouldn't be the only alteration now. This story will, among other things, form a record of various cuts.

You'll have realised by this time that we have started. We're up and running, albeit in a retrospective kind of way.

We'll take it for granted that Martin nips up for his sleep and the life of the house rolls gently along because on this particular day, only Martin and I are home. I cook and eat and throw away the scraps of dinner. I know without checking that what seemed quite a promising situation in many countries of the world beyond has slithered back into ignorance and spasms of random death.

That afternoon I might, for the sake of argument, recall that quite recently a friend has told me about a besieged group of soldiers broadcasting a tape to their besieging opposite numbers, dug in and waiting around one town or another in one war or another. Their tape had recorded proceedings while a young child was minced alive into small bore meat. My friend and I could not understand how such a tape could have been thought of, or how it could have been made, or how all the little technical necessities could have been seen to in the field. After a while, we found we were both laughing, in the absence of any more appropriate response.

I fill the kettle while the sun dips lower in what I am told is an irredeemably poisoned sky and I think of the distant damage I do, by boiling my water with electricity.

After the loudest of the birds have called on the evening – because even though I hardly see them, we do seem to have birds here always – I find myself very quiet, looking at a grainy room, dim, thinking of nothing at all, but slightly waiting. Then I hear movement above me, a gentle disturbance down the stairs, Martin on his way.

'Well do come in.'

'Ah. I'm not disturbing you.'

'Come in. Do you want to put the light on.'

'No, I don't. May I sit down and did you think about what you want and is what you want that I should speak to you?'

He moves to the table, surprisingly quickly, although perhaps that has to do with the lack of light and the drowsy way I'm watching him.

'Or is that too many questions to ask? Which is naturally another question more. It would be nice if you could answer one. I am afraid my sleep was not entirely serene and I am out of humour. Perhaps I should regather my force and meet you tomorrow.'

I realise just at that moment that I envy him his voice. I know a little about voices and his is very well placed: it has a round, open, dark tone which I like – an almost edible sound.

'Sit down, Martin. Relax. I know I'm not too relaxed myself, but that's just me. If you want to talk about something, talk. I can listen. I don't suppose I'll do much more than that. I'm pretty useless; if it's a woman thing, relationships, or money, I'm a bit of a disaster. But, I mean, I'm not trying to put you off. Martin? Martin?'

He is still standing, but now with his arms folded very high on his chest, hands tucked out of sight, head pulled down and forward. I can hear him making noises that I don't understand and little moves. The dark shape that his hair makes is shaking.

'Martin?'

Now it sounds as though someone is beating the air out of him with a stick. I have no idea what to do or why I would do it. Martin bumps his way to a chair, lets himself drop and fold into it. When he speaks he still does not raise his head and the words escape downwards in odd bursts.

'Please do not feel . . . I am so glad you are here . . . and so sorry . . . I am not sure, but I have the impression this is unlike me. I am not sure.'

I'm on to him by this point. He's crying and it has nothing to do with me. Safe. But also not safe because a peculiar thing is happening. I will find it difficult to describe, even having thought about it.

He lifts his head and the peculiar thing gets worse.

'Eh. I think this is passing. I think so. I do apologise.'

He rubs his face in both hands – I presume to make it dry. When he has finished, he looks up at me before noticing his hands and their condition.

'Ah. Does this make you afraid?'

'It might do.'

'Because I can assure you, it terrifies me.'

And he laughs, making the peculiar thing even more peculiar again.

A little advice here. If you find what I tell you now rather difficult to believe, please treat it as fiction. I won't be offended.

'This is one of the things I expressly wanted to ask you about.'

'No don't get up, just stay there. Stay where you are and I'll stay here and that will make me feel comfortable about this.'

'I am not any danger, I can assure you. I've tried.'

The kitchen is really quite gloomy by this time and it should be difficult to see Martin, but in fact he is far more visible than he has any right to be. When he opens his mouth for any length of time there is a pale gleam which reminds me insanely of the light from a self-sealing envelope if you peel it apart in the dark. An unnatural, static blue flash. His hands and face are simply burning.

That's exactly what it looks like. But with a silver burning, a chemical flame, fluctuating in and out of colour, running like mercury and then disappearing into air. When he moves, shadows boil away from him, they roll under furniture, hiding from his hands.

'Does it hurt? Can I . . .'

'No, there is nothing to be done. It eventually will fade. Except my mouth – that, at night when it is visible, that stays. This doesn't happen to you.'

'No.'

'To no one of your acquaintance.'

'No. This doesn't happen. This is a thing which does not take place. Tell me how you do it.'

'I beg your pardon?'

'How you do it. I can see it's to do with moisture – tears, saliva. What is it, a powder?'

'Ah, I think you misunderstand.'

'Because I can do a good thing with the striking surfaces for safety matches – you burn them and there's an oil left that smokes when you rub it. I learned that when I was a kid – from the *Quaker Oats Book of Magic Tricks*. Not as impressive as you, but it's all right.'

Martin was scrubbing at himself with his sleeves, partly extinguishing his face and leaving a soft, failing glimmer on his sweater.

'Jennifer, please, I've no wish to be alone with this. I need you to understand that I don't know why it is happening. I don't know if I am always this way, if something has changed me. I don't remember. The fire, the shine, whatever you would choose to call it – that isn't at all important. What I have to tell you which is the most important thing is that I can't remember. Do you see? Please sit down. I'm sure this is not contagious.'

'Why are you sure? If you don't remember?'

'Please.'

'All right, all right. Why not.'

'Bless you, thank you. Thank you.'

He snatches up one of my hands as I come within reach

and squashes it between his with a little burst of orange light.

'Oh, I am sorry. I didn't hurt you. Just made a surprise.'

There is an odd sheen on one of my palms, but no apparent damage.

'Don't do it again, though, hmm? I think I've had enough surprises for tonight.'

'Yes, yes, I can well imagine. I might take this opportunity to compliment you on your courage.'

'That's all right, I'm what you might call calm by nature. Being afraid would make a change, believe me.'

'As you wish.'

'But I'm going to turn the light on, because there's no way I can concentrate with you looking like that – even if you have started to fade.'

'Yes, when it dries, there's no light. Haouh, well, you see – oh, thank you, that's very bright isn't it?' He kneads his eyebrows for a moment. 'Now I am under a stronger illumination, I've gone. See?' He waves a hand experimentally. 'A candle in the day. Unimpressive.'

'More normal, anyway. Would you like to tell me what you've forgotten?'

'You may not like to know.'

'Catch me now, while I'm confused, you may not get another chance. I mean, come on, nothing you say could be any stranger than your performance so far. Or if it could I'm sure you'll correct me. Anyway. Go on.'

Martin closes his eyes and presses the knuckles of one hand to his lips. I can hear his breath. Then he looks at me and jerks out a smile that tightens into something slightly grim. 'I am glad you are here. We didn't meet before?'

'I think I would remember if we had.'

'Then chance is on my side, because I do think I need you to be here. This is what I would call a chain of incidence – a small something that makes sense when life . . . well, I have never known what life meant. I'm

14

sure that has been consistently the truth. The truth now is that I do not care in any point whether you are calm, or courageous, or unfeeling, or – and I beg your pardon – simply incapable of understanding your position. I will take it that you are brave, so that I can be brave also.'

'Hhrrrhf. I'm sure you can be brave all by yourself. Please tell me what you have to.'

So he does.

'If I begin with a very familiar beginning. Here, I take an apple from your bowl (if you will excuse me) and now we have a woman and a man and a piece of fruit with biblical dimensions which is a good way to start. To let you know . . . really what I mean . . . do you see this? . . . I can bite this. Hnn? Mmhm. Mn. So. I can understand that. This is not a very pleasant apple, but it does taste a little of apple, it has a colour which is the colour of an apple, tension in its skin and wax and shine and then sweetness and a very familiar flesh, although we can agree it is of a mediocre flavour. I remember about an apple. Good. I remember (as I said) vegetables and a variety of things, for example the sky and the grass in your little garden out there. I can remember how one should call to a cat in order to make it come.'

He works at the collar of his shirt and then licks his lips.

'Now please be aware that you are coming to this in reverse, you already know the last and very much the least singular thing about me, so put that from your mind and I will lead you to the main point of my discovery which is very simply that I can remember almost nothing else.'

His hands are beginning to quarter and layer the air ahead of him.

'Do you want to know the earliest thing of which I have any recollection? I can tell you that. I was asleep and knew that I was sleeping, I felt myself do it and was certain I would never wake. It was like a death without dying, Jennifer. There was a darkness cold and patient as the moon, without sound and without meaning and nothing more but my tiny thought of myself adrift along eternity. I was the black of an eye, a cold dry look pressed in against night, and I saw only the absence of God – a faraway disinterested ache, a faint taste of intellect on the edge of time.

'Even to remember it makes me numb – here – in my fingers, there's still a little blindness. When I am alone now, upstairs, do you know, I don't like to sleep. I lie on the bed and I am afraid I will go to that place again and not come back. I am like a child with more than a child's fear of the dark. It watches me and is hungry. I believe this was not always the case.'

He cups a hand over his forehead and rubs down. His voice suddenly smaller.

'This is making me sweat. That shines, too, in case you wondered. All of my . . . more fluid parts, in actuality, do seem to . . . Eh, but this is not even important, because it is not explanatory. So let me think . . . how long I was in this other world? I have not an idea. The whole condition of my being there made it seem to be for ever. For ever and an oversight, a moment too small for the warmth of attention to ever find it.

'And apart from all this, it was so tedious. Everything which was there (which was nothing and more nothing) was eternal. Do you understand? Fields and fields of nothing eternally. Dull. I believe Hell must be very like that. I believe I must have been there, in Hell, and without ever knowing why.'

He pauses, pursing his lips at something I cannot see.

'But very evidently my situation did change because now I am here and not there.

'So I'll tell you how I am released from, at the very least, Purgatory. I begin to feel warm. No brimstone, no burning, just warm. There is a little point of heat in the palm of my hand (right hand) and this passes into the core of my arm and – hopla – is at my heart. At the time this did not in one point please me. I recall that I wanted to be more dead rather than more alive and there I was becoming sensible against my will. You may imagine, I was, apart from anything else, extremely annoyed.'

He peers forward across the table like a very large bird, or a cat, muzzling at the emptiness between our faces. I can see a kind of shatter in his eyes, flaws of light in the blue and a mineral shine. Nothing unnatural, but quite striking. And his eyelashes are over-long.

'I am drifting, annoyed and lost, somewhere in the mind of an amnesiac Creator, or worse. Not an ideal position for anyone, but particularly not for me. I am, after all, very fond of me and care what happens to myself. But the changes are not over. I am aware of turning and rising, there is a rush of passing beside my ears and through my hair, what there is of my hair. I have never – I know this – had any difficulty with falling hair or becoming bald, I simply have too little of too coarse a type, in too desperate a distribution. None the less, I can hear and feel that I am in the process of plunging up and into a variety of morning. (At least I have the impression of morning.) There is the beginning of light and my whole skin is tickling with I don't know what, but it's something very pleasant, and I have a feeling of being not so terribly solitary as before. What is truly extraordinary at this point is that I landed. I came to a halt – boff – as if I had hit my head on a ceiling, except that the ceiling was a floor.

'So I am in a house which was never there before and which is spinning to fit around me so the bed where I am lying is slipping in beneath me and the walls to the side and everything is aiming for where it should be. Then it is there. Arrived. Now I can open my eyes and look at so many different things together it is quite painful. Upwards and downwards and to every side, there are things I can see.

'I found that very impressive and surprising for a considerable time.

'Softly, I know that I am somewhere, rather than nowhere. I know that I am lying in sheets, that I am cold but not uncomfortably so and that I am a human being, rather than perhaps an animal, half an orange, someone else's good idea. Then I begin to fall unpreventably asleep and I am without fear because this is perfect – all I want to do is rest. I have not been at rest for ever (as far as I can recall) so I am somewhat tired. What next? Eh? Night falls in my mind.'

He pats his palms together with a huge grin.

'Do you think I might have a cup of your coffee as a kind of intermission. It's very nice, that coffee.'

'You remember coffee now, then?'

'Not particularly, no. I think I had something a little bit like it once, but it was more . . . more dusty.'

'A pleasant surprise for you, then.'

'I'm trying to look on most things in that way, yes.'

I get up to make the coffee. 'I'll be mother.'

I don't feel that women should necessarily make men hot drinks whenever they are mentioned, but it so happens that I am thirsty, too. And I've already tasted the way Martin makes coffee. And it's a nice little excercise for me – probably as close to being anybody's mother as I'll get.

'Don't mind me clattering about, I'll still be listening.'

'Thank you. I have the impression I have always enjoyed talking. I like the way it feels.'

'Oh good.'

'Yes, and I didn't intend it, but this all binds in very well. Do you know the first thing I heard, safely landed and flat on my bed? The first proper thing, when my world was struck new and so remarkable?'

'No, I don't know. How would I know? You take lots of sugar, don't you?'

'I wouldn't say it was a lot of sugar. I would say it was just enough.'

'I'll bring you the bag.'

'But what did I hear?'

'I'm sorry, I can't even guess. What did you hear?'

'You. I heard you.'

'I beg your pardon.'

'It was you – you were talking about something. I could hear you through the floor. You must have been about where you are now. I lay up there listening and you sounded happy and you laughed. So there you are. That really would make you my mother, eh? The first woman I hear.'

'No. No, I don't think it would. Let me get this clear. The first thing you can remember is being upstairs in your room and hearing noises down here. There's nothing before that?'

'Nothing. I explained. This is the house I fell into. This is all I know.'

Which is the most normal introduction I can give him. I did consider avoiding a few of the stranger details until later, but that didn't seem possible. After all, I'm trying to give you as much of the truth as I can and part of any truth will be the order in which it arrives. One fact will trigger one feeling, while another will not, whole dominoeing rows of moles can romp off in entirely the wrong direction simply because of a distortion or omission in time. Far be it for me to mislead your moles.

For instance, you should now know the kitchen I described was in that square, grey house I mentioned – the one I shared with the three other people whose names were Liz, Arthur and Pete. In case you were wondering. Martin arrived at a time when Pete's room was empty, but a temporary lodger for it was imminently expected. It may be alarming, or disappointing, or just plain unconvincing that a major figure in this whole affair was a shorter than average man who glowed – more or less – in the dark, could only remember items of greengrocery, and came to himself in a conveniently unoccupied room. It's not what I would have chosen myself, but I had no opportunity to choose. And because Martin was a friend of mine, I would ask you to be patient with him. I wasn't the only one with no choice. He didn't even get to pick his name.

'What do you mean, you're not called Martin?'

'I mean what that would customarily mean. If anyone called me Martin, it was you.'

'Now you're confusing me again.'

'There's no confusion. I eventually felt safe enough to leave the bed. My surroundings seemed unfamiliar but not unlikely, if you understand me. I thought I should find out whose the voice was. First I walked to the window and found that I was on the first floor of a house – you see I didn't want to discover that this was a voice from, perhaps, under the ground. You can imagine, I didn't wish to be surprised again in one morning. Enough is enough.

'Now I had a problem. No . . . when I landed, I was not supplied with any clothing. Naturally, I didn't wish to introduce myself quite so personally and a search of the room provided an assembly of garments which I could guess might be suitable. I dressed as best I could and opened the door. To my huge relief, there was indeed the rest of a house beyond it and a flight of stairs. I walked out, a little as if I were trusting my weight to the sea, but all was well.

'The next door I opened was this one here, for the kitchen, and you were sitting at the table, reading aloud. And I am certain you can think what you said, if you really try. I am the one with the bad memory, after all.'

'You must be Martin.'

'Exactly. You told me that I must be Martin.'

'That wasn't an order, it was an assumption. We were expecting someone called Martin to take Peter's room.'

'I know that now. But you can appreciate that I was quite happy to agree with any kind of likely proposition that morning. Even a name. In fact, I hoped you might know me, have heard of me. I also had an idea that this must be the house where the newly arrived were given their names and instructions before they set out on their lives.' He gave me a large shrug. 'Well, I wasn't to know. You can't deny, it is always useful to have a name, even if not one's own.'

'You wouldn't happen to remember your real name now?'

'No. Sorry.'

'Just a thought.'

I HATE SECRETS. No, that's a lie, and here I was hoping to tell you the truth. Start again.

I hate to be on the blind side of a secret. That's more like it. Sometimes I'll be shown, let in on, something that seems a real secret to me, I'll be allowed to stand right up against it and look all I like, but I still won't understand. I might as well be staring at a length of algebra, an unknown language – it will have no meaning for me. Worse than that, I will know that it must have a meaning for somebody else. So I'm stupid. No one needs to hide this from me, it is, quite simply, beyond me. I am on the blind side.

I don't know if I grew up with this ferocious need to uncover the ins and outs of everything, or if growing up made me this way. I was an only child and it seems to me now I had nothing to do all day but be too interested. Because I had this odd frustration. My parents were not of the kind to avoid questions, or to slip me the type of tidy fable I would hear more distant adults and school-teachers palming off on children, or even each other. At home, we had nothing hidden. I could ask my mother and father anything and be answered with something solid and realistic. My problem was, I very rarely knew what they meant. As my years with them passed, I became more and more certain that I had an excellent grasp of the world around me, but that it would never make any sense.

Climbing the stairs to my room after Martin decided to tell me what he didn't know about himself, I walked up into a mood I had only associated with my parents' house. I could smell their furniture, the particular dry,

22

tickling air in their room. I was allowed in their room. Their bedroom. Even when they were there, inside there together behind a closed door, I was allowed to go in. They had a white door, which seemed to be like all the others in the house – flat in the modern way, with a white china handle and one or two long fat drips in the paint if you looked at it very carefully in the right light. I looked at it very carefully, because really it was different from all the other doors, it only appeared to be the same. I knew. It was a big, blind secret – I could stare at it for hours, until my face went numb, or I had to cry, and still I wouldn't understand it. Children are odd like that, they have an inappropriate determination, no way of identifying a hopeless case.

'Welcome to our starlight ballroom, ladies and gentlemen. The quartet is playing, your seats are being warmed by Philippino dwarves of your individual choice, and doing your thinking for you tonight will be Martin Wilson.'

You need to understand here – my parents were a hopeless case. You only had to listen to them, going on again behind their door, and you would know.

'What?'

'Specialist in paranoia, pain and perversity, graduate of the Sigmund Freud School of Charm and Social Scarring, your neurons are his playmates – ladies and gentlemen, I give you – guess who?'

'I wouldn't even mind if you could bitch without rehearsal. You know the trouble with that little effort? Your enunciation was too good.'

'Oh dear. My mistake. We're in detective mode tonight.'

'Don't strain yourself, will you. You're coming dangerously close to improvisation.'

'Fuck you.'

'Oops, there we go – straight into reality.'

23

'Yeah, yeah, yeah. Just take whatever you came for and fuck off.'

'But I can't remember what I came for. Now was it in the wardrobe, or was it under the bed.'

'You're pathetic. Pathetic.'

'You should think before you say things like that. I might take that to heart and be offended. Darling.'

'Fuck off.'

'No.'

'Fuck off.'

I didn't understand the way they talked. Looking at the words now, I work out some of the feeling, but it never was as clear as I would have liked. At the time, I almost thought they were playing, and then when I was older I thought they were fighting, and now I think I may have been right the first time. The way my parents were together was always very like a game, or a dress rehearsal for something that would be quite important when finally it was done.

Now Martin, like my parents, was a secret, but, unlike my parents, he was a friendly one. He genuinely seemed to find he was as much a mystery to himself as to anyone else and I couldn't feel threatened by that. There was something that made me believe the way he was. I don't know why, I'm not particularly gullible. Liars hope to make their lies convincing by adding emotional distractions which, of course, don't distract me. I once stood behind a sleight-of-hand artist and the effect was much the same – nothing to observe but naked technique, interesting but nowhere near convincing. Martin hadn't tried anything like that.

Even better, he was, in a way, my own private secret. No one else knew what we knew – Martin and I. Liz and Arthur didn't know. That particular night they weren't even at home. Friday night, we're all free people, what with work and its many alternatives, it wasn't especially likely that anyone would be at home. But I was and so was Martin and he had spoken to me. Rather a childish satisfaction, but I don't mind being easily satisfied – it can mean you're satisfied quite often and that surely can't be bad.

That night I got ready for bed in the usual way, but just a touch quieter than usual. The rain had stopped outside and the house had settled in the dark. There was no sound from Martin's room. I didn't know if he was sleeping, or holding sleep away, or just silently glowing in the dark.

You will already have considered the options I spun through once I was in bed. I have a very comfortable bed, perfect for undisturbed thinking, and designed to keep my back in good condition. It is a double bed because I am an expansive sleeper. I bought it with no one in mind but myself – I was the only person I could think of who deserved the benefit of such an excellent mattress.

I distributed my weight across the faultlessly engineered springs and imagined Martin with amnesia caused by accidents, chemicals, radiation, experimental gas. I imagined Martin as an experimenter, as an experiment, as an accident that happened on his way here, a random misfortune with delayed effects. I imagined Martin afraid of the dark and of sleeping. I thought of Martin struck by lightning, transported by lightning, as an illusionist, a circus performer, a natural phenomenon. As I eased down towards sleep, I imagined a great many further things I cannot remember now.

I couldn't work him out. I don't know why that didn't concern me. I can recall wondering if I should be afraid, all on my own and at night, preparing to sleep while no one knew what was only across the landing. As softly as I could, I got up and locked my door. Not because I was fearful, but in case I should act that way.

'Martin?' I still held the key when I shouted through my door, just checking. 'Martin. Martin?'

There was no reply which may have meant he couldn't hear me, or that he was sleeping. If he'd had any reason to be guilty, he would have answered to reassure me until his moment was ripe, and I imagined that if he'd been feeling at all apprehensive, he would have been listening, alert. I was glad he didn't answer. I didn't want him to be either guilty or apprehensive.

In the morning, Arthur came home early, wheeling his bicycle into the hall and singing. He woke me up.
'Jesus loves the atheists
Loves them for their gnostic twists
Honest doubt is heaven sent,
'Cos Jesus loves an argument.
Yes, Jesus loves me,
Yes, Jesus loves me,
Yes, Jesus loves, the postman tells me so.'
Arthur makes up songs.

This was an average start to the day in our household and, although this may seem unlikely, I had moved through washing and dressing and was putting on my shoes before I properly thought about Martin. I have often found myself unable to think of any really sizeable idea until my day has settled into a full beginning. This means that I am not above staving off the return of unpleasant realisations by staying in bed. Not that bad news isn't above simply snuggling in beside me.

Martin wasn't exactly bad news, more like a dull cloud floating behind my eyes until I bent forward to tie my laces and shook him loose. When I crossed the landing to go downstairs I found myself slipping a glance to my right. Martin's door peeled back and left him to stand in the shadows of his room. He was barefoot under crumpled jeans and a tired maroon sweater he must have found somewhere tight and dusty. Unless he'd brought it with him and then forgotten. I couldn't accept the idea that anyone arrived suddenly and naked at his age.

While I considered his costume for that day, Martin dipped his head forward and to the side, looked at me for a moment and then straightened up into a smile. There was a little glimmer of blue before he covered his mouth and coughed. His door swooped shut again.

Downstairs in the kitchen Arthur was digging at the butter with his hands.

'What are you doing?'

'Seeing if we've won.'

'Won what?'

'Oh, something.'

'I'm sorry, I must be having a slow morning. Why are you doing that to our butter?'

'This is margarine.'

It was. I call it butter because I use it to butter things, not because it isn't margarine.

'Are you going to tell me.'

'I am looking under the margarine because they write something on the bottom of the tub to tell you what you've won. I think it's money. And they give some of the price you pay for it to orphans abroad, or endangered species.'

'Same thing, really.'

'Mmm.'

'But couldn't you do that with a spoon, Art?'

'Sure.'

He placidly abandoned his quest.

'We haven't won. I can't see anything unusual.'

Using a teaspoon he scraped off the margarine from his fingers and pressed it back into the tub, slowly smearing the surface approximately flat.

We ate margarined toast together quietly while the radio told us that our new government was fearlessly adjusting reality's fabric with swingeing pamphlets. Europe boiled in the distance along killing boundaries, the redefined fundaments of several headline religions were redefined again and at home many bad people committed crimes, some

27

of them being arrested later – reality getting its own back for the pamphlets. I changed the station.

'*Well, of course, in Dominica, the giant frogs are known as Mountain Chicken and they certainly do make good eating.*'

Not long after this I went to work. I will tell you how I earn a living later, for now we'll move on to Tuesday afternoon when something important happened. I took Martin out.

'I have never done this.'

'You must have.'

'No.'

'At some point, you must have. To get here –'

'I fell here. Well, I am sorry, but this is how it happened. I am not in the habit of strolling up naked to the houses of strangers and then, perhaps, tickling their doors open (how did I get in here, do you know how I got in here?), finding a bed for the night, forgetting how I did this.'

'You've barely been outside of your room. That isn't healthy.'

'I am a little anxious with things.'

'A bit of sunshine. Up to the park and back. It's only round the corner, we can sit there for a while if you want to rest, or come straight back. I mean people notice things, Martin. We have a relaxed household here, but people notice things. In fact, I have to talk to you about that. Liz and Arthur thought I should talk to you.'

'Why? What's the matter?'

'Nothing too bad. Don't worry, I haven't told them anything about you.'

'Thank you.'

'No need. They wouldn't have believed a word of the truth and I'm no good at lying so I kept my mouth shut. Now, come on. Are those shoes comfortable?'

'How could they be, they aren't mine? And all of this, these . . .'

His hands waved in irritation as he stared down at his especially unlucky-looking pair of trainers.

'What?'

'I have never liked threading and lacing and these things when I dress. I prefer simpleness. Particularly, I prefer to have simple feet.'

'They're only shoelaces, for crying out loud.'

'Hmmn.'

'You hadn't forgotten shoelaces.'

'Eh, not forgotten – lost the trick of them, I would say.' He pinched at his already thin moustache. 'We have to go out now, hn?'

'It might be good to.'

But naturally it wasn't good because I'd forgotten that other people are prone to be worried or even terrified by things they don't understand. By the time we had turned on to the little road that would take us to the park, Martin had stopped walking. He leant one shoulder against the wall, a grey sheen on his face.

'We're almost there now.' I had decided to jolly him along. 'Nearly there.' A car passed us and he shied, jerking one hand high to cover his face and then softly continuing the movement, almost as if he'd intended to flatten his hair. I thought I should take his hand or just give him a pat on the shoulder, do something tangibly encouraging, but before I could think of the most appropriate gesture, Martin inhaled audibly. He straightened himself and began to walk forward again, carefully, as if he were afraid of overbalancing.

Once we had passed the park gates, he seemed to move more easily, pulling away from the path and heading for a little area bounded by low trees and a wall. He let himself fall on to the grass as if he had ended a difficult swim and wanted to hold the shore for a while and be certain that it wouldn't go away. Rather than interrupt, I waited until he flopped over on to his back and then called.

'Martin?' He made no attempt to rise, but swept up one arm and let his hand wave me over as it followed a sharp curve and hit the turf close by his head. 'Martin?'

'I must make my excuses – I am afraid I feel unable to move from here at the moment.'

'No, that's fine.'

I sat a small distance away, my shadow falling across his face.'

'Thank you.'

'Sorry?'

'For the shade.'

'Oh, no trouble. Hhrrf.' There was a silence during which a pigeon landed and paced away to our left. Martin must have seen it spin down the sky above him, sheathing its wings into angles for descent. He sighed as it dropped which I took to be a sign of contentment. 'Feeling better?'

'Hauo!'

I discovered I had drawn myself back while his pigeon and half a dozen others scrambled up the air and beyond the trees. Martin had diluted his original shout into something not unlike laughter. When he opened his eyes, the laughing stopped.

'I will never feel better.'

'Good, good.'

'No.' He snatched hold round one of my ankles. 'No. It is not good. I don't know what's happened to me. I can't get up. I can't walk in this. Dear Lord, surely I must have walked. Was I a prisoner somewhere, that now I'm so . . . I am so afraid.'

'Martin –'

'Listen.'

There was nothing in particular that I could hear.

'You hear them?'

'Um . . .'

'The children. They're playing over there. I won't try to look, it will make me dizzy, but I know they are there. They are playing. This is something that a little child is not afraid of, but I can't be here.'

'They're quite big children, really.'

'Jennifer, please. Listen. You hear things but you don't

listen. I do not think I will be able to get away from here. I will not be fit to face it. Can you help me. If you can't . . . I have no one else. Do please concentrate on my position.'

He was tensing his neck to keep his head driven hard into the grass. He rubbed his cheek against his outstretched arm. His eyes looked damp. I didn't like to notice that.

'I am listening, Martin, but I don't know what to do. Look, why don't you sit up?'

'I can't.'

'I'll hold your hand.' His fingers were taut. 'I'll hold your hand in both of mine. Just let go. I won't lose you. That's it.'

'I feel I will fall.'

'I don't understand. Tell me about that.' This is one thing I can say in my favour – if I have no idea of your mental state, I will ask you for more information. Many people base a lifetime's personal relations solely on guesswork. 'Tell me about that, help yourself calm down.'

'Oh, I – '

'Breathe, take some breaths. I'm holding on, don't worry.' I sounded convincingly safe – happy in my own mind that he wouldn't suddenly up and drift off like a helium funfair balloon, no matter what he thought.

'You're okay.' Perhaps a little of the tension left his wrist. Because of me.

'I believe you, I do. In my mind, I am convinced, but the rest of me is terrified.'

'Well think about it. Have you ever seen a man just up and drift bodily away? Do they normally have to weight you down at night?'

'I don't know!'

'Okay, bad question. But just because you're unusual in one way, it doesn't mean you're going to be a permanent bag of surprises. Now how do you feel? What's wrong? Are you ill?'

31

'I feel . . . I have the impression . . . as if I were about to fall off the world. So small and so on the surface. I – oh.' His voice suddenly firmed, settled. 'I have remembered something.'

'Well that's great.'

'Yes.' He almost smiled.

'So what is it?'

'Eh! Only a very tiny thing, but I am quite sure that when I was a young man I walked at some time between a high wall and some fields. There were dark, even rows of something growing there. Under a sand-coloured summer evening with a ripe, low moon. I had a soft road beneath me and my boots drove up the day's heat out of the dust as I walked. I was going home. I don't know where that was but I am quite sure I was going there, only pausing for a space because I was very tired, thirsty . . . when I took off my hat there was the cool of sweat. I looked up.' His hand suddenly snapped tight in mine. His eyes were closed, his face moving, as if he were watching a dream. 'That was it. The moon was darkening. I stood and watched a shadow slip over it as easily and quietly as if it had been my hand.

'Oh, and it was an impressive natural phenomenon, certainly, but I felt above all that to cast such a shadow, there must be something terribly huge and silent behind me. My logic tells me the huge something must be my own planet – I understand this – but I feel now an idea of the size of that planet. I am balanced on an enormous surface, but it does have a limit, it is only a surface. While I watch I can see the evidence of its shape and movement darken the moon whole, then allow it to light again. Intellectually I was happy to accept the principles of eclipse, but to know them in my heart, from experience, was something I found more mystical than scientific and more frightening than comfortable. I do not think any one man should feel the reality of his globe quite so personally. This is how I felt then and how I feel now. I don't want to fall.'

'That's wonderful Martin.' His head moved very slightly as he tried to look up at me.

'You're remembering. That must be a good thing. All this is, is a panic attack. People have them. It's not real.'

'I feel it.'

'Doesn't make it real. I'm here, too and I don't feel it. I'll be with you when you're ready to sit up and we'll take it from there. This is all very good. I bet you'll remember who you are soon. Probably this was a little shock and I'm sorry I gave it you, but it will turn out well in the long run.'

Odd, the things I've ended up saying in my life. Today I think I would be less assured of my grip on the future and the turns it might take.

In the park I was doing my best to be encouraging and was slowly able to coax Martin up and out of the park. It took us half an hour to make it all the way home, including a final slippery fumble at the front door as I tried to get the key in the lock left handed. Martin kept my other arm locked round his waist.

Once he was safely in the hallway, Martin bolted up the stairs to his room, calling a thank you over his shoulder that reached me along with the sound of his door locking.

I went down into the kitchen. Before I turned on the light, I could see the last shine of Martin, still on my hands and deep in the cloth of my shirt. There was something not altogether unpleasant about that. I can think of such little incidents from time to time and consider them memories of something good.

'Did you ask him?'

That was Liz speaking, following me into the kitchen and delivering a friendly blow across my shoulders as she picked up a teaspoon and headed for the fridge. You

33

haven't met her yet, but this doesn't make her a bad person, only one it's difficult to meet. I often wonder why and how I know her at all. We share the same house, that's been true for a long time, but she has developed being absent into her principal character trait. This can give her an air of changeability – between sightings she may gain or lose weight, develop a suntan, earrings. To be brief, Liz is the kind of person you talk about because she is so consistently unavailable for talking to. But then, you'll have noticed that yourself, by now.

'You didn't, did you?'

'What? Oh, ask him about the rent?'

'Mm. And all the bills and being careful with the immersion heater and noting down phonecalls and all of that stuff.'

'Yes, he did sort of fall through the net, as far as house rules go. But I'm sure, well, probably Pete filled him in.'

Liz closed the fridge door with her foot and began to eviscerate a yoghurt.

'He's messy in the bathroom. Not just messy – offensive.'

'No. He *was* messy, but Arthur sorted him out. It was more confusion than not being tidy. He's scrupulous now. I mean, he seems to be a tidy person.'

'Okay. But he needs to know about the bills – we don't want to end up with someone like that pal of Arthur's.'

'No. He was a bit much.'

'Never mind a bit much. If I ever see him again, I'll cut his bloody head off. That guy was a vampire. I kept expecting to come across Arthur handing him over his kidneys to sell.'

'Only one kidney. He'd need the other.'

'Yes, but this is Arthur we're talking about. He'd have been sorry he couldn't have handed over three. You will talk to Martin, though, won't you. I don't know him at all and he makes Arthur nervous. I thought you might have told him while you were both outside.'

The observant type, Liz, very hot on spotting our ins and outs. Only when she is here, of course. Perhaps she goes away to get a rest.

'I was going to ask him, but then he was ill. Well, not ill exactly – a bit agoraphobic.'

'There's nothing wrong with him, though?'

'No, I don't think so – he's just a bit sensitive.'

'Gay, you mean.'

'Sensitive. It's allowed for straight men to be sensitive now, I've read it in the magazines. Not that I know what Martin is, either way. It's not very obvious and it's none of my business.'

'Sensitive.'

'Sensitive. But don't worry, it's not infectious.'

'If you're implying that I am insensitive, you can fuck off. I'm in love, of course I'm sensitive.'

'Adolf Hitler was in love. Think about Eva Braun.'

'And all those Alsatians. Exactly. He painted in water-colours, too. Very sensitive.'

'It's just that we don't see that side of you because you're away so much – being in love.'

'Well, you'll be seeing a little more of me than usual while Frank calms down again. He will not understand that being in love and playing houses are not the same thing.'

'Men, eh?'

'Hmm.'

And all through this conversation I knew what you know –

Martin isn't Martin

Somewhere, there must be a real Martin

The more time passes, the closer to us the true Martin must come

As far as I can tell, our Martin has no money

Without money, I do not know a way that he can stay here

Our Martin is upstairs and may be lonely, or disturbed, or ill, or something else I cannot yet imagine.

I would like to tell you that I went upstairs to see how he was, just tapped on his door to let him know that he wasn't alone, but I did nothing like that because I didn't know how. I had no appropriate form of action or speech. The rest of that day passed without a sight of Martin, or a thought of him on my part. I think I watched a video with Liz and then turned in early, nothing more. I paused a while on the landing near his door when I was going to bed and then I walked on. I am not a good host, even now.

I have a feeling about that – I'm guilty. Guilt is of course not an emotion in the Celtic countries, it is simply a way of life – a kind of gleefully painful social anaesthetic. And like the dear, free-floating psychic ether it is, guilt pours around us, always readily available for no especial reason at all, but sometimes I do experience guilt because I am guilty. I am guilty because I wish I had done better by Martin and I would do differently now, given the opportunity. Which is, of course, the one thing time will always take away.

MY JOB. I said I would tell you about it, so here you are. I talk for a living. Don't act, don't move, don't sing, only talk. I am a professional enunciator.

Really. Someone has to do it. Radio prayers and poems, British voices for American faces, neutral voices for criminal faces – terroristically digitised – jolly encouragements to purchase who cares what and, of course, calm accounts of current chaos, who cares where. I've tried a little of almost everything in the vocal line because this is all I can do. I don't have any skills or talents, so within a very tiny field I try to be inexhaustibly flexible. Doing what everyone else can, only better.

For a long time I had an idea that most other jobs were not like this. At school, I was taught about trades and training and apprenticeships and the serving of time, during which lucky people would learn how to make things or think things, or both. Never having known what I wanted to think or make, I drifted into speaking instead. I was a failure.

Now I find that it is no longer admirable to make or to think. People take modules and courses and options, or don't, and then, in either case, they try to be inexhaustibly flexible. Just like me. Failures.

Sometimes I feel as if my generation was galloped one morning over a huge, metaphorical employment cliff and some of us were saved immediately, scooped up by angels or helicopters or convenient safety nets and given a useful and meaningful life. Some of us bounced a little further on, had to scramble to avoid the full drop. Then right down, just before we crossed the line into unprofitability and disaster, there were people like me, lodged in funny but quite comfortable places, overlooking the enormous mess beneath.

I would like to say that I am lucky in the life I have but my good fortune is so obviously arbitrary that it can also make me rather tense, if not actually guilty, or troubled by impending doom. Will they take it away or make me pay – for all this undeserved good fortune? That's something very like the question I always want to ask. In many situations, but most especially when I'm at work. At the time I first met Martin, my principal employer was a local radio station and every time I appeared there I would be drenched in my expectations of dreadful discovery – surely, in the end, they would find me out, throw me out. The longer I was successful, the more imminent my failure, that's how my logic went.

Which all sounds rather bleak when I fully intended to say that I really enjoy what I do absolutely. That's the truth. It tastes nice. I place something invisible into the air, just so, give it a tangible shape and somewhere, someone, a stranger, will get a word and the feeling in that word – both of them at once and because of me. I can do that.

Now when Martin found out about all this – and the broadcasting, in particular – he was very impressed. He didn't have a clear understanding of my position, or its limitations, and so he became very enthusiastic about its possibilities.

'Eh, but this is wonderful!'

I should say that we had this conversation some time after our outing to the park. In the intervening period, several things had changed – most importantly, Martin had begun to remember who he was. His real name and all that. He was becoming more talkative, larger.

'This is what you do? All the time? For your work?'

I nodded and eased down another gulp of fruit tea and honey. The glands in my neck had swollen to the size of apricots and were having the same effect as a strangler's thumbs. All morning my eyes seemed to have been bulging and there was a raw tension every time I blinked. But I would be all right if I didn't say anything until I had to, until I was at work. I would manage, follow the drill – a speaker knows how to look after a voice.

What I didn't know was that I had an abcess nestling in my throat and not just a cold or a 'flu. I would hold out, expecting the whole thing to pass, but becoming more ratty and feverish by the hour. I don't like to be ill, ever, but more importantly, at that time I felt I had no choice but to keep working. Things had been rather thin in the speaking line and I wanted to keep what work I had.

At night I would no longer know where I was and in the daytime reality would seem just the same as always but an eighth of an inch to one side. Everything I can remember from that time is smirred with confusion and slightly out of order. Which is why I'm telling you this bit first, even though perhaps you would rather hear about who Martin turned out to be. I don't mean to keep you waiting – I would love to tell you who he is right now – but I can only seem to focus on this particular afternoon and conversation. I may remember it so clearly because it was the first time I noticed Martin becoming more of himself. He was smiling and his shoulder-blades lay smoother to his back.

'Wonderful! You can speak to an entire city and the province around it immediately. No matter what you intend them to know, they will know it, hear it as if you were speaking their thoughts. There you have a position of remarkable power.'

I shook my head, which he either interpreted as false modesty on my part, or simply ignored. In half an hour I could take my soluble pain killer without risking fatal damage to my liver. Meanwhile the throttling in my throat was making my patience suicidally short.

'Ah, but that would be genuinely a wonderful thing. There would be no bounds on one's influence, no record of one's words; neither cost nor delay and no possibility of censorship because no one can censor a word in the air. And you yourself would be quite invisible. Marvellous.'

I shrugged with one hand.

'I have, for example, been giving madness my consideration for quite some time. The lunatic in particular has long been an enthusiasm of mine. You could ask almost anyone who knew me and they would bear witness to my close association with all varieties of lunacy.

'Imagine then my delight in finding that your own state and public functionaries not only share but excel my humble fondness for the insane.'

He had begun to pace, but stopped to grin over at me, slipping his hands comfortably into his pockets.

'Do you realise I could say this and – PHAOU – it goes, without a drop of ink, everywhere.

'Eh! So I can tell myself I am truly fortunate to discover I live in times of such genius. Precisely when your world and existence were so dull and commonplace and pitiful, your government – whom you have the wonderful opportunity to elect – has chosen to empty out the madhouses on to the streets. Now everything about our lives can be a question of interest and debate. Does a tree grow upwards, or does the ground recede? Who can be sure? Do I cast up my eyes in the night and see stars, or the eyes of demons, or cherubim, or God's silver buttons or horse's teeth? When the world is peopled by madmen (and madwomen) even the simplest matter can float merrily away from any divine intention into a sea of Jesuitical debate.

'I can only view my future here with delight for now every day will become new and unpredictable. How am I to know, among the people I meet, who are the lunatics and who are their keepers? Who are the lunatics without keepers? The lunatics who *are* keepers? Will the next stranger I encounter fall on my throat, or shake my hand, or offer to buy my soul? Adrift in this new community of the mad, I could be murdered or married at any hour of the day or night and no one would see any difference between the two. How exquisitely interesting.

'And what if the country should become alive with superstition and dread. This will surely provide cheap and ready entertainment for the otherwise idle. And what if some liberated souls should take to devouring infants at the roadside, or mashing in every fifteenth skull they see. We have people enough to spare and barely the work, or the bread, to support them. Our only other recourse to prevent rioting and sedition would be the gathering of men for war – an admirably insane but very costly exercise.

'Who will be sure, in that Babel of opinion, that infanticide and the other noble forms of slaughter are not the most virtuous forms of enterprise? I can foresee that we will embrace them as excellent means of saving weak or innocent souls from the hardships and temptations they might otherwise meet and succumb to in life.

'But how will your government survive when this supremacy of the demented is fully achieved? Let me tell you, gentle listener, it will walk among us finally unafraid to be itself. These are the men and women who are paid to improve your health by removing your physicians, to educate your scholars by removing their books, to shelter your people by removing their homes, to guard your souls by destroying your faith, to cherish the truth by hiding it in petty ignorance, who imprison the blameless, free the guilty, nourish your poor with starvation and let loose senility, terror and confusion in your streets because this will be to the benefit of you all. We are mad to suffer them and they are, most assuredly, true paragons of madness, every one.

'They are, however, to be blessed for taking evil from the land. Your language is turning pleasantly on its head and I find myself unable to remember the meaning of that small and singular word *evil*. I wonder more and more how there could ever have been such a wicked term to describe the glorious conduct of mankind. Surely, if there were evil in this world then the good would rise up against it, they could not bear its presence and power in their lives, they would condemn it, name it, drive it out. And as, everywhere in your country, there is only peace and amiable concord, one vast silence of agreement in the midst of an apparent turmoil, I am finally reassured that there is no evil. There is only the unfamiliar, and to this I may always become accustomed. At last, in my mind, all becomes good and well for the lack of any other definition.'

He paused, his palms caught on the turn, head back. When I nodded, he flinched back down into a simple standing position, utterly still.

'Of course, I would have prepared what I would say. I would wish to combine a certain immediate fire with a smoothness in the flow of speaking.'

I nodded and smiled.

'I have offended you. That was not my intention. I am sorry. I never have seemed to be content with anyone who has decided to govern me. I may, even on this point, still have an argument with God.' He tugged at the hair over his forehead and began to move for the door.

'No.'

'I can go now, this is not a difficulty.'

'No. Just. I can't speak. My throat. Saving it for later.' Catarrh was making me slightly deaf and wadding my facial resonators tight. Even aiming the words around the pain, I sounded terrible – thin, flat, breaking up across long vowels.

'Ah, I do apologise.' He pinched his hands together with a worried little flutter. There are times when I become too . . .'

I nodded.

'Yes, yes, you are aware of this by now. You will be able to, ahn, perform, today?' I made a praying motion. 'I do hope so also. What you do offers such opportunities, they carried me along for a while.' He kneeled beside my chair, a finger at his lips. 'Nod if I can tell you a secret? Only nod, please, I don't intend to cause any further discomfort.

'Thank you.

'No one knows this. No one alive. I can remember lying with a friend of mine on grass – we had been swimming and were letting the sun make us dry. Physically I could not have felt more at my ease, but I had something cold under my heart, it seemed there was only space inside my ribs and not the material of a man. I turned to my friend and I heard myself ask him, if you can imagine, "Do you think I will be famous? Will I truly be celebrated? When I am dead?"

'He only laughed and said – I'm not sure – that I was already monstrously on the way to living for ever, something like that. He was laughing because I had asked him this same question when we were boys. I think I often asked it.

'And this is the way I knew he did not understand me – this man who had been my friend for ever, we were very close. He thought I was looking for glory, for an assured income, perhaps for influence, when these things were froth, luxuries, they didn't concern me at any point. I swear.

'I needed to be famous to live, simply to fill the space that any normal man would take as his right. I needed to be mistaken for something more than what I was, for fear of disappearing.

'It is so easy to not be. I have seen a whole man stop, you know, many times. The body will move to a place and then fall away, it will go no further and there will not be any more of that person. This whole process can take an instant. I turn away to wipe my eyes, I turn back and you are gone. I reach forward with my hand in this line and I apply a pressure and you are gone. Your breath leaves of its own volition, you no longer have the force even to push it out. I can imagine, if I wish, the dark to be one shade thicker when that day's evening comes, but this is imagination and not one point more.

'Still I am here, although I am sure I have no natural place on this planet. In your world or mine. I feel constantly precarious and I need the weight of your attention to secure me and allow me to be justified. I cannot just be, I must also do and be seen to do and be heard to do and known to do and then I can live.

'My friend had never felt that way. Often we could seem as close as brothers, but at this point he left me to be completely alone. So, in summation, you understand why your occupation would appeal to me?'

I nodded and Martin smiled, a soft glimmer of happiness he quickly nipped away. His concentration seemed to drift for a moment and then he snapped into focus again and picked up a biro he'd been fascinated with all day. He turned it in his hands like a treasure or a knife.

Which allows me to say that once he held my hand in exactly that way.

The next thing I remember is his touch of, his respect for my hand. The day he tried to tell me his name.

Behind the house we have a square of shabby grass, hemmed in by a peculiar choice of flowers. Arthur and Liz and Peter and I each have control of one of the available, hostile borders. We hoped this might encourage a healthy competition in displays, or at least a guilty standard of cultivation. It didn't.

Martin and I walked out to a couple of kitchen chairs he had firmed into our apologetic lawn. He wanted to tell me something in private and, although I felt hot and choked, rather tired, I thought it might do me good to go out in the sun. Caught between the garden wall, the house and two leggy hedges, Martin seemed to feel secure enough to be outside. So we sat, quiet together, while behind us Radio Four dripped down from Liz's window and a golf commentary with Arthur's supplementary remarks grumbled away from the direction of the sitting-room. Full house.

'Well, now I know.'

'Hmff. Sorry, Martin?' He was shading his face with one hand and staring intently at the sky, almost as if he was expecting something.

'Martin?'

'No. Not Martin. But I do know who else.'

'You're sure?'

'How would I not be sure? A person either knows who they are or does not – the former being the most usual. There is no intermediate position. Other than I must say that my favourite part of my name did arrive first and then the rest. Yes, you could call that intermediate. Yes . . .'

'And?'

'And I know now. Who I am.'

'Yes?'

'Yes.' He dropped his arm and closed his eyes, letting the light fall over his head as if it were water, but showed no sign of saying anything more.

'Well, hhafff, Martin I am glad that you know about yourself, but if you told me then I would know, too. Wouldn't I?'

'You really don't know? It didn't occur to you who I might be? Perhaps something you hadn't remembered? I did have a certain . . . once. Nothing? My face?'

'I really am sure I would know if we'd met before.'

'You don't recognise me otherwise?'

'Look, enough is enough. I'm not at my best today, can you just tell me who you are and then we'll get on because there are things I have to tell you about the house and if you're a friend of Peter's – '

45

'No. I've never met Peter. I've never met anyone. I am, I am . . . do you think Alexander would suit me?'

'Eh?'

He stood up and I watched him pace and turn on the grass, his hands, the shape of his head.

'Martin, this isn't a matter of choice, or what suits you. Just tell me, it can't be that bad.'

'Oh, it's not bad, it's beautiful. I can't think how I couldn't have recalled it before now. I only, I only . . . You may not understand.' Oddly quickly he came to the side of my chair and took my hand, just as if it were a weapon or a prize. I jumped slightly.

'Don't worry, I'm no one that matters. Apparently. I'm no one to be afraid of. I can now be definitive on that point. As far as you're concerned.'

'I'm not afraid. I'm just fine. Thank you.'

'Oh good, because all of this came to me only this morning and I am so pleased.' He pressed my fingers between his. 'So now you will know me. Someone in this world will know me.' Then he dropped my hand, stood neatly in front of me, arms at his sides and weight on his toes. He looked at me as if he would speak but seemed to catch sight of something along the horizon before he could. He lifted his face to meet it with a small expression of gentle surprise and fell straight back, like fallen masonry – a dead weight landing with one leg a little bent.

WHAT I SEE now is Martin's face, his sleeping face, heavily set in a shallow slope of pillows. The small rise of his chin and the softness beneath his jaw. That's how I know he will be, at rest in the moment while I have to wait with all my attention on Arthur's voice.

'He has scars. Fucking horrible scars.'

'Scars?'

'Mm hm. But not from just now, they look old. One down from his shoulder, as if someone just decided to hack him with something, and the other one, in his chest, it's – I don't know what. I can't think of anything that would leave a mark like that. Except some sort of bloody shotgun. He must have had a bad time once. No wonder he's . . . the way he is.'

I had panicked when Martin collapsed and yelled for help. Arthur was extremely capable, checked for all the airway and circulation things and was very definite that nothing much had happened. I hadn't seen our Arthur as the first-aiding type, but then Martin had the knack of bringing out unforeseen details in almost anyone.

He had, of course, been less forthcoming with his name. And even that is on its way, incidents are aligning themselves, time is falling into place and soon you will know him very much in the way that I did. Forgive me for the delay. I should be able to tell you who he was without any trouble at all. I don't know why it makes me so uneasy to think of giving his secret away to you. Perhaps, because we had a certain privacy together, I am a little jealous with him now.

But I can, with a clear conscience, say that Arthur and I carried Martin upstairs after he fell in the garden and then I left them to do man putting another man to bed things. Liz had been making a phone call and had missed all but the last of the excitement. So, naturally enough, it was nurse Arthur who brought us the news of Martin's scars.

'How is he, though? Has he come round?'

'Oh, yes. He was just a bit dozy. I'll go up and see how he is in a while, but I think he'll just sleep now. He seemed exhausted. What's he been doing?'

'How would I know?'

Liz wandered in from the kitchen.

'Would you like a nourishing cup of tea, or whatever it is they have in crises?'

'Yes, thanks.'

'Mmm. Or hot water. Bad throat.'

Liz leaned in the doorway. 'I don't know. We always end up with them, don't we? I mean how long has he been here – nearly a fortnight and he's either loitering mysteriously or flaking out. I told Jen to talk to him.'

'I was going to but then he passed out. And why is he suddenly my responsibility? I don't know anything more about him than you do.' It hurt my voice so much to say that, my eyes watered.

'He's a soldier.'

'What?'

Arthur nodded sagely. 'He told me. I was helping him off with his stuff and he noticed me noticing the scars. He was in the army for a bit.'

'Any particular army?'

'Just the army, that's all he said. Oh, and he wanted to apologise to you, in case he'd given you a fright.'

'Mmm.'

'Nice of him, eh?'

'What do you mean?'

'Nothing.'

Liz sidled out of the line of fire. 'I'll just slip out and make that tea.'

'I don't mean anything. Except that it's probably good he thinks you're his friend. He seems a lonely bugger. He's obviously got rotten taste, but I suppose if you're desperate for someone to talk to . . .'

'God, I love living here sometimes, it's such a nourishing environment for my self esteem. Oh shit, I am losing my voice, it is really fucking going. Shit.'

'You know you like it here really.'

'That's what worries me.'

And all of that occupied most of a summer Sunday, making us creep round the house for fear of disturbing the sleeper upstairs as the blue of a long dusk slowly extended into night. Full dark had almost fallen when I went up to check on Martin, see if he wanted anything, say hello. It seemed to me that I should know how he was before I went out to work.

'Yes, come in please.'

The room was as Peter had left it, almost bare. The table lamp filled its corners with shadow and it echoed rather sadly. Martin's presence was signalled only by a neat pile of clothes on the single chair and even the clothes were Peter's. Martin himself sat up in bed, bundled into one of Arthur's pyjama jackets. A little cut close to his ear showed a ferocious red against skin which was almost translucently pale. He always was clumsy at shaving.

'Forgive me for being in this position, it is embarrassing. Perhaps you would like to sit. My clothes you could put on that coffer over there.'

His voice seemed lost in the physics of the room, baffled by bad acoustics.

'So I will talk to you, after my theatricality of this afternoon. For which you have all my apologies.'

'That's all right.'

I'm sure I said 'That's all right' or something to that effect. It was my intention to be reassuring, a calming influence for the patient, and so I am sure I said reassuring things, but I couldn't concentrate, not on him. I was distracted by the way he looked.

You see, I would rather not be in a bedroom where someone is lying in bed. I would rather not be near that picture because I know that when I do I will always see my mother, see my father, see most particularly Steven of all those who came after them. They will be there, each one of the people who ever came close, all lying with their hands above the covers and staring up into my face through the depth of the years, through the depth of my life.

I felt myself listen to Martin while my mind saw Steven, Steven who would do anything I asked. I don't think there are many things more terrible than having someone do that, day after day. It can turn your head.

'Please.'

'Please what? Why are you standing there, what do you want?'

'Please.'

'Steven, no.'

'Please.'

'You know what it would mean if I did it. You know what it would mean. You can't really need this to happen.'

'I do. Look. I do.'

'Get up.'

'No.'

'All right, then. Very well, very well. Then you stay down. But all the way down, I don't want to see your face.'

'Jennifer?'

'What now?'

'Thanks.'

Steve was impeccably polite – always ready with a please or a thank you – and all of that happened too often and then happened again. I felt tired. Impossibly tired. First thing, last thing, day-long, night-short weary. Not the appropriate emotion, I know, but the only one I could muster with any kind of consistency.

He would wake me before dawn, clinging.

'I have to go.'

'What?'

'I have to go now.'

'What time is it?'

'I don't know. Three o'clock, four o'clock. I have to go, don't you understand?'

'No, I . . . Four o'clock in the morning? Couldn't you go in a while, it's very early. Do you have to be some-where?'

'I have to leave. It doesn't matter when. I have to leave and not come back.'

'At least wait until I'm awake, I don't know what you're saying here. Why? I mean, what are you trying to say. Tell me why you want to go. And turn the light on.'

'Why? You know why. You've been telling me why. I don't . . . there's nothing more I can do for you.'

'Look, turn the fucking light on. What do you mean there's nothing more you can do for me? Ow, God that's bright. Now, you're saying things I've never said and it's the middle of the night and I'm barely awake and that's no bad thing because I should be sleeping. You know I hate to miss my sleep.'

'Something else I do that doesn't please you. Well I won't disturb you any more. Just let me go now and I'll get my things later.'

'All right, look . . . tell me what's really the matter. I'm listening. If that's what you wanted, you've got it. You have my complete attention. Tell me.'

'You know I would do anything for you.'

'I know that. I always know that. You always say that.

I would know that in the morning, too. It's late now, be sensible, please.'

'What else do you want me to do?'

'Nothing else.'

'That's what I thought. Goodbye, then.'

'Whoa, wait. There's nothing else just now. There doesn't always have to be something you have to do. Sometimes we'll be resting, surely and being ourselves. Sometimes we can relax.'

'Do you love me?'

'Yes, I'm sure.'

'Do you?'

'Yes, undoubtedly. That's the way I would say it. Will you come to sleep now.'

'I love you.'

'I know you do, you've told me. I know.'

Yes, indeedy, I knew. In fact that was everything I could think of, lying in bed and waiting for that other body to lie along next to mine, the dip and the sigh and then the fumbling of that. I could hear myself thinking, 'Yes, Steven loves me. Steven loves me, this I know.' I stared at the nothing which in daylight was my room and knew that he would probably never really go. If he loved me this much it was almost certain he would never, ever just go away and leave me be.

Well, what did you think? I gave up sex because that suddenly seemed like a good idea? I woke up one morning, exclaiming, 'Hmm, think I'll be celibate for ever and ever, just to see what it's like.'?

No, you didn't think that. You didn't know because I hadn't told you, that's all. I should not make assumptions on your behalf.

'Jennifer, you are uncomfortable? Or distracted. I can't think I am being tedious, because I am not a tedious person. Are you quite well?'

Martin massaged the slightly jowly skin under his jaw

with one hand. He grinned with his eyes. I tried to ignore the bed around him, to concentrate.

'I'm sorry, I was thinking of something else. It was rude of me. I did want to know if you were well.'

'I know, I share your interest. So we will both be relieved to know that my collapse is very easily explained. If a man does not sleep, he will eventually be forced into (at the very least) a sleeping position. I was afraid to be unconscious. In case it made me go away again. Forgive me.'

'Nothing to forgive.'

'I know that also. I never ask to be forgiven unless I have done no wrong. This gives us both the benefit of forgiveness without the inconvenience of harm. But now I do need to talk with you.'

Something in his tone of voice set up a cold little splash of nervous reaction tight under my heart, but I didn't think about it. I simply saw my chance to get in first with a few important points of my own.

'Talk. I'm listening. But before you say anything, I think you ought to know some stuff I've been meaning to tell you – all the things that Liz and Arthur have been asking me to tell you. Martin, your rent is expected and there will be bills to pay and maybe the real Martin will turn up. I don't know why he hasn't already. And it's high time Peter dropped us a line, what if he mentions something he shouldn't about the man who isn't you? I mean, I'm sorry, but this is very complicated. Now that you're starting to remember things, there are – '

Martin was sitting, eyes shut, head forward, all very closed and still, except for the tears. I watched and he cried without any sound other than the snagging rhythm of his breath. He wept and the slow sheen of his weeping quietly covered his face.

If I had said the wrong thing at the wrong time there was no way to unsay it. If I had been insensitive, it was only because I *was* insensitive. I meant him no harm. I suddenly wanted to say that I meant him no harm.

Slowly, he tipped back his head in the pillows, opened the soft dark of his mouth and let nothing out. I could perhaps have understood him, if he had shouted or spoken or sighed, but he only held still, in a kind of inaccessible, sculptural pain. He was gradually illuminated by the action of the air, a dark shine beginning in his throat and I knew again, freshly, that I had no idea of where he came from, of who or what he was. I waited until I might know what I could do and envied him a little for his passion which reminded me of something I couldn't quite place. We paused, both silent and together, for some time.

'Martin, Martin? Can I help you?' He opened his eyes. 'It's all difficult just now – seems that way – but it needn't be, I'm sure. Something. We'll do something.' He coughed. 'Are you ill?'

'No. I think I am not. I wish I were ill.'

'You'll have to help me with that, I don't know what you mean.'

'I have a number of choices I can make. Now I really do apologise for this.' He waved his hands over himself, as if he had become a problem, something to motion away. 'Perhaps I am too tired to be capable of thinking.'

'Try and see.'

'I have been trying!'

Even as he was shouting his hands were signalling, dispersing any offence, lifting in surrender.

'I am sorry. I feel too much alone and when I am alone, I am afraid and more than a little impatient. I have been trying to think, do believe me. And I have a number of choices. Either I am mad or in some other way very ill and disturbed, or I am dead.'

'Dead? You mean when you were hurt?'

'Hurt?'

'The . . . the scars. I'm sorry, Arthur mentioned . . .'

'Scars? Oh . . . oh no, I remember that. When those

happened.' He almost smiled. 'At least I believe I remember that – you see?' He slapped at his forehead. 'If I can remember and what I remember is true, then I was injured as part of the business of a war (two little disagreements with arms) and I would rather this never happened again, but I didn't die then, that didn't kill me. My difficulty is the time, I mean time . . . time must have moved . . . Where have I been for all of this time? Where have I been?'

He seemed at the edge of something again, his mouth moving uncertainly, but he swallowed, rubbed at his cheeks with both hands. Turning quickly to peer at one corner of the room and then at me. 'Do you know, I wanted to live to be a hundred? It seemed a very neat, a very memorable number. I don't look to be a hundred, though, do I?'

'No.'

'How old, then?'

'I don't know, I'm bad at ages. Maybe forty.'

'Not even that. Actually. Tell me, so that I can see if I am sane. If I begin at the very beginning to ask you where I am. This is the Earth, yes? This planet?'

'Yes.'

'This is a globe which revolves on its axis once every day of twenty-four hours and also each year makes a circuit of the sun.'

'Yes.'

'Accepted knowledge? Fact?'

'Yes.'

'Oh, good.' He seemed a touch disappointed that his information had come as no surprise. 'No argument there.

'We are in Europe?'

'That's a matter of opinion, but geographically speaking, yes.'

'And we are how many years after the death of Christ at this point?'

He avoided my eyes.

'One thousand, nine hundred and ninety-three.'

'One thousand nine hundred and ninety-three. And the calendar is?'

'The calendar.'

'What kind of calendar? Has it been changed?'

'No, not for . . . I don't know. Hundreds of years. I can't remember, it's named after a Pope.'

'Naturally. Unmarried women, prisoners and popes – always have an interest in time. But which Pope? Julian? Gregory? Who?'

'Well, he sounds familiar. I mean, I really don't know, but we've been using this one for ages.'

'Then I am the loneliest man in the world.'

Which is the perfect place to end this section because it looks so conclusive on the page. Except that we didn't finish there, we kept on, two unfictional people speaking in the emptiness of a small room. If I could, I would write his voice so that you could feel it the way I did, dark and simple. Also good, very pleasant to hear – except for the chill of confusion under it that left him speaking from somewhere I couldn't touch.

'I have no one now.'

'Don't say that.'

'Believe me I would rather not, but spoken out, it sounds much less terrible than it does here in my mind. These are thoughts I do not wish to be alone with. I am out of my time or out of my mind, which seems such a simple choice, but I cannot make it. Tell me, did you enjoy when you were a child?'

'Oh, I . . . parts of it.'

'Yes. I can always recognise another – another partly happy child. I enjoyed parts of my childhood also. Do you know what I thought of this morning? No, of course you don't, I am inviting you to be with me in this, not really asking a question.'

'I know. I'm with you.'

'I'm glad. I am glad of that.' He snatched a look at me to underline his meaning. 'Well, I watched the sun move across these boards here on the floor this morning. I watched dawn opening and then the movement of the light. And I remembered sunlight hanging in a plum tree, caught in round little yellow plums, making them shine like liquid.

'Then I am out in the gold of the sun and running along a path away from water. The path is made of big, hot stones and passes a wooden door with a huge lock in it and eyes. Mmm, oh yes, I see a door with eyes. Someone has cut them, up high in the wood, sad sloping-down eyes, black. If I was tall enough I could see through them into the black space beyond, but I can't, I can only look up at them, looking down at me. I was always afraid of the eyes in the door. It was the only bad thing in all of that place. I would – bouaff – kick it when I ran past, being brave. I was a very brave boy, always. The way you can be brave if you're used to getting only partly happy and very afraid. You have good intervals in your past like this?'

'I suppose.'

'No, you must know.'

'All right then, yes I do.'

'But are you sure they ever happened? Are you sure?'

'I think so.'

'You see, I don't want to be sure. I would rather have lost my past. I wish it was gone. Can I ask you an unusual question?'

'Well, why not, it's been that kind of day.'

'Do you believe in heresy?'

'Believe in it? Seriously?'

'Yes.'

'I'm not even sure that I know what it means. In fact I don't.'

'That you go against God. That it is possible for a person to offend God. Heresy.'

'You weren't ever a priest, were you?'

'Ha! No, no I was . . . hardly that. I think you could say that I had a certain difficulty with belief. I have always found it hard to believe in most things. For example, my own existence appears very unlikely to me at the moment. But I did think I was with God, I never thought I was alone or against . . . not against. How can a person be against God. I am such a small thing in the universe, I can't think I could be a disturbance at any significant point. It would be like a moth offending a mountain: ridiculous.'

'I'm sure.'

'To let you understand at least a little, I can say that I was a soldier for some time. Yes? Arthur told you, I thought he would. Well, on the edge of a battle, in that thick, heavy waiting when you watch for tiny signs to tell you what will happen and such and such a buckle must be fastened in the right way, the right order, fitted with all the other orders and habits and words that meant you didn't die the last time. It's a very secret place, to be with men there, their lives burning away into moments. They are all here and now and love and quiet. In that place, I would pray. Or, rather, a friend of mine would pray and I would listen.

'I would believe him absolutely. He told me:

' "We make our allegiance to the Kingdom of God. We are soldiers of the regiments of the Kingdom of God and our lives are of those regiments and no others. We may never betray God's Kingdom or commit any treason against it for the sole amend of treason is death, the death of our souls. Our souls are soldiers in the regiments of God. We are of God and with God and God must surely keep us for we are true."

'I can feel myself kneeling in the grass with my hands holding other men's hands and all of us holding those words. A sour wind would rise from another world and blow in about our faces and we would shiver, kiss, embrace, walk away and be ready to kill other men.

'Sometimes I would say the prayer in my head to myself, or I would make poems. Right in the thickened red heart of siege, there is nothing like a poem for giving light, a pleasant kind of transportation, freedom. But now I don't know about freedom, certainly about freedom from death which it was my intention to cultivate. I didn't die then. I believed it was a good thing that I didn't die. Now – '

He let his eyelids fall, exhaled, 'I am sorry, I have a terrible ache in my head.'

Which made me know what I should do. When somebody has a headache, I know what to do. You walk up and cup your hand at the back of their neck and you feel the heat of their blood under their skin and you support them. Tell them to close their eyes. Tell them not to speak. Hold them. Press at the forehead and temples with no more than your fingertips. Watch their face clear and empty. I've done that for a lot of people, my mother taught me how. It's easy and emotionally neutral, doesn't mean a thing.

'Thank you.'

'Sssh.'

'Why do you think I am here?'

'Sssh. I don't know. But you need to go to sleep. I let you talk too long. We'll sort things out in the morning. No, don't say anything.'

He swallowed and smiled and slowly said, 'I would only like to say that I do believe that God still keeps me, because I was true. I was Savinien de Cyrano de Bergerac and I was true.'

So, there you are. I was the first one he told it and now I've told you. Savinien de Cyrano de Bergerac. Odd name. A big name – literally big on any page and enlarged by familiarity and a certain kind of popular use. I must say I didn't quite know what he meant by using it. I didn't quite understand. I intended to ask him if he'd mind repeating what he'd said, but he was drifting out to sleep, already beyond me. I rubbed my throat and swallowed, looked down at his sleeping face, heavy in the shallow slope of pillows. I moved my hands away from him, from the delineation of his forehead, from the familiar pattern formed out from his particular bones and I made sure that I didn't disturb him.

When I drew the door closed behind me, left him alone, I felt a peculiar constriction in my chest. Even as I prepared myself for work, swallowed the last of my soluble pills, there was an unfamiliar tightness keeping snug under my scarf. I blew my nose. It didn't help.

AT WORK IT was quiet, it always is. I sat at a felted table, in a muffled room defended by two sets of double doors. The doors at work are smooth and heavy and peel softly away from their frames, they are impossible to rush through or fluster. Nothing disturbs the heart of the station, nothing you can hear, in any case.

Every thirty minutes, I was required to tell a fat, black goosenecked microphone about traffic irregularities, mutilated children, the wreckage of peace in Europe and the weather. I felt the syllables warm and open against my teeth, I licked and pushed and breathed them, kissed them goodbye. It was almost moving, even with a crippled throat.

But in the intervals between? I sipped on my thermos of honey and lemon and thought of the night that carried my voice. Potentially I was going with it everywhere, through walls and under buildings, into all the little corners of my city and several more beyond. Very few people were actually listening of course – other back-shifty workers, the taxi-cruising, night-watching types, professional seducers and policemen, the lone insomniacs.

Whenever I spoke I had the insomniacs particularly in mind. I would tell them, and really only them, if it was raining or if anyone special was dead and I would once again wonder how many hundreds or thousands of them had masturbated themselves into compromise relaxation, coincidentally listening to my voice. Nice to be of service.

A caring female sort of woman once shared with me how she had learned to appreciate herself as a caring female sort of woman by discovering her own body. By this I take it she meant showing her own body a good time, rather then waking up screaming one morning, shocked by the unmapped expanses of her, for example, inner thigh.

I think she hoped, in a kindly but evangelical way, to encourage me into exploring and discovering Good Times of my very, very own. This would, eventually, turn me into a caring female sort of woman, too. Or not.

Hoping to appear quite caring already I thanked her for her concern and smiled a lot. I nodded. She smiled. I didn't tell her that myself and I already knew how to get out the good times and roll. And as it happened we hadn't found this liberating, or an unalloyed joy. We didn't like to be the only people who genuinely knew which was what in the technical sense. We were even slightly sad that we couldn't be sure why this was – if we were the only ones we trusted, or the only ones ruthless enough to really get things done – either way, we made us lonely. There was no romance about us. We didn't send flowers, we never phoned, we made it abundantly clear we were only with us because we were all we'd got. The minute that anyone better came by we'd be off – no tears, no goodbye dinner, not even a note. We did not improve our self esteem.

It's remarkable what you can think of while your mouth is saying something else. I find that's shaken the last of my faith in conversation as anything other than sleight of tongue. But I don't doubt the words, never the endless, unappreciated fact of the words. I perched in front of my microphone that night and, through in the booth, my voice flicked over needle dials, stacked and dissolved the lighted blocks of graphic sound displays. This is the only place in the whole wide world where everything moves according to my breath. Just now and then I like to have that much power. To see how it feels.

And of course the power is relative – I have no say in what I say or even how I say it. I spent the first hours of the morning in another soundtight room filling its aeroplane-quality air with precisely the prescribed number of seconds on a private health care scheme. The job was less than delightful. I was very tired and almost hoarse, intermittently deafened by the miseries going on in my nose and throat, but still doggedly trying to edge out the caring female sort of womanly tone I had been asked for.

'Light but warm. You want us to share the good news.'

'Good news, for only a moderate outlay you can buy the peace of mind a welfare state would probably provide if our national priorities were not entirely fucked.'

'Save your voice. That was about the tone, though. Apart from the words.'

'Isn't this what we pay our taxes for, though? Or have I completely lost the place. This isn't even insidious, it's barefaced trading on fear. Protection money.'

'Could we just get this over with.'

'Of course, of course. I do understand the principle – nobody appreciates what isn't paid for. If our unsolicited lives are given to us free, we won't ever learn what they're worth so it's perfectly reasonable that we should pay for their healthy continuance. We should always have paid – fancy getting away with it for so long.'

'There's the painkiller still to do.'

'Any free samples.'

'Starting on my signal, light and warm.'

'Okay, Steve.'

Yes, Steve. The same Steve – the same Steven – the one that I used to know better than I do now. For a while he worked in the station, sometimes with me. God has a funny sense of humour. In a way, I even helped him get the job. (That's Steven, not God.) He wasn't interested in radio until I met him and then he got very keen. I encouraged him. (Also Steven, not God.) Something like a year had passed since we'd split up and then there he was in the studio one morning, quite at home and ready to record. (Once again Steven and not God. I'd split up with God a long, long time before.)

Which is what I thought while I closed my eyes and then lightly and warmly recommended the low cost of good health and mental wellbeing. For only a small additional fee, my listeners could safeguard their teeth and eyesight and have children, all of their own and delivered at source.

The painkillers were even more reassuring and also sexy. There was just a suggestion of 'Yes, tonight dear, I've got a headache.' Which would have suited Steven right down and on to the ground. I could be as husky as I liked for the public's benefit, but what would make Steven's motor run wouldn't be me, it would be thinking of possible pain.

Each to his own, of course, and there's nothing like a touch of fantasy, a ritualistic element to stave off that nasty old sexual ennui. Pain was an interest Steven had before I met him, but I will admit, I did encourage him. I was a very encouraging partner, all round. It made him happy to be hurt so I made him a game to be hurt in. We played at Captain Bligh, 'Very well, sir, you shall kiss the gunner's daughter.' Snibbed together close in the dark we were Captain Bligh almighty and the Stupid Sailor and it was fine fun. At first it was fine – all salty and striking and fierce. I had no objections to my part and Steve, my hapless seaman, my gladly unfortunate pun, was nothing if not happy and if he was happy then, my goodness, I was happy, too.

No. I was happy anyway. Steven enjoyed himself, he got what he asked for and more, but I was happy anyway. He'd let me into somewhere I hadn't found before, a compensation for other less satisfying areas of our relation- ship. After all, I could never have done on my own what I did with him. Only politicians are able to sit by them- selves and still make other people hurt.

Of course, these things are not quite as manageable as

they might at first appear. In the end, our situation was far from ideal. Our roles had developed a life of their own, far more intimate than anything we could achieve without them. I worried we might damage each other permanently somehow and so we ended, winding the whole thing down to the ultimate cliché – the one where the masochist waits and trembles, at the absolute mercy of the sadist.

'Hit me, then. Go on, hit me.'

'No.'

So the irony of my position as I purred about paracetamol and instantaneous relief did not escape me, but the job is the job is the job and it has to be done.

'Thanks then, Jennifer. That last one was fine. Lucy will call you when they have some more.'

We were nothing if not professional, no involuntary body language, no casual meeting of eyes. I only noticed how tired I was as I walked out to the bus stop. My spine felt compressed, tender, and I was reminded again what an effort it takes to sustain a convincing indifference.

Now what I should have done then was to come home and go straight to bed. That would have been sensible. I had gone through a more than averagely disturbing day, but for someone like me, a calm person, that really needn't have had any great effect. I should not have done anything out of the ordinary, out of character, but I did.

I'm trying to say that I don't understand what happened next. But then, why should I? My life had always been fairly incomprehensible, why should it change for the better that morning, why not for the worse? I didn't understand my father or my mother. I didn't understand my country, its past, its present, its future, its means of government or the sense of its national anthem and flag. When I was young I didn't understand the other children and the adults were just as bad. Then I became an adult and nothing had changed. I didn't understand Steven, or anyone else of my intimate acquaintance, up to and of course including me. I never did really understand me.

Still, it's nothing to get upset over, is it? This frightening lack of comprehension is balanced by a wonderful absence of fear and on I go, just as capably as many more apparently normal people do. So at the faint blue beginning of that particular day, I travelled perfectly predictably from the station to the bus stop, to the bottom of our street, to our house and up and in.

I remembered I had to be quiet, with everyone home and sleeping, and snugged the door behind me against the few experimental chirps and bronchitic engines of our city's dawn. The lock slapped back in place, I took off my shoes and creaked gently up the stairs. End of a tough day for little old me, not feeling well, feverish and light-headed and I should be going right to bed but I'm not. I go into Martin's room instead.

He's there, not actually sleeping, but not entirely awake. He is sitting up and staring at the thin pewter light from his window curtain. I watch while he yawns like a puppy, damp-eyed, and pats at the side of his bed with one hand. This is a gesture I have not seen in years, but I know exactly what it means and am already walking towards him.

'Is it the morning, Jennifer?'

I am ready, leaning in to hear him because I know that he will whisper. Only whispering will suit us now, because we are exchanging secrets at the outset of our day.

'Yes, it's morning.'

'Good. Good morning, Jennifer.'

'Good morning. Whoever you are. It's very early. You should be asleep.'

'Certainly. But you have something to tell me, I think.'

'Yes, I do. I would like.'

'You would?'

The words were sticking in my chest for some reason, they weren't making it all the way up and through to my mouth. It was ridiculous to be nervous, so I felt ridiculous. Probably that's what I felt.

'Hum, I would like you not to worry.'

He curled his forefinger against his lips for a moment. 'Not to worry. I would also like me not to worry, but it does present a method of occupying time, when one is utterly powerless.'

'I know it doesn't sound very sympathetic, or constructive. I just would like you not to worry. And I will do things to help you not to. I will take care of, well, of some of the problems.'

'You need not.'

'I know.'

'I haven't asked you to do anything for me.'

'I know.'

'Which is an excellent way to encourage unsolicited assistance, but this is not why I have not asked.'

'That's fine. I don't really mind, either way. I think I have to go to sleep now.'

'I would agree. So we will both sleep and not cause ourselves any worry because we will both be asleep and what harm can we come to in our sleep.'

I found it oddly hard to resent the tiny white spots of fatigue that were firing away in grand style at the backs of my eyes – the way they like to. I nodded and was moving to go when Martin took my hand, lifted it to his mouth. 'Thank you for all your attentions.'

Back out in the dark of the corridor, the print of his lips shone very slightly along my fingers, and disappeared gently as I sat in my bedroom, unbuttoning my blouse.

AND NOW WE'LL leave me there for a while. Nothing too much will happen while we're away. I will rest and become more ill and then much better. I will sleep and be afraid to swallow and then sleep again and be visited by a doctor as if he were also in my sleep. I will be told, I think by the doctor, but maybe by Arthur, that I will neither die nor go to work for a week because I have been given a certificate to that effect. More importantly I have an officially recognised abscess on my tonsil which means I must take several daily pills. I will do this and be cured. I will move from being sick to being not sick in the most clear and beautifully comprehensible way. For one whole day I will be happy just to be well. Then because I am not only well but also human, I will forget how good this is and life will become less fresh, but much more normal.

This chapter will roll its way forward in other times and places and, when I feel ambulant, I will abandon my room and go roaming about downstairs. I will see that the kitchen has survived without me – it is perhaps cleaner than normal. Slightly disappointed that I am so domestic-ally dispensable I will spend almost a week about the house with Liz in Cornwall for no good reason at all, Arthur working his strange shifts at the bakery and Martin who isn't Martin. Martin who isn't Martin doesn't go out, he stays and speaks to me. He has barely said a word to anyone since I fell ill and now he is making up for lost time, for lost years, for a whole lost lifetime of conver-sations. He is talking his world into existence and I am listening because I have very little else to do. I risk a few expeditions to the garage for milk and crisps, and I listen to Martin who isn't Martin and I am quiet with Martin who isn't Martin and I find I am almost constantly in the company of a person who is not me. Not such a terrible thing, I know, but very unusual in my life.

All of that talking and medication will swill about together in my head, but first I must have a fever. I have banked myself up on a wedge of pillows because I feel that if I lie flat I will choke and drown and that fever is rising close now, rocking and twirling at the brain. It waits until I'm drowsy to come right in. It gives me the clear idea that I am not in bed and sitting up for important reasons that I have misplaced. Or perhaps I am in my bed, but without the familiar room around it for important reasons I have misplaced. I should find all those reasons. Or at times I feel somebody looking at me, the feel of their looking is green and the same as a headache only longer.

I do not, to be honest, hallucinate in a full-blown way, but my dreams go roaring and crawling all night and on into the day. They are unstoppable and include in their florid procession an atmosphere I knew a long time ago. It passes through me and I shiver from a hot sweat to a cold.

Do you remember that little movement Martin made a while ago? He patted the side of his bed with one hand, just his palm landing lightly on the coverlet, two or three times. Well, something very like that happened quite often when I was much younger. Thirty years much younger, even a touch more than that. Remembering made me think and brought on that old atmosphere.

Now this section, you needn't read or really bother with. It won't add to your understanding of the book, or of the story it's trying to tell. Here is where I'll put something down that's for me, a corner of all this writing which is only mine and not a confidence I'm going to offer, not part of my calculations. I really would like to say what I have here to say.

I would like to take a part of my past in the past and set it down so it will stay. I will let it go from me and keep this record here because I wish to. Here I will see and understand this thing and then I will put it down. This is heavy and has come too far with me already and now I am tired and I am going to put it down.

Here.

I am behind the white door, my parents' white door, which has the china handle and that door is shut. We are all together in the one room, my father and my mother and me. I watch.

Pat, pat, the hand at the side of the bed. Come closer, stand here, sit down and be so near to us you will breathe our smell.

They had a mad kind of seaside and eggwhite smell that made me sick. I would taste it when it wasn't there.

I have forgotten how we began to be the way we were. It may be that I never knew, that plans were perfected before I could catch a trace of them and that I moved within them, never aware until the room was opened and I was taken in.

She was my father's second wife. Definitely my mother, the only one I'd known, but his second wife. I don't know if that was important, a determining factor, or not. I think that he loved her. I think that I did, too.

There was, of course, a time when I knew that something was wrong. A time to decide that no one should ever come home with me. I had started at a school by this time – the way that children are supposed to do – and it was accepted that school friends would visit each other at their homes – your invitation would follow theirs and vice versa. Before I had fully considered why, I knew that friends should be avoided, that no one should get in and see us, find us out. And friends are not so difficult to make, it took a good deal of work to escape having even one. Later I thanked myself for my efforts – they earned me a great deal of peace. I believe I have always liked peace.

Christmas was the first time, I'm almost sure of it, because the whole proceedings were presented as if they were an extra present, something saved for Boxing Day.

They called me, they made me laugh and run up the stairs. I was out of breath when I stopped running, the blood knocking in my ears and I had fear all over me. Not just the pitch in the stomach – that had happened before because children are always afraid, they don't know enough not to be – this was prickled down the side of my face, crawling at the backs of my legs. It was a kind of horror, moving on me.

I didn't understand it, naturally, not for a couple of years. I was frightened by their shapes and their colour and most of all by their noise, my mother's noise. I thought she was hurting.

Sometimes he would be hurt, too. All I did was watch. I knew, when they looked at me, that they couldn't tell how I was inside, unless I showed them. They were trying to see what I thought, but I didn't let them and once they were really started they had no interest in me. I was left alone.

Outside their room I was generally safe, unless they gave me those looks, or asked me questions. But they could be too keen on occasions, too anxious to be at each other, I would find them in other places. Which was how they made my house unsafe. Their gritted teeth, their damp faces, inquisitive eyes – there they would be, in ambush.

I can only suppose they may have needed me to be there, wanted me, but I didn't know that then. They did what they did for their own, closed reasons and I waited at the end of it every time, wishing they wouldn't come round, wouldn't move again. I wanted stillness and no voice to tell me, 'Go on now, go away.' No voice.

There is a little of myself I may have left there. If I

could reach back and get it, let myself out, I would do it. I would tell me that it was all right now because they both were a long time gone. I'm safe. There is nothing that can tie me to any of those days and hours but my mind and my mind is my friend. I am the best friend I ever could have in the big, broad world. I look after me now and am careful to know what could and could not be my fault. Naturally, I am sorry for my past. I let myself down there, was not on the ball, but I don't blame me too much for that. It most likely wasn't my fault.

Not anyone's fault, in fact, just some of the stuff that families do – certainly not the worst I've heard about. Except that it happened to me and so is, evidently, the worst that I have known. But any after-effects have been minimal. I'll get a twinge of recognition when I come across an over-familiar gesture or an unlucky order of words. And if we ever had to share a house, Lord knows I would respect your privacy as much as I humanly could, but never make love so loudly I can hear you. I don't like that. That makes me play music and slam doors and do things inimical to a mood of undisturbed romance. Which is why Liz spends most of her love-life elsewhere, even leaving us when she is here through extensive nocturnal abuse of our telephone. Arthur, on the other hand, is easily quiet about sex, very physical and liniment-smelling in other ways, but quiet about truly entering into sex. I sometimes think he would rather eat or lift a weight than fuck and I personally can't say that I find his decision in any way strange. But then I wouldn't, would I?

Talking of our household, I think we'll go back to it. Intermission over and we have reached the point where I am all better and taking two baths a day to soak the smell of illness out of my skin. My voice is back, unscathed, or perhaps even improved by its little rest and if Martin was talking the clock round, I must admit, I wasn't far behind him.

We paced out circuits of the garden, exclaiming on

its walls and earth, its fifteen overbalanced antirrhinums. There was more than enough time to count them. We noticed how tree leaves, generally speaking, were in colours complementary to the sky. Along the passages of our house and through the kitchen, at any step on the stairs, we could find ourselves overwhelmed by a fresh sentence and glad that we had someone handy to hear it out. We did not even need to be together – from anywhere to anywhere we could shout. We made the place ring.

This expanded our small-talk, but left it essentially unchanged. Small. No souls were unburdened, no levels of communication were plumbed and breached. We didn't touch. I would have noticed if we did. And we didn't. Still, there was something going on.

I think it took three days, or four, and then we hit Friday, the day before I would have to go back to work. Friday in the morning.

'Jesus loves the Eskimos,
English and Arapahos,
Pigmentation is no bar,
He loves us for what we are.'

'Is that you off, then?'

Arthur grinds his way through a round of black toast while tying his shoes. He goes to stand over the sink and brush the crumbs from his sweater, wash his hands.

'No, this is me just in. Three hours off and then it's back to the hot-plate. I think I'm going to jack it in soon. Before I become unable to talk to anything but scones. And front of the shop Mary. The way she rings up that till can make you hallucinate.'

'At the very least.'

'She dresses all in that dark blue with the little apron and the name tag. Like a confectionery nurse. I've started having dreams where I cover her with floury handprints. And I don't even like her. We don't speak. Except for 'Any more scones there, Arthur?' She doesn't even say that nicely.'

'I'd never really seen you as the baker type.'

'Well I'm mad as a baker.'

'Mad as a hatter.'

'No, mad as a baker. I'd have to be. I am going to pack it in soon, though. A couple of people want murals for their kid's bedrooms. I might have another go at doing that – see if I can keep the orders going this time. I thought two velociraptors disembowelling a ninja turtle might be the thing. Or Bambi kicking hell out of a psycho android.'

'For infants, is it?'

'Mm, you're right. Bambi shagging Thumper and Barbie knocking hell out of Ken.'

'Sounds great.'

'Maybe if I went back to driving the cabs.'

I usually enjoy Arthur's company – he is comfortable to have around, non-abrasive. But I want him to go away this morning. I want him to leave me alone, or to leave us alone – me and Martin de Bergerac.

'Oh, and my mum said she got a spirit message for me from my Auntie Bet.'

'Uh huh?'

'Yes. Said she'd had a definite presentiment that I was about to become superstitious.'

'Mm. And I hear gullible's being removed from the dictionary this week.'

'Really? Gosh.'

'That's my boy. Go on to work now.'

'Okay. And glad to see you looking better, by the way.'

'Thanks.'

'How's Martin?'

'Fine.'

'I see he left the money for his rent.'

'Yes.'

'Quiet type.'

'Yes.'

'Aren't we all, though. Today I shall construct a monster out of scone. The perfect man.'

'Self-raising, you mean?'

'Sssh. The sweetness of treacle, the brain of a raisin and the strength of a potato. They said I was mad, you know. Mad. See you later.'

He goes and I realise what's happened. For some reason, certainty has fallen into place. I could literally feel the idea drop and just run down the back of my neck, close to the spine which is always the sign of quality thinking for me. I understand. Whatever I choose to call him, I'm getting used to Martin. I am starting to see being with him as an activity in itself, one for which I need no other company. I wouldn't put it any more strongly than that, there are no specific emotions involved, but I undoubtedly like him being in our house. I like that whole experience enough to be paying his rent. Cash.

(Which I knew was a short-term solution to a long-term problem, but it seemed the best move I could make, all the same.)

And it is still Friday and each of those end of the week heavy minutes are chaining together and hauling in the rest of the morning, all under a dingy sky. It will probably rain later.

'Good morning, Jennifer.'

I can see in Martin's face that the tide has turned. We won't talk about nothing today, we are going to speak to each other and it will take some time.

'You're looking very serious. Are you all right?'

He shrugs with one of his wrists, something I now find myself doing. 'I am not unhealthy, but I would appreciate – I must hesitate to ask you again for help because you have helped me so much. You have all of my excuses already and I have nothing left to give. My thanks are inadequate and again I am asking you for something.'

'I can only say no.'

'You can say no.'

'That's right, I do it all the time. What do you want?'

'Listen to me.'

75

'That's not hard.'

'It may be.'

'Tell me who you are, then. Really.'

'Savinien de Cyrano which is the truth. I promise you. I swear on everything I no longer have that my name is my only possession. I am neither mad nor mistaken, I am only impossible. Men who tell lies will always say impossible things, but all men who say impossible things need not be liars. I would maintain this rule remains unaltered when we consider *being* impossible.'

'All right, whatever. I'll suspend my disbelief.'

'Oh, that's good. You have a fine way with phrases. That's very pretty. Original?'

'Yes, I just made it up on the spur of the moment. The suspension of disbelief. Nice one.'

I know he knows I'm lying.

'Truly?'

He knows I know he knows I'm lying.

'Mm hm.'

I know he knows I know he knows I am. Lying is good like this, it becomes a truth that only the parties included can understand and nothing to do with deception.

'You have not said yes or no.'

'I know. Tell me what you want to tell me, I'm listening now.'

'A small favour first.'

'What's the favour?'

'Very small, smallness itself, in fact. You must say yes and then I tell you what it is.'

'That isn't usually the way I operate.'

'But for me, you will make an exception.'

'You are an exception, never mind making one. All right.'

'Hn?'

'Yes.'

'Eh! That's wonderful. Could you please, then, say my name. Not this Martin, this is not me. Say my name. Only the first one. Sa-vi-nien. It's like if you eat something and it tastes good and then better, best at the very end, Sa-vi-nien. You look at me in my eyes and say that. Please.'

Which was oddly difficult to do, perhaps because in meeting his eyes, I understand he isn't looking at me. He is staring at something nobody had seen in lifetimes, trying to reach back. Nevertheless, he has asked me to say his name and so I try.

'Savinien.'

He sucks an instant or two of air in through his teeth and makes something like a smile. He nods, looks up and then over to one side, tugging the grey hairs at his temples, smoothing them back with his thumbs.

'Was that all right?'

'Oh yes, that was all very right. That was a point. You know points?'

'Possibly not.'

'Well, it is a very complicated word, but also very simple.' He's getting ready to speak now, properly – he is about to expound. I find that I know the signs, that I am actually looking forward to sitting back and seeing him run his brains all the way through whatever idea he's decided to tear apart. He leans back against the table, crossing his legs at the ankle, angling his head. Then he pauses, winks. 'I could tell you about points, if you would like to listen.'

'I don't mind.'

'You're a good listener.'

'I just have trouble thinking of things to say.'

'I don't think that's true.'

'I don't care. Tell me what you're going to tell me.'

He leans forward, flickers his tongue between his lips. 'I am slightly like free theatre, a private performance.'

'Thank you for saying I don't have to pay.'

'Very well.' Inhaling, his head moving with it, making it a good breath, hungry and slow. 'The point. When a point has been made you will feel it like nothing else and any explanation is no longer to the point – it is beside the point. Which is a beginning of getting an impression of the true point.'

'Mm hm.'

He walks away. 'Weak start, it gets better.' Turns. 'The point is that single moment when you truly touch another person. You reach to them with a word, a thought, a gesture, an attack from the third position that flicks to the fourth and slips through, hits its mark. And within the point which is a very brief thing (not enough time for your heart to beat) two human beings are one. The speaker and the listener, the writer and the reader, the man who bleeds and the man who makes him, they are the same thing. We are the same thing. You, when you say my name – there – that's a point.'

'I don't think I would like that.'

'You wouldn't like what?'

I can feel the beginnings of a nervous cough, but I swallow it down. 'Points, they sound uncomfortable.'

'They are alive. Don't you like to be alive. Ah no, I forgot, you are mostly oblivious.' His hands flutter their fingers together and he peers. 'Alive, this isn't attractive, just in some corner of Jennifer. Touched by life.'

'Well . . . No, not really. If I have to be here, then I have to be here, you know? I don't think I have to be touched as well. Tell me about this Cyrano.' If anything was a point, that was one. Almost unhealthily changeable, he swung steeply towards a padding, soft intensity.

'This Cyrano is me. You know another?'

'Then if he is you, tell me about you.' And now he sits down with his arms folded and looks at the ceiling. From his expression you might think that his voice is appearing without his consent. He is listening, waiting for his words to see what they say. 'I was born in Paris and I was the second son which meant I didn't get my father's name. Abel, my brother, he had that pleasure. Along with having the good fortune, of course, that I wasn't called

Cain. Our house was in the Marais, near the rue des Verreries. Very thin, high streets, like paths in a very dirty forest. In the courtyard, we had our own, narrow column of sun that would slowly pinch itself out into night and torches. Our own sun, looking down at us like an eye at a telescope.

'I could not say I was so delighted to be there, I never liked the city or its variety of summer perfumes, the continual stare of its streets. But I was very young then, you know, and not entirely aware. I did not, for instance, know how close I was there to the heretics and witches. The more things change, eh? Every crime on earth was being either considered or committed in the Court of Miracles (a terrible place and really terribly close to my house); assassins, thieves, beggars, necromancers, treasonists, they were all there, no doubt with a few evil spirits thrown in. A demon or two. Naturally, my mind must have been coloured by their thinking when I was so young and so soft and so near to them, their doubts and their dark prayers. Meanwhile the appropriate authorities are using Les Halles (again, hard by my birthplace) to make spiked pork of anyone they choose. Malefactors are elongated and truncated and bled and scourged and diced for the enlightenment of the curious mob. The air I breathe until I am fully three years old and driven off to the countryside like a tedious wife so that my father can be further from people and closer to his dogs is thick with the ash and smoke of grilled sorcerers. I inhaled so much blasphemy and heresy and original thought that naturally their atoms and mine became combined, as is wood with fire. I was alchemised.

'It is no great surprise then, that I grew to be a man with, uh, dangerous enthusiasms. I found it difficult to live my life well, it seemed not to be entirely my best fit. I seemed to grow away from my life's proper shape. And now I think, it was so ungenerously provided. If I had been permitted only another five or ten years, I might truly have become accustomed to the world and achieved something. I might also say, I could have lived with more care and perhaps gratitude, but I did feel then that care would not make me a name for myself. Being careful had no point.'

He seems to pause for thought and then lose himself.

I guessed – wrongly – that he might require some comment from me. 'Maybe you didn't do so badly.'

'Badly. I must have been a catastrophe – He made me come back.'

'I know the name Cyrano de Bergerac. If you're saying that's you.'

'That's me.'

'Then I've heard your name.'

He can move very quickly for a man of his build and he rises and holds my shoulders too fast. I flinch.

'Why?'

Jumping back, apologetic hands.

'I'm sorry. But why have you heard me, of me?'

'It's a play. You're a character in a play.'

'Do I look like a play?'

'You don't look like Cyrano de Bergerac. He's always – '

And then I look at Martin, just as he turns his head. It all depended what you meant by 'like Cyrano de Bergerac', it all depended how you thought he would be and it all depended how long you looked.

'He always has a – '

'What, please?'

'He's always an actor. The way he is, is different every time. I mean, I don't know. I was just thinking and the name was familiar and that's why. Maybe they stole it, it's a nice name, maybe they just lifted it for a play. Maybe you read it somewhere and forgot about it when you forgot about everything else.'

'No!'

This time he doesn't apologise, even though I flinch.

'Don't even suggest . . . You really cannot have been listening if you can believe that I am not . . . Do you think I would choose to be so out of place? After a lifetime of finding my world as hospitable as the moon I would elect to be this different again?' He goes back to his chair, something hesitant now in his walk. 'Jennifer. Please. Please don't make me be no one. You know me, you know who I am.'

'But this de Bergerac, he's French.' I keep talking, even though I see from his eyes that he is looking at me for sympathy and silence. I can't quite find either of them.

'But of course.'

'You're saying you were born in Paris.'

'Yes.'

'Your parents were French.'

'Yes, this is obvious. Everyone was French, we were always French in my family. Now we are all French and all dead, dear Lord, even my bad little nephew Pierre, all dead.' His voice is breaking up, he shouldn't push it any more, he will hear it and break up, too. 'I have no doubt that we should all be buried in France if I weren't up and walking and breaking with tradition again. I am French.'

'Then why aren't you speaking French?'

'I am.'

I have a reaction ready for this. 'Well, look, I think I'll make us some tea. Are you all right.' He isn't. 'Are you all right?'

'Yes, yes.'

'Just say if you're not, but I'll make some tea for now. Say if you're not all right, it won't worry me.' Pat his shoulder. 'I'll be over here, filling the kettle and then we'll see what's what.'

Playing for time, you see, playing for time. I am inadequate, but also practical.

AT AROUND THIS time my hands started shaking. Not just occasionally nervous jiggles, but an unmistakable, all the time tremor, rubbing the air. I didn't fully notice this because I had my mind elsewhere. I now believe I was being disturbed by the facts prevailing in my life and my body was doing the best it could to tell me. Some people come out in rashes or fainting fits. I shook.

'Atoms. The sole explanation. Atoms.' Martin, or Savinien, stirred his tea solemnly, I don't think I've ever known anyone like tea as much as he did, he was almost reverent with it.

'Oh I see, of course. Atoms.' Something about his matter of factness was almost irritating.

'Mine and those of your country, your tongue and your air, your self. We have mixed. I am now a fraction more than me. This is the only reason for my never noticing a strain, an effort at translation. I have been added to. It's logical.'

'Ah.'

'You are hearing but not listening to this, hn?'

'You're bloody right I'm not listening. Atoms. You're telling me atoms are what let you speak a language you don't understand. You are telling me you are not only – what was it? – three hundred and seventy-five years old, but also dead and luminous and French, but atoms make all of that fine! Just how stupid am I supposed to be here! Remind me!' I wasn't angry, I was defending myself. Because I believed him.

No one should believe in impossible things, it causes hope. Oh, that's a very cynical thing to say and hope is admirable as an idea, or an inspiration. I know that. But hope does no good. As Martin/Savinien talked, I knew that volunteers in blue muddy overalls were digging thousands of bodies out of crumpled Indian buildings and no doubt those bodies had once experienced all kinds of harmless little aspirations, hopes which might have been driving them on in spite of the money they never ever had and their fragile health and the shoddy construction of the homes that would fracture and fall and kill them in just the way that similar shoddy buildings had done just one generation ago. Perhaps the builders had hoped the earthquake would be different this time. No doubt, at one time or another, all those involved had smiled in the teeth of their lives, hoping for the best. Even the men and women, digging in the rubble, they must have been hoping, too. In fact I seem to recall that one of my broadcasts said so.

In just the way that I used to hope. All the years I spent with my parents made me despair, but I still had hope. Certain other times in my life have had much the same effect, creating pain alongside hope. The pain and depression I found unpleasant, but you must understand that what made them unendurable was hope. That tension between my situation and my hopes for the better – not for the best, just for the better – can eventually only do what tension does, it causes splits and tears, a degree of loss. Hope is tyrannical, hope will not settle for anything but change.

And when the hoped-for future finally appears, I would rather not see what it brings because hope has already robbed it, mortgaged it to the bone. Hope ruins the future, fills it with clumsily balanced disappointments, every one ready to fall. Which means that I do not want hope, I want peace. No impossible things, no believing.

But I believed him.

'Why are you angry?' He had one arm folded high across his chest, the wrist wrapping round at the back of his neck and pushing his whole head forwards. He looked at me up and sideways, smiling warily. 'You are usually so calm and tranquil . . . although I know that women are more changeable in their natures than men.'

'Balls.'

'Would not be in their nature, if I understand what you mean.'

'It is not in my nature to take the blame for something simply because I am here and female. This is not my fault at all and it's absolutely fucking not my fault because I'm a woman. This is your fault for being impossible. Your fault for being you.'

'I know.' He turned slightly to the side in his chair and took a mouthful of tea. 'I know.'

'I'm sorry. I don't suppose this is very easy for you. I mean, it must be worse for you than it is for me.'

'Being me?'

'Yes, being you.'

'So I am me?' He glanced at the window and rubbed his finger down along the bridge of his nose. 'I beg your pardon?'

'Why beg my pardon, I didn't say anything.'

'Ah, because I did ask you there if this all might amount to your saying that I was myself. I thought that you might have some answer for that.'

'Yes. All right. You are. What you say.'

'I beg your pardon again.'

'You heard.'

'Yes. Yes, I did. Thank you.'

So I simply gave up hoping he was someone normal. I think I may have said as much.

'This is a compliment?'

'This is as close as you'll get.'

I let Martin turn into Savinien in my heart while time lets him be happy now. The whole year is rocking from summer to autumn, back and forth between pale sun and unexpressive rain and soon the trees will turn and the nights push in and little things will die. But he will be happy.

In the car park behind the railway station close to our house two young girls find an injured pigeon. Almost all of its tail is missing – only the feathers are gone, but it cannot fly. For several days, I see it as I walk to get my train. The pigeon is being adopted, men and women from the houses round about are feeding it bread.

Then it isn't there any more and I don't know who to ask where it has gone. I like the flats by the station better, though. People who are pointlessly kind to injured things live there.

First and last times for this and that pass by unnoticed and life happens in the world. I tell people all about it through their radios. Except I don't mention the pigeon or the people who helped it because they are not the kind of thing I am meant to speak about. People, individuals, are to be avoided in case they seem more important than the big lies I have to retell. I am glad this aspect of my work is unable to make me unhappy and when I come home, Martin/Savinien is there, being very good at being happy.

I might say it was even frightening to see how happiness could get a grip of him, how it left him open, undefended against pain. I'll show you him being happy from later on in a place where it was sunny and, I suppose, considerably more attractive than Glasgow and Merkland Street where the crippled pigeon lived.

Paris. This is a memory I have from Paris, because I did, in the end, have to go there. You'll hear about why. I am on the Ile Saint-Louis which is small island shaped like a stumpy rowing boat, moored to another larger island by a single hoop-backed bridge. Unlike a rowing boat, it does not move – the Seine slides tight around it instead, supporting other, more moveable craft until it becomes the sea.

We came here because Savinien remembered it new, could stare at the waterfront buildings and think of them under construction, raw stone. He found that he wanted to call on friends who could not be at home and I waited while he walked round the small garden at the island's head, composed himself, looked at the sky, scuffed his shoes across the countless hieroglyphic sparrow tracks in the pale, sunny dust.

All that afternoon, we walked slowly round and round the island, crossing in and out of the sun. It seemed to ease Martin/Savinien to be on the move and there were very few cars here to worry him. On one circuit we noticed a man and a woman lying. They were in the shade of a small sunken courtyard, next to a flight of seventeenth-century steps, and were fully occupied in being a pair of Parisian lovers. Not actually having sex, but both were deeply engrossed in each other, silently writhing, artfully unaware of the straggling tourists photographing them and moving on. Having no cameras, we simply looked.

'There you are, then. What Paris is all about. Meant to be.'

Savinien closed his eyes. 'We are like dogs now. This is all so much the same in the buildings, but now the people are like dogs, to fall on each other in the street. Come away, they would like us to watch and I have never enjoyed that kind of entertainment – to be staring or to be stared at in the street.'

'I'm not so terribly fond of it myself.'

'No, by here.' We walked down, off the pavement and on to a slipway of sloping butter yellow stone that gradually disappeared into the brownblue river. The sun sprang at us from the hot flags and the honeycoloured embankment.

'You think I am shocked.'

'No.'

'Nothing can affront me, I assure you. No action. The

setting was a surprise, nothing more. Eh, but I always did say that if men were to walk abroad every day with their swords to hand (such dangerous things these blades, all pressed together into a city with tight-fitting play-houses and cabarets and streets) then why not display their other, more peaceable weapons. I see no offence in this, only pleasure. Obviously my compatriots have taken to heart my advice, their rapiers and daggers are gone and very soon, I would guess, they will reveal their less cumbersome replacements.'

'It's an interesting idea.'

'It does at least get to the meat of the matter.'

'Very subtle, yes.'

'I never could support these terrible outbreaks of versified mediocrity and soft broiled brains that were meant to display undying love. Probably quite sane men and women trading sick little couplets, all prettiness and dying flowers and mildewed ornament when what they wish is to fall on each other like dogs. These stillborn misconceptions they insist on nursing and dragging through the streets to fling into each other's arms – they have no point.'

'Not everyone is a poet.'

'I know this! Why pretend, then! Why not do what they do and have done with it as best they can and let those of us who are able exercise the public points.'

'Don't tell me, you're really North European history's greatest lover and you just forgot to tell me. And you know how I enjoy meeting experts. Tsk, tsk, tsk.'

I leant against the slipway's fat retaining wall, felt its heat licking through my shirt while Savinien turned to face me, one of his feet faltering with a slither of damped sand. He lifted one hand to block out the sun.

'Lover? This has nothing to do with loving, any kind of loving, this is a point!'

'Another point.'

'This is a combat of hearts, a delicate, demanding

expression of virtuosity in the point. Love was a real illness, then. At the very least a fever of the brain producing phantoms, fasting, evil humours and whitened hair. My hair only became rather thin, it was the best I could do.'

'Is this serious?'

'Serious? This was a vocation. Men could spend their whole lives being in love. And besides, a point is always serious, you should know that by now. I will show you. An Exercise in Love. A point.'

'Sssh. We'll get a better audience than the couple by the stairs.'

'Yes!' And he suddenly stood somehow taller. He did something that meant he was taller than his natural height, balancing on his toes, his arms lifted to either side, as if he might begin conducting an orchestra, or simply executing a forward roll. 'Now! You should watch, this will not be something you have previously seen. For three hundred and seventy-five years this will not be something Paris has seen. Do you love me?'

'What?'

'Do you love me?'

'I can't answer that.'

'If you truly loved me, if you truly did . . .' He turned his back and began to walk to the end of the slipway.

'What are you doing?'

'I am proving love. I shall continue to walk and this will be a proof of love.' The water lapped at his shoes and then over them. He turned to face me. The light sparking and rolling on the water made him almost a silhouette against a sheet of irregular white. He placed his hands on top of his head. 'If you were true to me, I could walk on this water. If you loved me. I shall place my trust in your love,' a shuffling step backwards, 'and that will bear me up. I believe in you.'

'Don't.'

He had shuffled to ankle depth and now let the water

inch placidly towards his knees. 'I cannot stop. If I stop I am dishonouring your love, I am showing I lack faith.'

'That doesn't matter. You're being ridiculous.'

'Tell me that you love me and my passion will answer yours. The fire of my emotion will roast the Seine into clouds of vapour and together we will walk its bed. Huoh!' His arms flailed out as if he might fall.

'Careful!'

He smiled and folded his fingers together under his chin. 'I've proved you do care then? A tiny measure of care, for when I stumble and fall to my death? Because I am well able to swim but the currents here are strong and treacherous. How soon, do you think, before this stone falls away and is only water. One step more? To my knees?'

He moved as if to start another step.

'No! Don't.'

The head cocked to one side, the profile suddenly intent, almost sly. 'No what.'

'No, whatever you like.'

He sprang forward, up the slipway, genuinely slipping as he came, wheeling his arms to save his balance and laughing. 'Eh, you see? The testing of wills, of true hearts and, in an instant, there is the point.'

'Well, you didn't have to make it with me. And look at you.' His trousers clung blackly to his shins, rolling with river water while his shoes bubbled in silence. He assumed his most patient expression.

'We are in France, this is a country with a functioning sun. A person can be wet in the open air and not die of it, one simply becomes dry.'

'Don't do that again.'

'It was an exercise. I had such a lovely day today, I felt I wanted to be alive.'

I patted his shoulder. 'I know. But don't do it again, okay. It could be worrying.'

'I wanted to be alive.'

89

As we rose again to the pavement and its slim trees an old woman in a print dress stared at us. Then she smiled and flapped her hand, sucked in a little gasp with a tick of her head.

Savinien shrugged his mouth and nodded, 'Je sçay, je sçay.'

I've never liked public discussions of love. I've never liked pointless things in general and why spend so much time whining and obsessing over something no one can define. There's absolutely no point in that. I mean there isn't a common or garden point. Or even a French one.

There's a useful addition for the good old vocabulary – Improve your Word Power with The French Point. I used to try and describe it to people but now I don't bother. As you may have guessed, there's no point.

But I could give you my personal definition of love. Or I could at least tell you what it makes me think of. Not roses, bells, hearts, even broken ones. I think of a thin, round black leather case which was lying at the bottom of my wardrobe with the shoes, last time I looked. And in the case?

Clickilicklick, every trip. Snug in the leather, curved together one on the other, a nicely heavy metaphor for many things, but to me they mean only love.

Ever tried them? Handcuffs? They are such an indelible cliché, they will now always be automatically far more than themselves, loaded with sleazy authority, unexpectedly harsh. The three thick chain links between the cuffs really don't give the freedom you might expect and the fit of the bracelets is indeed firm, tight, can even be painful. Given its way, the hinged arm of each cuff would swing right round, only your wrist, or some other inserted interruption will stop it.

These are not gentle things, these mean metal against flesh. They cannot give, may in fact even enjoy an element of struggle, allowing them to bite. Set into each lock is a little switch which can be flicked over to prevent the cuff closing too tightly and nipping the skin, compressing veins, rubbing the bone and nasty goings-on like that. Beside each switch is the word STOP.

Clickilicklick. STOP.

Because you should stop. Although they are so small and amusing, so very readily available and not even embarrassing to purchase publicly, quite a joke really, you should stop and not buy them at all. If you are like me. They are the door you will open in order to go too far.

For us – for Steven and I – they made Captain Bligh much less pleasant then before. And, goodness me, Bligh was already getting more than out of hand. My performance was beginning to be painfully pointless: for Steve. I was, as they say, feeling no pain. One or both of us might have quibbled that Bligh never was – in any historical sense – anything like a lady. But then again, neither was I.

'Very well, sir, very well. The gunner's daughter, you shall find, is waiting and you shall be restrained.'

Our accuracy was physical rather than factual. Steven squealed when I snapped on the cuffs with that quick flip-click you see in the films which takes a little practice but is worth all the effort, believe me.

'That's . . . I'm sorry . . . that's too tight.'

'What was that you said?'

'Ma'am, that's very tight, ma'am.'

'Are you questioning my decision, sir?'

'No, ma'am.'

'Good. It would go hard with you if you were. Wouldn't it?'

Oh naturally, of course, this wasn't all we did but this was what I aimed for, this was my consolation while we shared out all the landlubberly, preliminary stuff. The pedestrian rolls in the tedious hay were more or less proficient I suppose, but somehow they failed to impress. The good Captain was always impatient to get out.

After all, what did all that penetrative pitch and roll amount to? In the end? You know as well as I do. The graded variations on that particular, same old, theme:

Cunt + Cock =
Cock + Cunt =
Cunt + Mouth =
Mouth + Cock =
Cock + Mouth =
Mouth + Mouth =
Mouth + Breast =
Breast + Hand =
Hand + Cock =
Hand + Cunt =
Cunt + Cock + Arse + Thumb + Mouth + Toes +
Hands + Knees + Boompsabloodydaisy =
Cunt + Cock =
    All That Other Stuff = All That Other Fucking and Wanking Stuff.

You know. That stuff.

People write about it all the time and it never does a thing for me. With Steven, I would lie or sit or stand beside or above or below or in front or behind him and have never a thing done for me, thinking, 'You shall be sorry for your faults, sir. I shall make you.' Excellent motivation, that – never failed.

So, Clickilicklick. STOP.

But don't stop. And off we go.

The best thing was to fasten him across the kitchen table. Naturally, we would require an empty house. I have never liked to trouble co-tenants with even conventional disturbances, knowing how sensitive I was myself to such intrusions. Sensitivity breeds sensitivity.

Our proceedings were more than averagely disturbing. A broad belt, vigorously applied, truly does swish in an endlessly fascinating way. It will not crack as a whip might in the air, but across the back, buttocks, legs, stomach. 'And where else shall we go, sir? Will you trust your Captain tonight? Will you?' That's the game. Wherever the Captain and I thought fit, there we would go and crack away remarkably. Re-mark-ab-ly.

With thought, we might have avoided the inevitable. I might have. I had, after all, known my emotional deficiencies for many years by this time. Given a situation I found so interesting, so releasing, I would naturally find it hard to concentrate on another person's pain. I would forget they were there and be in danger of doing them harm.

'Take this in your mouth, sir, and bite. I'll not have crying out, there. I will not.'

I would see the shiver of his muscles, the plum and scarlet bruising, the sheen of fear on his skin. Sometimes I would only swing the belt, or stroke his back, and he would flinch. If I only inhaled emphatically he would flinch. I could make him flinch just by breathing. Nice.

Oh, and he got to come. Naturally. Being a good, brave sailor and doing his bit for the two we had to be to tango. And he came because I wouldn't let him not – there was always that to be considered, having the power to satisfy. Pipe aboard the Captain and no hands are needed at the pump.

Not that I was utterly numb myself. I had a reaction or two, even calm old me. I'm still blood and flesh, I was affected. I wouldn't be honest if I said I didn't, in the end, enjoy what we did, relish it. So much so that away from him, I wouldn't think of what we did. The images I could recall – and remember that I did have the best possible view – were too strong, they would slide away from me under their own steam, showing me where they might lead next. It was far wiser to forget about it all until we were together again. By which time, the Captain would take charge and relieve me of my responsibilities. I always found the Captain a great relief.

And if all this were not enough in the way of monstrously damaging fiascoes, please bear in mind that the naked human body, in itself, is not something I find endlessly fascinating. I do not find it especially easy to look at. It is messily put together and has altogether too much skin when compared to other animal forms. I should know, I grew up watching both the male and female model put exhaustively through their paces. I do know.

Naturally, if you beat a man, you will eventually be looking, not at him, but at what you have made of him. But looking at him before you have caused enough of change on that body, in that body, this may be a problem. What will solve your problem beautifully and for ever will be the handcuffs – love, as I understand it. Fix your man securely and you need only look at him when you wish, you will already know where to strike.

I am ashamed of the cuffs now, they are like a bad old friend from another life and I'll not use them again. When I look for shoes I am half aware of the case. I push it further into the shadows and leave it be. The leather is slightly mouldy now.

Do you know, now that I've given this thought, it feels right that I should just throw the case and the handcuffs away. I'll do that. I'll wrap them up in a carrier bag and dump them – go for a walk and leave them in a public wastebin or a skip where I can't get them back and no one will know they belong to me. I'll do that now.

ALL GONE, all done. My little parcelled wickedness is now sleeping in a skip along with half a dozen furtive empty bottles, the fruits of an interior upgrading, and some dead mattresses. Probably there are some abandoned syringes in there, too. We have passed the time when anywhere in this city will be entirely free of used syringes, of our public sicknesses.

It's also rather cold out. I'm better off in here with the radiators on, quietly putting paid to the atmosphere with profligate energy use.

There's nothing like a good symbolic act to give you a sense of achievement. Buying a poppy seems almost as good as preventing a soldier's death, phoning a radio programme seems nicer than taking part in democracy, and throwing away your handcuffs feels just like being free. If you happen to have a past like mine. Just as I have no physical reminders of my parents, I now have no concrete proof of Steven's existence as part of my life. More importantly, our mutual friend Bligh has been dropped ashore – I really couldn't face that performance again. Everything gone, better now.

And leaving me far more room to think about our household's resident dead Frenchman. Slowly, we all started to get used to the person everyone still referred to as Martin. It became unremarkable to find him in the living-room, eating an apple with a knife and fork, or to watch him pacing the garden round, humming high unfamiliar tunes. He had a remarkable adaptability, walking out with me quite calmly, managing traffic, overhead aircraft, billboards and bicycles with only a famished curiosity. Soon, he was setting out by himself, returning with lists of questions and sometimes objects he'd found on his way. I bought him a little notebook which he began to carry with him everywhere in the pocket of Pete's abandoned East German Army parka, along with a huge supply of biros. I don't think his devotion to disposable plastic pens ever faded.

And often he would ask me to go with him to the park round the corner where he had been afraid once and I would do that.

'Thank you.'

'It's all right. I like a walk sometimes.'

We sat on one of the fireproof red metal benches provided, folding our hands under our armpits against the mounting cold and looking at the dribble of traffic falling down the Crow Road. We were surrounded by the strong, bitter smell of dead leaves and the occasional detonation of early autumn fireworks.

'That's us cold, then, ah?'

'Mm hm.'

Conversation wasn't particularly part of the proceedings.

'It reminds me.'

'Yes?'

'Perhaps you don't wish to hear this.'

'I won't know until you've said.'

'I cannot deny that. No I cannot.' He rubbed his front teeth with the ball of his thumb, watched the pale cloud of his breath drift gently and lose its shape.

'Well?'

'Well, I am reminded of another time as cold as this, colder, and I am on the field, or in the field near Saint Germain. It was morning, I had just seen the dawn and the air was full of the end of the year, like this, and there was a darkness there which the sun could not drive out. Frost was in a glass across the meadow and the grey dead leaves, lying as they are today. We could not walk anywhere without crushing something irreparably. You must understand, I hate the winter, waiting for it to come, like a sleeping death.

'It was fitting to think of death because my friends and I were waiting to kill a young man. He and his friends quite naturally had the opposite intention, which is how these things proceed. But this gentleman, I did not wish to kill him. He was a boy, a yellow-haired boy with a soft, clear brow, wonderful eyes and such a desperation to die. He believed he was on a course to establish his honour and I could love him for it because he was so much as I had been when I first became a cadet and would have murdered the whole city to prove my existence. I was so small and Paris was so enormous I could do nothing but wash it in blood. Do you know in Henry's time four thousand similar gentlemen died to gain the honour they had always had? The honour which was neither dependant on a fine suit nor a good horse, a full purse, or one's sword? Did you know that? Of course you did, these things don't change, not at their hearts.

'On the morning we are discussing I was a terrible old duellist – I was like a musket ball, just swimming through the morning until I hit him dead with both our honours unconcerned, unaffected and I think more and more with our maker squinting down from behind the sun and finding us too ridiculous for words. "Haoh, you don't learn, my little ducks. I had no need of your crusades and I now have no need of this. Your souls are mine already, there's no need to keep throwing them back. I could find that discourteous." But I knew this and the boy did not and there was no place for love, or he would kill me.

'You see he had approached me in the plain view of all the world and given me "the opportunity to prove my courage". Now my health had been less than perfect for many months. Having become accustomed to walking abroad and finding myself daily bombarded with casual and formal and polite and ridiculous challenges from dawn to dusk, suddenly I had to contend with unsteady limbs, an old man's weakness, a constant enemy in my breast. I had kept myself miserably out of company in order to preserve what was left of my life and to save the world the sight of me shuffling under the sun supporting a face the colour of old cod. I looked as if I had . . . a particular disease.

'Fortunately I was somewhat recovered when this boy, whom I might call Guy, courted me, coaxed me, pursued me. Day after day he casts insults against me and my friends and although I am careless of myself when he threatens those I care for I have to act. No choice.

'Poor Guy, he only wanted to live for ever. Like the boy . . . there was a boy who challenged that lunatic's lunatic, Chevalier d'Andrieux. "Chevalier, you will be the tenth man I have killed," he says. The Chevalier smiles and gives this small, mad nod he had. "And you will be my seventy-second." The Chevalier duly dispatches his opponent and nothing of the youth is immortalised, beyond his stupidity. I haven't forgotten his name, I never knew it.

'These ridiculous, posturing conversations, they came to sicken me. Each man using the other to prove God's special grace for himself alone. "Save me Lord, now that I choose to risk my life in taking another's without even asking you if this is prudent (never mind a very likely sin), prove that you love me more than him." Arrogance. We were such children.

'I asked my God to forgive me that morning. Just very quickly, it doesn't do to think much of heaven at these times, it diverts the will. Guy was stretching his arms, warming his limbs like a stupid veal calf in the sun, letting me watch his confidence, and I knew I would have to kill him because he would not be stopped in any other way, he had too much spirit and he did so want my heart.

'He had an odd style, hardly effective. He would leap up and forward to overcome my guard like a very predictable bird, tiring himself. The cold grass turned greasy underneath us, he weakened, grew more and more incautious and also dangerous as he abandoned his technique, fought with his body and not his mind. I could always see his mind, but his body, well, his body might surprise me. His conclusion was less than glorious. He simply slipped and I could do nothing but stab him in the throat, spike through hs neck. I watched him drown in a meadow with his hands searching for apposite phrases in the grass and his beautiful eyes reflecting a colour better than the sky. One of his friends closed them and was about to push me away before he stopped himself, because he knew that if he touched me, I would have to kill him, too.

'Someone gave me a bottle of cleared wine and I had stopped drinking wine then, but I took it and I walked away, stared off at the frozen windmill. I filled my mouth and even as I did that the dark in the air sank through my mind until I couldn't swallow. I had to spit out. A breeze had drawn up and it caught the neck of the bottle and made it almost sigh and at that time, when I had already killed far more men than Chevalier d'Andrieux ever did in all of his terrible life, I knew I would never kill anyone again. Except perhaps myself.'

'I was staying on the rue Saint-Jacques then and I went home there and washed myself. Then I walked almost to the river and went into the church of Saint Julien des Pauvres and made my confession. I was not a great man for confessions and found I had very little of any usefulness to say. After that I had my breakfast, my life continuing while Guy's did not. Do you see this, am I clear?'

I coughed and told him he was clear but not always easy to understand.

He would often ask if he was clear, if 'it' was clear – whatever 'it' was. I became used to that, Savinien checking his point had slipped home. I became used to the way he would clap his hands together when he stood, his early morning exclamations when he woke to find himself still there. I learned that in periods of depression he would hide in the bathroom, lock the door and sit. When both of us must have been barefoot one night I accidentally set my feet in the imprints of warmth his own had left at the base of the toilet bowl. I generally have cold feet. If I consider those weeks now, I know that I spent them forgetting the difference between being with another person and being with more of myself.

When I came home late, I would catch Arthur watching the updates on a prominent game of chess. An Englishman and a Russian were playing and playing against each other and, as the games progressed, the Englishman began to speak as if English were not his first language, he paused and searched for words, he grew an accent, hardened his stare. The Russian turned soft, developed ineffectual little gestures in his hands, a bashful smile. They sat and thought at each other, the Englishman losing while the Russian won, their identities extending, exploring, exchanging. I've never really liked chess – my parents played it – but I couldn't help taking an interest in those men. I understood where they were going together because I was going there, too.

Of course, nothing tangible happened between Savinien and myself. What could happen between the professionally calm and the long-term dead? But I knew I moved my hands the way that he did and I knew he had one of my laughs and I knew I didn't care. There was nothing to stop us being together so we didn't stop.

In fact I genuinely started to relax. I'll tell you about that.

There's a difference between calm and relaxation. You'll be aware of that. The former is still, while the latter is unwary, and in domestic situations I had, for years, been used to being wary. I learned I should be wary and, yes, a child must eventually crawl out from beneath its mother and father and make a few decisions in its own right about itself and the world against it, but these things take time, they really do. Particularly when you have been taught so well in early life to have leanings in one direction and not another. It makes me uneasy to relax. Unless it happens very slowly, softly like a leaf fall. The way it did with Savinien.

'Martin?'

'No. We're on our own. I beg your pardon, who did you ask for?'

'All right then. Savinien. I just don't want it to be a habit and then have to explain. To the others.'

He presses my hand between his. 'Sometimes perhaps I need to be too precise. I am sure, after all, that *we* know who I am. What did you want?'

'Why don't you put your hood up. It's getting cold. You don't want your eyes getting blurry whenever you go outside.'

'My hood? In the . . .'

'The parka.'

'Mm. The parka.' He manufactured an entirely insincere smile.

'Or you could get a hat. I think Pete had a hat, but he probably took it with him. It'll be cold where he's gone.'

'Now a hat, yes. Something to make me appear in some way less like an indigent agricultural labourer.' One hand waved a neat little denial. 'Although I have almost no interest in my costume, like so many other people in your country. (Please believe me, I feel most sartorially at home here.) But yes, you've a reason there. You've a reason for a hat. Is there one – something a little more generous than the current mode?'

All very domestic and humdrum, but think about what's happening there – right up at the beginning, before he gets all bound up in how politely he can loathe his parka. Do you see? The third little paragraph I say? I know the cold will affect his sinuses and put his eyes out of focus. I know it without asking. Every change of air pressure can send my sinuses into a nervous rumba of congestion and fug. I did not have to check we agreed on this point, I was already certain. Without thinking, I assumed that, in this point, Savinien and I were the same.

So you have the full picture now – my principal constituents at that time were calmness, relaxation and assumption. I don't know about you, but when I roam around unchecked in that condition for any length of time at all I don't need to ask if disaster is likely – it's already on the way. If I only look up, I'll feel its shadow on my face.

I learned that particular lesson one evening in the snow. Broad, slow snow was falling and I was young and still living with my parents. As I've already outlined, home life with Mummy and Daddy was what you might call theatrical. I think of it now as Life With The Lions, if that isn't too dated a reference. When I found myself alone with both my parents, I tried to be aware of available exits and how best to take them. And it wasn't so bad – they were really very predictable if you watched them closely, Ma and Pa. When trouble was on the way, they would start to get a shine around their mouths, or something in the eyes would tick slickly into place. Paying attention to their voices – I worked to develop a good ear – I could often pick up alterations of tone, the seeping in of low notes, slackened consonants. Time to go.

But outside, in the world, we were all of us very well behaved. I assumed there was an unwritten rule that whatever insanity we suffered from would never leave the house with us – was not for show. I assumed.

Then came the evening with the snow. We had been playing at families, out all day, taking part in a surprise trip to Glasgow. My head was filled with the grizzled air, the bruised colour of the buildings and the huge, roaring streets. The city seemed sprung for darkness, waiting to be busy in the spaces between lights. Living here now, I can look down at the peaceful haze of frost in my empty, aimless street, quite contented, but this is still the city I felt suck around me, swirling my brains with the cold, bright threat of utter indifference. I was, of course, right in my impressions the first time and I am, of course, right now. It is impossible to be wrong about a city – it will be anything you do or do not want, quicker and harder than you can think.

Walking between Mother and Father, even holding their hands to be sure the bad streets wouldn't get me, I sneaked up a look at the sky and found it, remarkably, ashy green. The snow, still skating down, was black and then white and then lost in the churning pavements. This was what the city offered instead of night. We would have to go back to our car now and drive home. I assumed this would be a good thing. Safe.

The car was a big, brave beast. The heater hardly worked and on one or two occasions the engine had caught fire, but it was still my friend with a brown leather back seat where I could stay on my own. I was still short enough to sit with my legs flat ahead of me along it, if no one was looking, and taking my shoes off to prevent mess. The engine numbed out my parents' voices and we ground slowly beyond the shops and house lights. I fell asleep.

Until a cry in my dream pulled me up awake. We were slewing and toiling in a thin track of packed and mashed ice. The carriageway was mad with snow, it boiled in a mist just beyond the windscreen, dragged against the jerking wipers and made wild elongations and reflections in every trace of coloured light. There was a great deal of light. Red tailgates, naked white headlamps, swaying and bouncing, and to either side of us, bright tableaux of throbbing orange and crimson and blue, set out at the foot of skidded pathways, flicking illumination across impacted metal. In one place I saw a small fire winking under a pillar of black smoke, in another an entirely dark car, apparently undamaged but splayed across the hard shoulder and already deep under faultless snow. In the centre of a curve of vehicles and men, one woman sat up straight, her coat and the snow hidden in the darkness of her own blood.

'Now?'

'Yes, now.'

'How fast do you want it?'

'How fast do you want to go?'

Father was wheedling at Mother. She was gripping the steering wheel hard, compensating for twists and slithers, every now and then breaking out with an odd short laugh. Then Father laughed, too.

We were accelerating into the fluming tunnel of white and headlight and speckled, sheering dark. Lost in all the varieties of noise, my parents' voices only surfaced now and again, but I knew they were planning something. We hadn't got home soon enough, whatever it was would start here in the innocent world beyond our house.

I asked them to stop – an admission of feeling, of defeat which I regretted immediately – but I think they did not hear. They showed no sign of remembering I was there while I wondered what I meant them to stop. To stop driving, to stop speeding, to stop being so together, to stop being. The car rocked and slipped while Father finished with Mother's breasts. I saw the shadow of him slip under her tensed arms as he dragged up her skirt and then dropped his head against her thighs. She said something and I closed my eyes to prevent seeing out of the windows.

It may have been their intention to kill themselves that night. I would have been their unfortunate bystander, a chance casualty. Instead, they accelerated me from a condition of terror into one of stillness and the dumb assumption that I would die. By the end of the journey I had discovered that I would always be correct in assuming that I would die, anything else would always be more doubtful, disappointing.

So I was lucky, really. I might have returned with nothing more than bargain Christmas presents – instead I'd found out the beginning of a whole Philosophy. Which was much more uplifting than it might seem – quite naturally, if I was going to die, they were, too. They were older, they would go first. I looked forward to that.

'Have some attention, here.'

It worried Savinien that his past had been so violent. He imagined it might disturb me.

'I am paying attention.'

'I was not as I would wish to have been. I was a fine writer, a fine playwright, a fine friend. I do believe that. Nevertheless what I did best was to kill. I created myself in that.'

'Hrrf. Well, that was your life then. Things were different.' I understood about wanting to kill and about wanting to hurt, which he never actually mentioned, having a more pragmatic and unsentimental attitude to death. 'I mean, your past is over. It doesn't affect me. It needn't affect you.'

'I made myself. I trained and drilled and trained like the novitiate I was, dedicated to the early dispatch of souls. I took dancing lessons to ease the passage of my feet, I parried and broke ground, advanced, beat against time as if it were a man against me and I made a whole city careful how it looked in my face. I developed a not entirely comfortable reputation.'

'But if you have anything now, it's a new start. No one need know what you've done, or why. Listen, I have to get on, though. I'm due at the studio in an hour and I've still got to eat and have a shower and pay our rent.'

'And pay our rent.' I said it without thinking, full in the face of a man who had often told me how much he loathed imposed dependencies.

Savinien let the air gather back over my four stupid words before he spoke again.

'Ah, yes. Of course. Good bye, then. Good bye.'

He nodded, stood up and away from the bench, paused with his head a touch forward and to the right. 'Good bye, Jennifer.'

'Hm, see you later.' I moved off towards the park gate, the grass giving wetly under a thin bite of frost. For no reason I can think of, I glanced back up the rise and saw him still standing, kicking with one foot at something in the leaves. He was ankle deep in leaves.

When I left for work I was calm, I was relaxed, I assumed I would return the following morning and all would go on as before.

Wrong. Wrong. Wrong.

For Jennifer, My Dearest Friend,

Already irredeemably in your debt, I must make one final demand, that you should lend me enough of your language to hold my thanks. You should be warned that as my thanks are infinite, this will be no small request.

Be sure I am a thief at heart, for there I shall keep hidden every good effect of your connaissance. Your patience and welcome restored me no less to myself than to my health. Your own and your household's numbrous kindnesses leave me a guerrier defeated for I have not the slightest means to repay you, other than by removing the source of any further depense, the man who remain always,
   Your Servant,
   DC DB.

The note was on the kitchen table, deftly folded around itself with my name marked in a clear, high hand, the J of Jennifer enlarged with florid care. The lines inside were neat and regular, rather small, with each of the t's crossed savagely in long sweeps that sometimes overran the page. The whole effect was politely ferocious. Or ferociously polite.

I looked at the paper and the letters and the black biro ink and hoped this would stop me reading what all of them came together and said. Their information was not possible, it was too abrupt. They appeared to be saying he'd gone. Martin had gone. Savinien had gone. He'd gone.

There is something about sudden things that can make

them seem impossible. As if there were nothing in nature that happened suddenly, arbitrarily, without being in any way noticeably just. But in spite of my thinking, or my incomprehension, he had gone. I checked in his bedroom – he'd taken all his pens.

Stupidly, I ran out and up to the park, as if being back there could loop up the flow in time. Perhaps I would surprise its mechanism somehow and simply start out there from where I'd left off with Savinien standing in the grass.

I was only a day late, not even that. Leather-black leaves skidded under my feet on the slope and I was only a day late. If I had paid attention more to how he was I would have seen the signs of his departure and turned it aside.

The chilled air ached in my throat while my breath steamed around me and I turned slowly, seeing nothing but an empty park, still with cold. I walked and turned and walked and I was a day late and he was gone and I leaned under one of the trees and then walked again and then stood and waited and then went home.

For the whole of that day, my mind would open and close against the one idea that I had become alone. This meant that for several days it was quite hard to concentrate and I began to dislike sleeping. Night and morning, those soft edges in and out of the day, would open me up. Consciousness would drop its guard and pain would dig in, like the black little mole it is. On some days I felt I was nothing but tunnel inside.

Good for a shaking experience or two, though, isn't it – life? I think it means no harm, it's just too big not to be brutal from time to time. And this was where it taught me what happens when I come across someone indivisible from myself. Or when a trick of personalities encourages conjunctions I should not risk. When I meet someone who needs no acceptance, because they are already home. They are not a change, but an expansion, like the flavour of a kiss, where one mouth finds another and presses into somewhere not new but warm and familiar and much more than before.

I learned about being alone. There was more of me to be alone with now. It hurt.

Don't worry. He comes back.

Although, naturally, I didn't know that at the time.

'Jennifer?'

'Mm?'

'What's up?'

Arthur was wearing his best solicitous face. I couldn't be sure how long he'd been looking at me, my mind having been elsewhere.

'Up?'

'Or down. What's the matter? If you want to talk about it. I mean, I know we only share a house, there's no need for us to get all family about things.'

'You and Liz will never be anything like family, believe me.' He gave a tiny flinch and I realised he must be offended. 'I mean, you're far too pleasant. I like you.' I'd never thought about it, but that wasn't a lie. Liz was so seldom there she couldn't cause offence and Arthur was a nice man – the kind of nice and still quite young man who was probably already thoroughly tired of being called nice and reliable and helpful and someone you could talk to in a crisis, but perhaps not at any other time because then you wouldn't notice him.

'Do you want to talk?'

There, you see, he said that the way a good doctor might – interested and genuine, but aware that he's said it a thousand times before. He may even be overacting very slightly because he finds himself unconvincing through simple force of repetition. Something about his sentences droops.

'It's not compulsory, but I am here. Good listener. My

mum always said that. I wish I hadn't listened when she did.'

'You do fine, Art. Honestly. Hhhrrmm. Sorry, catarrh. Hhuhuff. Yes, it's nice you're here.'

That genuinely surprised him – I would have thought he knew how useful he was, but then again, people are generally quite unappreciative of themselves. I know I am.

'The thing is, you see, this is the problem – there isn't really anything to talk about. Oh, I'm fed up, yes, I'm certainly fed up, but the time'll go on and then I won't be. That's how it works, isn't it.'

'Mm hm. Where is he now?'

I thought about asking who he meant but there was no point, so I got straight to the lie. 'Right now he's probably all tucked up in bed, being looked after like an orchid and getting paid for it.'

'Tell me how he managed it and I'll join him. Separate beds, naturally.'

'It's one of these new medical places.' I'd seen it in the cinema and taken note of the details for later use. 'You go off and they give you doses of new drugs. Experiment. In the photos it looks like a big supermarket – out in a science park – they give you food and lodging and fifteen quid a week. I think he said fifteen.' It doesn't do to get stories too perfect – the truth never sounds that neat. 'Something like that.'

'He be there long ?'

'I'm not sure. He might be going on somewhere else afterwards. He was a bit vague. You know how he is.'

'Yes.'

'He said thanks for all your help, by the way.'

'Oh. I didn't do anything. I gave him some stale Danish pastries once. He made a big fuss about them.'

'I didn't know you did Danish pastries.'

'Oh yes, we bake anything – as long as it's flat. Management policy. I try to see it as a challenge. Pastries are flat.

I lent him a razor, actually, now I think. He didn't happen to leave it around . . .'

'No. I don't think so. It might be in Pete's room. Take a look.'

I already had.

'I already have.'

'Ah well, sorry.'

'Och, it was only an old one. Listen . . .' Arthur walked over to the window and blinked out at the dying garden. It was raining. A wet, bitter winter was blowing in. When November came, we would have early snow for the first time in years. It would surprise us. Lingering vegetation would burn black with frost overnight and I would think of how Savinien was managing, if he was safe inside, keeping dry. There was no way of knowing. I felt I might have prepared him better, told him we have a sly climate, unforgiving.

And that wasn't just the mood I was in, making me think on the black side, that winter no one was having too much fun.

As Arthur fidgeted with the curtains, it occurred to me he must be well on his way to saying something difficult and I could either let him or change the subject, perhaps leave the room.

'Listen, Jennifer . . . who was he?'

Having been powerless to take a decision I found I could no longer go.

'Who . . .'

'Martin. Who was he? Did you know him?'

'Know him. No. No I did not. I didn't then and there is now no reason for me to know him. I didn't know him. You make it sound as if he's my fault.' I also had no reason to be angry, but there I was, being it anyway. Poor old Arthur, I made him jump. 'All right, yes, I knew he wasn't Martin, that was our mutual mistake, but who else he was . . . I don't know, he said he didn't know. Well he said . . . I don't know anything about him

Arthur. He shouldn't . . . I don't know where he's gone. Or why. It's a mess.'

'Oh.'

'How did you know? Or when did you know. You didn't say anything.'

'Peter sent a letter from London, just before he left – he said Martin couldn't take the room and we should find someone else.'

It's funny, I'd never thought Arthur capable of having secrets until then. He looked me carefully in the eye and then away again.

'Well, we did, didn't we? We got a different Martin. I liked him, he really was, well he was enjoyable to have around.'

He stopped himself from becoming any more like a farewell oration and sat down alongside me. 'Probably he'll . . . well, you never know. Shall we keep the room, we could for a bit, leave it free, anyway . . . anyway.'

'Well, I'm not in the mood for thinking clearly about it just now, Arthur. Or anything else. I'm not having a clear time at all. Sorry. I was irresponsible wasn't I? With this.'

'No more than I was.'

'It felt right, though.'

'Yes, didn't it. When you're in the mood, we'll talk to Liz. Tell her something. There's no need to do anything now. We'll keep it between us, eh? Less fuss that way.'

He smiled, very successfully drawing a kind of comfort into his eyes.

I leaned over towards him, 'Give us a feel at your skull, then.' Arthur's brush cut is just long enough to separate him from anything fascist or even slightly threatening and I have the impression that total strangers quite frequently come up and rub him for luck, never mind those of us who know him. His scalp has a thick, slightly teddy bear quality.

'Och, all right.' He dropped his head and I ruffled through the warm, clipped hair.

'Ta.'

'Anything to be of service.'

'You're a mug, you know that.'

'Aye, but I'm happy with it. Except that's enough, now – I'll end up bald.'

'Bald and happy.'

'No. Just bald.'

You can even push a teddy bear too far.

Writing from my position today, the next winter weeks and months seem to be only the time I had to pass until Savinien reappeared, but then, I was almost certain that I wouldn't see him again and so I occupied myself in adjusting to my new condition. The pain, fresh every morning, delivered right inside your door. And I did what most people try to when their lives take an uninhabited turn and they rattle about their days feeling something lost. I worked.

When I wasn't buried in the station, I worried out voice-over jobs in the little studios round the city, helping ginger up the listening world for Christmas's unchristian expense. Rain would brawl up the streets, lamps would be lit and then extinguished and I would exchange one gently beige suite of rooms for another in soothing lilac or Italian washed-out blue.

Pints of hurried filter coffee, left to distil all day on evil little hot-plates, began to give me a new reason for sleeplessness and I stayed awake, thinking only of striking the ideal tone, of adding or losing that second or two requested and of the essential musicality to fake and make. My breathing was clear and round and utterly invisible. I stood or sat, all attention, in dead telephone box cabins and gave just whoever was asking more than they could possibly pay for in obvious joy, infectious glee and solder-tight trustworthiness. I promise you, I ran up and down the octaves like a rat in a greasy drain, I turned accents by minutes within the degree until they were more themselves than they had any right to be. If you want an overriding obsession then the attainment of absolute vocal perfection isn't a bad one to pick. It will keep you busy.

The voice was standing up for it, too. No one had any complaints, not even me. Well, no technical gripes, anyway, what unsettled me were the silences.

Obviously it is in everyone's interest to keep the studios clean free from extraneous sound. Very often I felt an enormous relief when all the doors were closed and even the low voices – the funeral parlour hum those concerned with sound can often produce – when even that was gone. But then I would be alone with the down-to-the-bone picked air, shut in a sound vacuum and suddenly under pressure to mumble and shuffle and hum to myself, anything to fill the gap and know that time was passing because I could hear it go.

While we recorded, each word would emerge with nothing but itself, a courageous little assembly of sibilants, fricatives, plosives – lips and teeth and tips of tongues. When I work I listen hard, inside and out, and all I could hear was loneliness, slipping and smoking under every phrase, one great lack of the noise of any other living thing. I would stare through the coloured haze of my reflection in the booth glass and feel like an astronaut peering down over the edge of for ever. When I closed my eyes, nowhere unfurled around me in a thick and silent arc.

Of course somewhere in that arc, out in the dark of my imagination, there was Savinien de Cyrano de Bergerac and sometimes I thought of him safe and sometimes I thought of him in danger and sometimes I didn't think at all but he was there, like a difference in the quality of light. He wouldn't go away. This suggested to me that excessive work would not, in itself, solve my problem. In fact, it was causing a few.

'Is that you out again?'

'Yes, Art.'

He laid his hand on my shoulder, half jokingly, 'Come home, your friends miss you – the old hound dog don't do nothing but howl all night. Isn't that right, Liz?'

'Mm. It's starting to feel like a hotel round here. Yes, all right I know, I always like to use this as a hotel – '

'But you'd prefer it if no one else did. Well, I'm sorry, it's just a busy time of year.'

'No need to get stroppy.'

'She's over-tired, not stroppy.'

'No, she's stroppy.'

'Don't talk about me as if I wasn't here.'

'Why not, it's what we're used to?'

I needed another option. So I began to spend even more time down at the station, drifting around its pea-green cafeteria and reading abandoned newspapers. I was not unaware that the most absorbing activity next to work is usually sex. I was not unaware I had found this to be the case at other times. This was a possibility to consider.

'You must have developed some new habits.'

Steven.

Steven – exactly the same size as life and absolutely bang on cue. I'll swear some people have radar, they only appear when you're liable to do something you'll regret and it's liable to be with them.

'What do you mean?'

'The amount you must be earning at the moment could pay for some serious eccentricities. Then again, you're working so hard, would you have time for them?'

'Well, that's my business isn't it?'

'Oh yes, that's all yours. All yours.'

Thirty: Forty, new balls please. I kept to my table and he flounced off to his, all was well.

That is to say, no, not really – the damage was done and nothing was well. Believe it or not, that was the first time we'd really talked about anything other than work since the terminal collapse of what I might loosely have termed our relationship. Those were our first unchaperoned innuendoes and had involved us in glimpses of a certain willingness in each other's faces, a less than hidden inclination to try something more. For old times' sake. The first moves had been made and it was now too late.

Either one of us could, with very little loss of honour, have decided to take no further action, but frankly this was unlikely. Or rather, it was an option I did not wish to consider. I wanted to be seriously distracted and, to be honest, Steve had a nice bum. I watched him walking away with his nasty, police-issue cup of nastier coffee and I could not help being aware of the niceness of his bum. It seemed, if anything, a little firmer than when I had known it. The whole effect of his retreating rear made me remember the muscular tucks close in above each hip bone which had been at their most pleasant when he sat, slightly tense and nude in a hard chair, as requested.

A few days beyond that point, I polished off an achingly well-pronounced bulletin in which a prominent parliamentarian calmly explained that widescale public misery was unavoidable, given his party's emotional attachment to ever-decreasing income tax. Finally, public spending would disappear completely up their ever-decreasing arses, but they could not bear to be anxious while it did.

I longed to add a suggestion that wholesale aversion therapy might solve the problem more sanely than humouring the policies of the financially retentive. A whole electorate cannot nod and smile and back away for ever. I said nothing, however, and only thought wicked thoughts inside – it's sometimes a kind of relief to write them down here, they may not be useful but at least they're getting out more, seeing the world.

Steve was watching my delivery from the box. He smiled and his eyes shouted, 'I knew you couldn't last without more of me – we have a Special Relationship, you and I. Go on, admit it, you're less of a person when I'm not there. Claim the major prize and lose the game.'

I claimed the major prize.

And even while we made our arrangements I knew it was all a huge mistake, but even a huge mistake would keep my mind busy. It might even be more diverting than something nice.

I would have loved to tell Steve that particular truth – 'By the way, I'm really hoping you're the blowtorch for my zeppelin – my unrefundable ticket for the *Marie Celeste* – the flea on my plague rat – the open manhole I can fall for, so to speak. No offence.' But wiping the smirk off his face so soon might have been counter-productive.

In the end I had three hours to kill before I went over to a flat he'd acquired since I'd known him. He didn't have to share with anyone. Lucky Steve. Sexually active Steve. Three hours began to feel exactly long enough to go off the whole idea. For no reason I was aware of, I decided to walk the minutes away, all 180 of them.

It was a frosty night, the sky high and sharp, pavements sheening over with a dangerous gleam. I climbed to the fat, pedestrian-friendlied street that leads into the heart of the city and found the benches. I hadn't known until then I was looking for them. Looking for him, for Savinien.

My adopted city is, like many others, breeding Street-people. They have always been here – made a different colour from other people, a different shape, with faces that are not like other people's faces. Disinterested pedestrians have always glanced at them from time to time and known in their secret hearts that Streetpeople can never have been young, at school, indoors, in love. That they were only misfortune's experiment in self expression: more a kind of uneven poetry than a kind of humanity.

Now my city, like many others, has made its moves to take what was a kind of embarrassing hobby much more seriously. We have Streetpeople who are undeniably young, very vulnerably insane, clean, sad, sober, osten-

tatiously human and even talkative. They are now impossible to ignore and, on some days, it seems they must
inevitably become self-propagating, a whole, sealed world
of Street. It is likely this world will be angry and demon-
strably ungrateful towards its creators.

The civic hobby was showing that night and I walked
past doorways piled with blankets, cagey glimmers of
reflective foil, the private movements of shallow sleep.
Figures waited in the street corner lea of coiling gusts of
rain. Or, it would be more accurate to say they stood,
because there was nothing they could be waiting for unless
it was each other. The benches held men, smoking, talking, drinking, sleeping men giving demonstrations from
a forgotten, furnished life.

Without knowing the city or any way of living in it,
Savinien must almost inevitably drift to Street. Unless
something happened before he could find it. I slowed my
pace and glanced at hands, the curve of shoulders, the
gentleness in a bowed head, something I might recognise.
Perhaps if he coughed – I would know his cough.

In this way, I passed almost the entirety of my three
hours. I arrived on Steve's doorstep a casual ten minutes
late and he answered the door at an admirably offhand
pace.

'You look cold.'

'I am.'

'Coffee?'

'No. I'm not here for coffee. What else have you got?'
I thought bloody-minded would be the right tone to
develop. A bit late now for the soft sell. Steve was, as
ever, slow to catch on. Unless my intonation was off-
beam, but I don't think it was off-beam, I think it was
fine.

'There's tea or whisky, then.'

So we weren't going straight for the main event, but
whisky might be a good move. Possibly ideal.

'All right, a whisky. Where do you want to drink it?'

'Here.'

The little sod was going to keep me standing in the hall. While I hadn't been paying attention, we must have decided to out-humiliate each other. I knew I'd have the losing hand on that front – it's always tricky, humiliating a masochist – and so hard to tell when you're done.

'Bring me the bottle, then. If you want to fetch and carry.' That just sounded ridiculous, far too Joan Crawford and I haven't got the shoulders to carry it off. Never mind, I supposed the forthcoming proceedings might turn out almost bearable if I was drunk.

God, I shouldn't have gone there. Why did I go?

It wasn't really whisky he brought, only Canadian Club, but it helped me beat down a few of my final defences. It's odd how cagey my brain can be about utter foolishness – somebody back there has no sense of fun.

I took a long swig and then an unlucky guess and ducked past him in around what turned out to be his bathroom door. With his best peckish labrador expression, Steve followed me in. Good boy.

You can have your own guess on the rest.

Horizontal sex + bathroom floor = carpet burn + bruised
vertebrae
tsk, tsk, tsk

Not the most satisfactory equation I'd ever run across. Or been run across. And I wasn't drunk enough. I had, however, developed a strange and very slightly euphoric determination that I *would* become drunk enough, have an adequately good Good Time and make a mess of the bed he was obviously hiding somewhere for an unsullied sleep when I'd gone. We had both provided ourselves with a baroque quantity of condoms in what I found an almost touching display of combined bravado and paranoia. Maybe we weren't so unalike after all. But back to business.

'Bed.'

'Mm.' He'd collapsed into a gundog drool with his head underneath the sink.

'Where is your bed.'

That had done it, the spark fanned wolfishly behind his eyes and I sat up to improve my membership of the Canadian Club.

I've noticed that three-letter words with a central 'e' will always hit the right libidinous spot.

Bed

Let

Pet

Get

Set

Wet

Even, God help us, Jet.

And of course, of course, of course, the ultimate – Sex.

See what I mean? They all work.

I had occasionally wondered if this was some kind of reflex and perhaps any convenient grouping of letters would do. If I lovingly/breathlessly/teasingly whispered 'ned', or 'pej', 'zez' or 'dep' at appropriate moments would these do just as well?

Steve didn't turn on the light in the bedroom, possibly to avoid any comments on its tidiness. There was a distinct atmosphere of sporting underwear and fust once we'd both barged each other through the doorway. Still, the bed felt presentable as we floundered on to it for round two.

For some reason the whisky and darkness were making my hands feel at least twice their usual size, they seemed to plane and flap in the air like partially anaesthetised fins. As I adjusted to this sensation, Steve and I grappled and hugged manfully, loosening clothing where possible while I was suddenly, forcefully reminded of my first time ever. The occasion of my Losing It. Lying, exhaling more or less rhythmically under the pressure of Steven's chest under Steven's T-shirt, I could see myself in the dark of another grainy, grubby room.

My position had been very similar, although my partner was different and it was his shoulder and back I had been crying on to for several, in flagrante, minutes. I did this silently so that my tears were only noticed when the main event was over. At which point my significant other happily performed the cinematic manoeuvre of kissing-away-the-loved-one's-tears, between contented, hormonal grunts. This made it clear he had identified the cause of my weepings as his delivery of a mind-altering experience, excelling every possible one of a young girl's (forbidden) dreams.

All of which made me even more lachrymose because I knew the truth. That I had cried simply out of bewildered gratitude because It had happened at all. With anyone. That I had cried because It had been so uninvolving and fucking brief. That I had cried because, having started crying, I was now leading his ego to believe a lie about the wonderfulness of It which I would not alter – he did not understand me and this was only the beginning of how far apart we could be.

Meanwhile Steven was nearing the point of delivery for another little rubberised sperm donation and I did my best to get mentally in gear, to really join in. I cupped and gripped the flesh of his nice arse while imagining bad poems, good poems, newsreaders, rugby players, magazine articles, dead actors, live actors, old actors, fat actors, young actors, tall, temperamental, tuneful, uglymugged, black and white and technicoloured actors. I exhausted Equity, Actor's Equity, The Screen Actor's Guild, and then slewed rapidly across the entire Musician's Union and dreams of a boy I might have fancied, had he ever, ever lived next door.

It was no use, naturally. My imagination failed even to move one square inch of earth. I blame the Canadian Club – it's a very unromantic kind of ethyl alcohol.

So never mind the weather, just get it together and breathe and twitch and breathe and sigh and fake it till you make it, not that you ever necessarily will make it. This is, naturally, a cheat, but a fair way of cheating because the cheater is the one who loses most. I finished my maple leaf attempt at whisky and Steven suggested a thing I might do with the bottle.

Thanks. But no thanks.

At which juncture it seemed to me this was not the best way to go on. Here I was, with alcohol finally loosening my joints, unpicking the tighter corners of my brain and making me ready for something when there was very little of anything to be had. Which I mean as no criticism of Steven, I expect he was doing the best that anyone could. This was my problem.

I rolled on to my back, feeling my head give a tiny, warning spin. If I didn't get very active again soon, I would simply fall asleep. Without thinking, I flopped out an arm and inadvertently slapped Steve, I think on the thigh. He gave a doggy little snort and I did it again. Once more the sound of a happy pooch, gratefully disciplined. I did it again.

'Permission to speak.'

He honestly didn't know what he was doing.

'Permission to speak, Ma'am.' He wanted me to row out our old friend Bligh again. Yes he did, indeed he did. He wanted to see the Captain. Dearie, dearie me.

I hadn't even thought of Bligh in months. When I stopped being with Steven, Bligh stopped being with me. I hadn't for a moment imagined he might pay us a visit that night. I was sure we both remembered that in his later incarnations he had played more than a touch rough, but there Steven was, hailing him to come aboard for all he was worth.

Well, I certainly couldn't resist all of that marine enthusiasm for too long. And my alter ego, having been called on, also seemed keen. Extraordinarily keen.

'What, do you want to see the Captain, then?' That wicked, old seafaring voice appeared in the dark like the sparkle that starts the fuse. In my mind, Bligh always had a tang of sulphur, beneath the salt.

'Yes, Ma'am.'

'Are you sure.' And, even if he was sure, was actively requesting ill-treatment, it didn't matter because it is impossible to give one's consent in these situations. I had already asked the opinion of a lawyer acquaintance of mine on this very point – only out of academic interest, of course – and she had set me right. Even between willing partners in the privacy of their own homes this was criminal, this was a felony and could not be consented to, this was a crime. I knew that. So I knew I was about to commit a crime.

'Very well, then. Make ready the Captain's table.'

'In the lounge, Ma'am.'

'Then make ready yourself and I shall await you at the appointed place. And be in good order or you shall have to make amends. D'you understand?'

'Yes, Ma'am.'

But he didn't and nor did I. We couldn't foresee the effect of Canada's finest, of all my many months of non-violent abstinence, or of all my many years of somewhere wanting very much to do what only Bligh could do. Or, to put it another way, nobody could have predicted that I would be so unpredictable when I came to take the helm.

His lounge was small, scruffy in a boyish way, with a low coffee table stretching the length of his sofa. Just right. But I left off preparations for a while and walked to the window, separated the curtains and stepped inside.

I loved to do that when I was young, to close myself in the thick, chill space between the window glass and the curtain lining and look out without showing a light.

Steven's flat was on the third floor, that tiny bit nearer a sky which had turned the colour of milky tea. Lazy clots of snow were wandering down past me, rushing ahead of the breeze and falling again. I did not think of Savinien, of his being out there. Instead I felt oddly peaceful, smoothly approaching the brink of anticipation, excitement. One always should, after all, feel excited when preparing to commit a crime.

I decided to draw the curtains and turn off the lamp – I've always found the bounds of possibility grow more flexible in the dark, particularly with regard to bad behaviour.

And when I remember this now, I know that Steven was happy when he came in. Oh, he was trying to act naval and contrite, we were each of us playing our very familiar parts, but his personal contentment had room to show through – this wasn't exactly Shakespeare, after all, only S and M. (Which I often feel should stand for Seedy and Mad, but that's only my opinion and, Lord knows, I'm in no position to criticise.)

We seemed to be rediscovering two old friends, like a Variety double act taking one last turn. Of course, Steve had never tried his hand at a definite role, like Fletcher Christian, but that seemed only right, we were much more cosy and safe when we kept it simple. Setting Christian up against Bligh would have shifted our balance, made the relationship too equal, if not actually mutinous. We were both very happy with Steve cast as the powerless hand on deck and myself as the mad Ahab, bad, glad captain of his body, and never mind his soul. Something in us had waited until we could meet and be this for each other. And do this to each other.

Steve smothered a giggle which I found instantly annoying. I wanted this for real, to demand full concentration. No more fun.

'Take them off, everything off.' He hesitated for a moment, fumbled at his underpants, and I realised he hadn't known quite where I was in the dark of the room. I had the advantage and I was going to take it.

'Off. And put the makings on the table. Thank you.'

While I fastened him to the table, as though he were hugging it very tight, I could feel that he was an extremely jolly tar. The room was not cold, but the flesh, his really almost feverishly hot flesh, shivered merrily. He lay, the perfect, obedient sailor, allowing me to make him almost completely immobile. My flipperish hands were behaving themselves quite well, although my eyes had begun to project huge blooms of sanguine colour on to the darkness – something I found quite disturbing at first.

My aim in thus securing him was not to obstruct the circulation of his blood, but to make sure that twisting or writhing would prove highly uncomfortable. Simply lying at rest, he would also have a constant reminder of his very vulnerable position. Those bright, tight handcuffs would have come in useful, but I found I was managing to make do.

Tremors in his legs made it quite tricky to bind them, particularly when the table only extended a touch below his knees. Still, he'd thoughtfully supplied me with a generous variety of neckties that did the job.

'And now, you shall wait, sir. You shall wait until it pleases me to begin.'

So I stood at the window again with the other thing he had given me close to hand. I could hear Steve breathing hard, a small tremble beginning in his jaws on each exhalation.

We reached the space a moment or two before my first blow. Blow, stroke, lash – all wonderfully suggesting, ambiguous words – somebody wicked got there before me with each of them. I knelt down, bending my mouth snug above his cheek. His face was turned away from me and I could smell his shampoo, his heat and manness, a trace of acid sweat. And I was so close to him then. There was no necessity to touch, because I was already covering his bones, threading the pulse in his heart and racing under the pale corrugations of his brain. I licked his neck and heard the table creak its whole length in response. So then I kissed his ear and whispered.

'This is the time. This is the time and I shall touch you now. You shall kiss the gunner's daughter and not forget it. And you shall have need of this.'

I stopped his mouth with most of a rather woolly tie and held it in place with another and then went too far. Because where else was there?

I can recall just enough to wish I knew nothing at all. The floral patterns continued to explode behind my eyes, especially when they were closed, and I began to look forward to each sickly purplish detonation. At one point Steve had started to make a repetitive, mindless kind of noise which I had not heard before and wanted to stop. The sound of what I did was there also.

In a tiny way, I never did actually stop what I did. It carries on. I feel the movements of it in me now. I know that the swing in my arms continued in time with the ache of my breath and I uncover that feeling under my heart and along my spine of finding an edge and stepping beyond it and finding an edge and stepping beyond it and gripping that edge and throwing it away. But then I caught myself. As if I had dreamed and then jumped myself awake by taking my own hand and holding it still.

I was sweating. I felt sick. A huge silence swayed out under me and I discovered I was afraid to turn on the light. The shock of illumination when I did made us both cry out.

He wasn't really bleeding, not seriously. I heard my voice tell him that several times. What I saw mostly were raised, rust-coloured blisters, subcutaneous eruptions of blood. And do you know what makes me feel the worst? I almost wrote 'the worst about what happened' when of course I mean *what I did*.

I do sincerely intend to take up my full responsibility here.

So above all, the worst thing about what I did was the

fact that I untied his mouth last. I didn't want to hear what he'd try and say, what noise he might make.

Strangely, we both behaved as if some crazed stranger had broken in to do this while we were engaged elsewhere, which had more than a tiny ring of reality about it. I laid a blanket for him on the floor, lifted his head for sips of sweet tea and paracetamol, set the central heating as high as it would go, ran a bath with a tiny amount of antiseptic which was a terrible, terrible idea and I do not wish to consider what I had to observe when he eased into that water, the hands clinging to mine, his mouth, the whimpering, none of that.

I also, in the course of that night, said the word sorry perhaps a thousand times. Neither he nor I could even hear it in the end.

WELL, I ONLY told you I was calm. I never even suggested that I was nice. There would be no reason to believe that, just because I'm writing you this, I ought to be any worse or better than anyone else. Than you.

In fact, if I was you, that whole *writing a book* thing might make me wonder just what kind of person I could be – spending so much of my time on this, to the exclusion of other, healthier and perhaps even outdoor pursuits. There's something a little bit wrong about doing such things. I should get a life.

Still, at least I'm honest. I really did set out to be and I'm keeping my word. Even if I end up falling pretty much into the mould of those people with mad cow eyes who come up out of nowhere sometimes and, very calmly, insult you and your family and your most deeply maintained beliefs and relatives yet unborn and then say, 'Still, at least I'm honest.'

But let's get to the point.

Do you still like me? Did you ever? Need to? Maybe not.

Perhaps I should simply say that we'd come so far together, I thought it was time you should know of my criminal past. Now you'll understand why I found it so strange to hear Savinien talk about violence, killing, even war, with such love and regret. Although he had confiscated the lives of two or three times as many men as Charlie Manson, there was a tenderness in him I'd never managed to find. Then again, he also had a pain about him I didn't want to feel. Tenderness is dangerous, softly cataclysmic and never in the places you'd expect.

All of the above only providing another reminder that little comes more naturally to me and my kind than guilt. Devoid of feeling, yes. Devoid of guilt, never. I'm sure even Scottish sociopaths are soaked with remorse, it's in our air.

Confession time again, then. Here we go.

Steve called in sick, saying he'd been beaten up by a drunk while I winced in the background, knowing this had, indeed, been the case. I toed and froed between my various works and his flat, partly out of a sense of responsibility and partly out of a craven fear that he would call upon help other than mine and the whole, sad episode would lurch into the light of day. Thinking back, I suppose he might have found the good Captain's activities almost as embarrassing as I did. Then again, I might just have beaten him into a corner. To coin a phrase.

We never mentioned that night – I even washed every one of his ties that first morning after it happened and gave them a particularly vicious ironing, as if the removal of any knots and wrinkles would lighten the burden of emotional evidence, to say nothing of my appalling hangover. Steven at this point was, of course, still nothing other than an entire body of evidence.

So I cleaned and fussed and kept myself as far away from Steven and how he looked as I possibly could. He took a rather peculiar pleasure in calling for help to move to the bathroom, to change his position, to stand up. Every little pained sip of breath, every grimace was very justifiably aimed in my direction and each one hit its mark. I was grateful he spent a good proportion of his time attempting to sleep.

Then after what I recall as being the space of four days, he answered the door to me and said, 'No, thank you. I'll manage. I don't think . . . I think you shouldn't come back. Yes, don't come back. Don't ever.'

This was delivered in a nervous rush, his eyes darting beyond me and away. I lifted my hand to brush back my hair and he flinched visibly. Which told me far better than he could that I ought to leave my paper bag of guilty groceries and go back down the stairs. I considered saying sorry again and decided against it.

I was left back very much where I'd begun, with nothing but overworking and further proof of my status as an interior cripple to sustain me. Along with one more memory, a sharp black edge for my mind to rub over in the night.

Want to see it? Close your eyes now if you don't.

I'm back in Steven's living room, hard up inside that sweating dark with my brains alive as cordite and a belt secured round the fist of my right hand. His own belt. And now I'm not playing any more, I'm not being anyone but me. I pause and stand, more than warmed up now, really into my stride, and I look down at Steve where he is lying on the table. Possibly he is coming, undoubtedly he is close to the point on one side or the other. His breathing is hoarse, he moves as much as he is able in a private rhythm of his own and he gives out soft noises of a comfort I cannot understand. There he is, alone with his pleasure, and it seems I can do no more than push him even further beyond my reach. I feel all alone.

I know I should tell him how angry this makes me because that would set my anger free where it could do no harm. I do seriously consider speaking to him as my mouth fills with saliva and I swallow and swallow and find I have begun to cry so that I have to use my free hand to rub at my eyes. I think how unusual it is that I should be weeping this way and that I should be so utterly furious. I find it rather pleasant to feel, all at once, so much.

I unwind the belt from my hand, wipe the sweat from my palm against my stomach and then take a good hold on the leather again, this time with the buckle end free. I want to be nothing but angry and I am.

Because dreams do come true, if you want them to.

But that is no longer one of mine and I promise you I did regret it very much, almost as soon as it had come. I am aware that I cannot regret it as much as Steven must have, but I try my best.

For those of you who weren't watching, you can open your eyes again now.

I disappeared into my work with nothing on my mind but sore things I dearly wanted to forget. I shuffled through December on a sea of coffee and roller-coastering blood sugar in my role as life-support system to a voice. Not that I was ungrateful, my voice did at least return the favour when we weren't dawdling together in a variety of waiting-areas and subsisting on a diet of chocolate and scribbled-on tabloid remains.

I hadn't read the papers for a long, long time and they were coming as quite a shock. In the first place I tried to keep myself separated from images of the news I had to broadcast. It was all very well to talk about gassing whole villages, publicly anatomising children, cosmically and domestically designed disasters – what I didn't want to consider were the faces of those involved. Now here were all the images I'd avoided and more. A plastic toy suitcase, a coloured fancy hat, the light of intelligence in a pair of eyes could make a photograph instantly unmanageable. I could neither look nor look away.

Fortunately many of the pictures on offer would be of sturdily grieving relatives offering health and beauty tips, of kissing or tripping, vomiting or waving, smiling or fornicating celebrities by birth, celebrities by occupation or celebrities by act of will. They helped to see me through until even the most distressing snaps became, after a while, part of my expected insensitivity. I could pick up any headline

SECRET JACUZZI SEX LIFE OF NECROPHILE
VOYEUR – PICTURES

with not even a shiver. I had been successfully numbed.

Enabling me to enjoy the finer points of the editorial

comment on offer. Apparently my country was in the grip of an extraordinary phenomenon. The public as a whole, and in particular the criminal classes, has lost all ability to discriminate between fact and fiction. No misdeed, however ghastly, could not be traced back to a horribly obtainable novel, film, popular song or comic book. This made for far more exciting reading than the usual tedious bulletins on mass unemployment and hopelessness, including as they did a spicy variety of Hollywood scenarios and pin-up pics of movie stars, now called on as stand-ins for a positive horde of unphotogenic perverts and murderers.

The next stop was obvious. All our enlightened leaders needed to do to salve all our social ills at a single dab would be to institute a strict public diet of nothing but Beatrix Potter, Walt Disney and Richard Clayderman. Our national stiffening handful of tabloids were doing their little bit by offering tempting displays of body parts and libidinous fables to distract the otherwise discontented mind, but even tits and gossip can only do so much. The church and academic establishment might have been expected to take a lead in governing public thought. Sadly their minds must have been irrecoverably clouded by prolonged exposure to incestuous, cannibalistic and murderous so-called classics by such as Homer and Shakespeare, to say nothing of the incestuous, licentious and utterly bloody contents of the Bible (King James and Good News versions, I don't know which is worse).

I even found myself wondering one morning – as I waded through two nasty little murders and a Putney love nest – whether my own sexual irregularities had been caused by early exposure to Charles Laughton in seamy Sunday afternoon matinee black and white. And then I decided this was very likely to be a load of bollocks and that reading too many newspapers was clearly affecting my mind.

Still, the papers did keep me fully informed on the

looming Festive Season. Liz was going to spend Christmas away with her mysterious new man, which almost entirely scotched the idea I'd had that any partner so intensely clandestine must be married. Arthur was, as usual, going home to his mum. This meant I would be all alone in our cold, square house at the top of the road. Because my parents are dead there was no possibility of going home to them and I couldn't muster any other relative or acquaintance I would dream of spending time with, particularly not at such an overfed and sentimental time of year. In fact, I was looking forward to spending a few quiet days with myself, courtesy of a minuscule Yuletide break from the station.

So I said goodbye to Liz.

'Goodbye.'

'Must run.'

'All right then, off you go.'

'Oh, well, have a nice time.'

'You too. Don't do anything I would.' Not that Liz was the type to even consider it. A long weekend of bad television and romping about in a cosy hotel would be more her style and good luck to her.

And I said goodbye to Art.

'Cheers, then.'

'You won't be lonely? Here on your own.'

'No, no. I'll be fine.'

'I'm sure, I'm sure. Um, about the room, Pete's room.'

'I've paid the rent.'

'I know, but – '

'We can talk about what to do when you get back, when you're both back. Hhhffur. See what happens then, eh?'

'Yes, probably, well, who knows what might turn up.'

'At this time of year, I hate to think. It will probably involve reindeer. Go on now, you'll miss your coach.'

He gave me one of his finest clumsy kisses on the ear – this time bumping down to my cheek – and shuffled off under a rucksack and two haemorrhaging bin liners filled with surprisingly inexpensive Tibetan cushions he thought his mother might find useful.

And then I closed the front door, trying to resist the first wave of Xmassy memories. For some very odd reason, Arthur's shambling retreat down the icy front path had summoned up a burning recollection of Christmas past. My first public annoucement of world news. It was admittedly rather old news, but still had a fine ring to it. I'm sure that, without checking, I could write it straight out, here.

'And there were at that time, shepherds abiding in the fields watching over their flocks by night.'

Or something very like that. That was all I got before some other high and wobbly contender picked up the passage and hobbled on with their part of it and then the reading was over and I had to crocodile back to my seat and yell out a carol in the traditional manner. My fragment of glory was all done in far less than the full Warholian fifteen minutes.

As my father drove me home, he glanced across at my short body, rattling between the safety belt and the leathered expanses of the passenger's seat.

'What's the matter?'

I was feeling slightly disappointed by the whole affair for no particular reason. Maybe I'd expected a better audience reaction, a few favourable reviews.

'I don't know.'

'Yes, you do.'

'Well . . . now that I've finished I wish I could do it again.'

He allowed himself a whoop of knowing laughter.

'Oh, yes. I always thought that. Never a near enough perfect performance. I know how you feel. Oh, yes. I know exactly how you feel.'

It was a perfectly humane and reasonable comment – now I listen back to it – I suppose we all do feel roughly the same on these occasions. First we are too nervous and then we're in the thick of it, mouth working without us like a soft pink word compactor, and then it's over, where did it go? But at the time, at that time, I felt my father's knowing, his attention approaching my private self. I was completely determined that he shouldn't be able to tell how I felt, ever again. I would rather disappear than have that. So I did.

I suppose it was a kind of resolution – too early for the New Year, of course.

NOW I'M GOING to cheat.

We are high on the lip of the new year, just looking down at January rising into sight, we are almost dizzy with time. But December is still here and dug in tight with its own peculiar glassworks slithering down pavements and stiffening the earth ferociously. This is our first bitter winter in some years and we have forgotten what to do with real cold. While I wait in a seasonally swollen post office queue, an elderly lady with purple hat and face grabs at me.

'Is this not terrible? Och, it's awful, so it is.'

'It is December.'

She takes a breath and then stops, begins a small, grim smile. 'Well I suppose we should not expect better. No indeed, dear, this is all we could hope for. December, yes.'

'Be nice when it's spring though, eh?'

'Oh, aye. It'll be lovely.'

And so it would.

She strode off, blackly reconciled to the gusting morning that tore her out through the door and worried at her hat.

I closed my eyes and thought about the spring – I do that sometimes, they can't touch you for it, harms no one.

And here comes the cheat, because this is where I'm going to start the year. At least a fortnight early, walking over the hill and down towards home I will tell you that an old thing seemed to stop and a new one began and I stepped through a change of time. This happened later in the same day as the post office queue.

Although I had no way of knowing it at the time, I can tell you now that Savinien was also out at the edge of my city, trying to lose himself in what began as a densely foggy dusk. We were out there together, sometimes a few blocks apart, sometimes taking the same street in different hours and half hours. Had we understood how close we were, we might have backtracked, paused, met. Instead we were feeling alone.

After something like two months of habit, I hardly noticed that I never simply went out and walked any more. I went out and looked. I caught myself asking meaningless questions of the people who sold the home-less magazine, I searched at faces, I checked my bulletins, combed the local papers for news I didn't want to see. I discovered there are numbers you can ring to register your confusion at a disappearance. You can offer information to the Salvation Army, or Missing Persons, if you have enough information to offer. I didn't have a photograph, a history, a relationship. I was told my search might not be easy even if I did. I was told how many other persons were missing, that it seemed a popular choice, one of the few available fresh starts.

The mist that evening was unpleasantly cold, almost choking, and made it almost impossible to look for any-thing. When I breathed I didn't get quite as much air as I needed and my mouth began to taste of sour metal, but still the experience was oddly relaxing. I had wanted simply to walk and pass my time, pacify my mind, accept-ing the general assumption that even in this day and age pedestrian pursuits are intrinsically soothing, but I was coming close to losing my bearings and beginning to feel ill. Houselights simply thickened the overall cloud, sounds jumped and distorted and claustrophobia writhed greyly over anything that was still moving.

I decided to pick the shortest possible way home, concentrating precisely on my route, leaving no room for panic. The temperature fell steeply. I continued to move forward. I glanced up. I stopped. I found I was standing beneath a phenomenon.

Perhaps you know all about this, but I did not. I had never seen mist frozen clean out of the air before. I was suddenly surrounded by a sparking, mineral dark that rained down ice powder in long, light drifts. Each street lamp supported a kind of fish shoal halo, shimmering past like mica or grey silk.

Within less then a minute, I could breathe again and tarmac, concrete, car roofs, the whole horizontal world was covered in a fine grey fur of frozen moisture. The pavement leading home was as alien and wonderful as the first I had ever seen hidden under snow. I caught myself tiptoeing, as if I was walking the back of a whale.

I can be very easily satisfied by weather.

But only in the way I might be by an unexpected busker, any kind of free, open-air event. Climatic change does not normally lead me to expect further, more personal alterations. But this time it did. Perhaps I was tired, perhaps I was indulging in wishful thinking, I don't know – either way I came in from a night that was quietly silting itself clean and found I was completely certain this could be my fresh start, too. The Year could be New from now on, it would take just a suitable little nudge on my part to get it in place. Somewhere out of reach the future was waiting and I only had to work the combination that would set it all configuring together, clickclickclick, in a beneficial lock.

Something like that, anyway. Even the gently shifting house, now comfortably empty, had a lightly charged atmosphere. It was waiting for something and wouldn't tell me what. I felt I was walking around inside an enormous Rorschach blot, trying to make sense of it.

THE MEANING OF THIS SHAPE IS YOUR FUTURE, WHAT FUTURE WILL IT BE? PLEASE THINK IN THE SPACE PROVIDED.

I went to bed instead and had the kind of dream that might be expected at this point, because when you miss people you really do dream about them. I hadn't gone through the 'I see your face in every crowd' palaver yet, but my sleep had been very thoroughly invaded with little snaps and snatches of someone I wanted to recognise. This was the night when he made a full appearance.

There wasn't a nauseous search for him through dwindling Escher labyrinths, I didn't watch myself trying to call him from melting telephones, or semaphoring invisibly through one-way glass, none of that. Freudian melodrama was avoided altogether and I slid from adjusting my head against the pillow, settling and growing warm, into something very simple.

Savinien was there. Back. With me. I was happy. We were happy.

We were in a small, bare room together where we were perfectly able to step forward and let our arms go around each other. Both of us wore long, black coats that slowed and muffled our movements, but we did take that step, we did cross and close that distance until it was pressed away.

We embraced.

No we didn't.

We hugged. Definitely hugged.

I knew, in the manner of dreams, how both of us felt the little crackle of tension, the shiver of muscles pulling in tight. We constricted each other's breathing, let a hungriness run along our arms and closed our eyes to fix our concentration at the act of holding on.

Most of all, I realised we were relieved. We were more relieved than I had needed to know was possible.

Pathetic, eh?

A dreamer can do anything, can run several amoks simultaneously and whoop it up no end without the slightest nibble of conscience. What did I get? Hearty hugs and overcoats. Then again, perhaps this was the result of running a tad too amok in reality. The subconscious is nothing if not obsessed with balance. From what I know. Sometimes it tells me things, sometimes it won't.

Not that I didn't feel better for all my Crombie-covered and platonic hallucinations when I first woke up. Then, of course, I developed a clear sensation of being all on my own. Which is the problem with squeaky clean and emotionally committed dreaming, it'll always give you a terrible kind of hangover in the morning. I'm always much better off with faceless sex and violence, or trying to not dream at all.

I made the best of my situation and occupied the day very gently with breakfast and lunch, tidying over carefully between them.

I stood and looked out of the window as the street dimmed down and its lights lit up.

After that I couldn't be interested in eating again. For a while I sat and watched an irregular area in the carpet until I couldn't see it at all and had to switch a lamp on.

The phone didn't ring and no letters came which was hardly unnatural for Christmas Eve, but left the day feeling very unbroken. I shortened the evening by going to bed.

The following morning, Peter came home.

'I MEAN, THE poor fuck, you're meant to pick up hitchers and get a good story out of them, but he wasn't expecting that. He wasn't expecting me.'

Peter laughed and seemed much older and much younger. You might say he had suddenly grown into his face. Also he had cultivated a fawnish moustache; a full, soft and very European-looking moustache.

'Oh, you don't know how lucky you are. I think I talked all the way from Newcastle to the exit for Great Western Road. He got the worst of it and this is just what's left. All over the country, there are people talking too much about Rumania. Sorry. I must be really boring.'

'No.'

Three hours solid he'd been speaking, ever since he'd arrived, with only a break for coffee and a very long bath. I was toying with the idea of stabbing him in the throat, even though it beat staring at the carpet and I'd always liked Pete very much and, goodness knows, respected what he was doing. But I was discovering I'd liked him because he was quiet.

'I suppose you were looking forward to a quiet couple of days on your own.'

That wasn't intentional, it just happened that way. I was thinking of how quiet he was and then he started talking about quietness. I smiled and his eyes rested on my face without seeing it at all. I don't know if he was really seeing anything.

'I used to love it here for that. The quietness. Away from the road, just the odd kid, the odd wean. They're all odd round here aren't they. To be truthful, I'd kind of forgotten you didn't go away for Christmas. Well, I'd forgotten it was Christmas. Christmas Day – I knew the time of year. I've seen the Christmas decorations of all nations on the way back, but I've lost a day somewhere. D'you know?'

Peter had clattered his key in the lock while I washed up after a sandwich and a bowl of soup. I'd made the soup more for the work it would generate than out of any appetite and was looking forward to staring out of the window. I had already cleaned the cobwebs from most of the ceiling corners with a duster on a stick and rubbed the layer of black from the top of the skirting boards. Such excitement.

And I hadn't wanted it to be him. You understand? I had not in any way wanted to suddenly hear someone coming into my house and discover that it was Peter. I wanted to turn my head and lay down whatever I had been doing and walk into the hall and see someone else. Not fucking Peter. I had thought, in the way that really very sane people can, that I would get what I expected, who I expected. All I had to do was expect it powerfully enough.

Instead, I got Peter, bless him, a very good man, recently returned from doing admirable humanitarian work in Rumania and deserving of a warm welcome and every courtesy. Except that I wanted him to fuck off. I wanted him to fuck off and leave me in my big house on my own, waiting for something I wasn't sure of. No, I was sure, I was absolutely, overly specifically sure and certain of what and whom I hoped to see.

My efforts at being polite to Peter were managing to reduce my conversation to the level of the absent-minded grunt. I had a relationship once where that happened quite quickly, but that was because I didn't really like the man involved at all. I think we lasted two months. It felt like lifetimes.

'Bucharest, we were there for quite a while. You

wouldn't believe . . . they said it used to be a fashion capital. Paris, New York, Rome, Bucharest. Sometimes I tried to imagine models and photographers in the streets, doing an outdoor shoot. Things is, I *could* imagine it. Everything there is an outdoor shoot.

'It's crazy. Sometimes, if you couldn't hear – you know, voices and noises and that – if you tried not to hear anything, you could walk a bit seeing nothing but all right-looking buildings and everything okay and you'd think it was anywhere. It used to be anywhere. The people all used to live there as if it was anywhere. They must have gone to the shops, run about with their kids, talked about models, communism, I don't know. Maybe it would have been like here. The people aren't much different. Pretty much the same fucking weather.'

I nodded, because nodding took less effort than grunting.

'I mean, it's different. Like having money-changers come up and hassle you. Bucharest, they've got the worst money-changers, though. Real fucking macho bastards, try to slip these big rolls of notes on you with fuck knows what kind of shite in them. I mean, you feel sorry for them. It's pathetic – they're trying to act like gangsters while the whole country's melting around them and nobody gives a fuck. Nobody cares if they make however many dollars' profit they're trying for – nobody coming in and screwing things up, nobody with an army, with an aid budget, any kind of fucking budget.

'The same all over, though, isn't it? I was thinking that. We all stand about or whatever, doing our stuff and thinking it's really significant and everyone with any . . . what . . . *influence* . . . could care less. Then again, a sniper could take any one of *them* out and they'd be pretty non-significant pretty fast. We wouldn't care. Fuck, I don't know. I'm thinking too fast, or something, but I can't really stop it yet. I think I've been not thinking too long, or something.'

'Yes.'

'Not that it's bad. You weren't getting shot at, or any-thing. It was just different kinds of people dying. I couldn't believe it, how easy it is to die. People would pass through, or you'd hear stories, this one woman had been somewhere really heavy in Bosnia – and she was a tiny wee woman, too, nothing to look at – she was talking about hearing a sort of 'pop' away off in the distance and that was a gun, or there would be just a wee thump next to you, a thud, and that was a bullet. Nothing dramatic. Too fast to think about. I couldn't have been in among that. I couldn't. Looking after kids, that's all I wanted to do. Make sure there are new people coming along. Hope they don't want to shoot anybody.'

I wanted to make another cup of tea, but I couldn't shake off his attention to move up and out of my chair.

'Coming back . . . you're mainly glad to be leaving. Miss people. Yes, you miss people, but you're coming home. I rang my mum from somewhere, somewhere near Hanover I think, does that sound right? The van got lost for a while and that would really have freaked me out, but I didn't care, nobody cared, we all kept riding, going to sleep, singing songs. I can sing offensive or incredibly sad songs in five languages, I should learn some before I go back, not let the side down.'

Something tripped in his memory, I could see it coming down in his eyes. His mouth parted slightly and he rubbed his knuckles across his forehead while his eyes closed. He was used to having his private moments in company now, didn't rush the pause before he started up again.

'Anyway – I phoned Maw and said I'd be back for something like Christmas and I was glad about that. And things look terrific over there . . . Europe, it's so . . . there are bad patches, yes, but . . . once you're over the North Sea. Do you know how bad this country looks, smells? For what we're supposed to be? For what we think we are? You wouldn't believe the crappy little dribbles of money we send out to anywhere that actually needs it over there. Oh, we get it right sometimes, but, shit, the fuck ups. They think we're crazy. Nothing personal, they're sorry for you when you're there – they like Scots but they're sorry for us. And they have . . . their opinion of Britain is . . . interesting. Do you think the Empire was like that? You think? Have we always gone abroad to majorly screw up? Is that what we're for?

'The least they think is that we're crazy. Over here, we've got no idea. No idea. Oh, God.'

'What, what's the matter?'

He flapped his arms around his head in what turned out to be a yawn and for an instant or two I thought he might be about to confide some particularly harsh reality he'd brought back with him. But it was all right, he just wanted to go to bed, suddenly completely tired. Like a child.

'Do you mind?'

'No, not a bit.'

'Where can I sleep?'

'In your room, there's nobody there.'

'Aw, sorry. I thought Martin would be fine, but then it turned out he got somewhere closer to his work. You got somebody else, though, didn't you?'

'Yes, we did. We got another Martin, but he's away.'

'Would he mind, if I kipped down there? I'll head for my mother's in the morning. I just needed a break before I saw her. Then I'll be back over there next week.'

'So soon?'

'I'd rather have it like that, really.' He began to shamble towards the door, tugging off a sweatshirt as he went.

'You wouldn't like to put some washing in, while you're here? I could probably get it dried by maybe lunchtime tomorrow.'

'Naw. That's what mothers are for. Another Martin, eh? Very ingenious.' He closed the door, having given me a look which led me to believe that he and good old Art had been in a more extensive and speculative correspondence than I had imagined.

True to his word, Pete left slightly after lunchtime, having spent the morning trying to get an Indian takeaway sent round. He'd woken up with a sudden urge for a traditional Glasgow Chicken Tikka Massala and was disappointed by the available response.

'I'd started to dream about curry. Still, never mind. Seeya. And give my best to Art. Oh, and Liz, of course.'

'Of course. Need anything for the journey?'

He slung up his back pack, jogging his knees, and looked puzzled. 'No, what would I need?'

'I don't know, Pete. I really can't think, now that you ask. You keep in touch now.'

'Mm hm.' He was already concentrating on the journey, the best hitching strategy. Maybe he was further ahead than that, thinking himself back inside the hospital with the quiet children and the flat earth yard where they used to hose the madmen clean.

I went back to the kitchen and checked how many tins of soup we'd got.

Now let me tell you something. I used to be sad sometimes when I was a child and if I had the peace to sit and cry. A point would come in the hot indulgence of it all when the crying continued although the sadness did not. I would listen to the unhappy noises I was making, feel sorry for myself and join in the weeping again. I could drift up, free of the feeling beneath the action, pretty much at will and then slope down again.

In my clear-headed moments I would consider how depressing the whole situation might seem to a calm observer and how pointless it all actually was if there was nobody to see, to be affected. Nothing was truly happening here. I wanted to be so sad that something could be made of it. I thought of someone overhearing me and coming to help, or, on one of my highflown days, that my miserableness would imprint on the house, on time, and that this section of my life would remain behind me like a sad ghost. I was probably a tedious, horrible child.

I mention all this because I have only once been at the opposite end of such an arrangement. Once and once only, standing outside a closed door and hearing the sounds of someone else's pain, I have hesitated and hesitated and hesitated until the force of gently setting my hand down to close it around the doorknob seemed to rock. I thought I might fall. I was there to be affected, a voice not far away and sobbing in at itself because there was no help it can think of that will come.

It was the 27th of January, safely over the boundary and into a fairly New Year. All aboard for '94. The nation had recently heard that the author of its government's new moral policy was, in fact, a faded – and unelected – romantic novelist. This was patently untrue from the outset, happy endings of any kind being nowhere in evidence.

There were gales and a cold snap was threatened in changeable skies where the full moon hovered like a watermark on the day.

It was time for me to go home. Steve had come back to the station and a civilised frost was maintained between us, but on that particular shift we had not even met. I had the feeling he was taking steps to avoid me and was not offended, only relieved. All was calm.

I headed home, looking forward to a pot of tea, toast if there was any bread left, a nice sleep.

When did I know something was different at the house?

I'm not sure. I would say that when I opened the front door the smell of the hallway had changed. I remember I felt a prickling sensation along my arms and across my back. It crossed my mind that we could have had burglars, but there was no sign of any disturbance. There was no sign of anything until I stopped moving and my breathing settled. Then I heard the sound from upstairs.

The bathroom door was locked. It did not give to pressure and the noise did not stop.

'Arthur? Is that you?'

No change.

'Liz?'

It couldn't have been Liz, it was a man's crying, the sounds of a crying man.

'Arthur?' I knocked on the door and there was silence. 'Arthur? This isn't Arthur, is it. Please, is this you? If you can say – it's you. Isn't it you? Martin? No . . . Savinien? I haven't forgotten. What's wrong? Please. IS IT YOU.'

I remember what happened at this point because it seemed all to be extremely slow and so it has been very easy to keep hold of. Nevertheless, some of the images are out of sequence, some clear, some very unfocused and this leads me to believe that I quickly became too involved, too much a part of the proceedings, to be of any use either to myself or to the other individual concerned. This happened even though I wanted very much to be of use, believe me. I haven't often wanted anything more.

Someone came softly to the door and drew the bolt free. I heard them move away and then pause, stand, and I couldn't – I couldn't anything. I could not do anything.

At some point I must have moved into a kind of concentration, because the tug of the doorknob against my hand sent a shudder the length of my spine and I probably made a noise.

'Jennifer?'

'Yes. Yes? Is it – '

'You are holding the door. Let go please.'

I did as I was told. Of course, I knew the voice, had no thought that I was mistaken. Savinien was there. It would be possible to see him, to touch, to shake hands, hold hands, I didn't know – it was confusing to think so much in so little time. And I already knew there was something not right. I could hear something new when

149

he spoke. His words seemed small, dry and, as he swung the door away from me, I could hear a shiver in his breath.

Now I wanted to look at him and couldn't.

What I could see, I didn't understand. There was a dark heap of what I presumed were clothes in the middle of floor. The bath was empty but lined with a thick, dull stain. The sink was also stained and there was something like a brown dust everywhere. I disturbed a little of the layer with my feet as I stepped over the threshold and realised that it was hair. The floor was covered in hair.

'Do not come any further. I would talk to you from here.'

'What?'

He had closed himself into the space between the door and the wall.

'I truly had hoped it would be you . . . the first to come home. But I was wrong with the time. You are too soon.'

'No, it's all right. It doesn't matter. I'm here, there's no one else. Look, is there something wrong? Do you want something?'

'This all should have been ended . . . finished. I wanted to be clean . . . to . . .'

His words fragmented and I found myself pressing against the wood of the door.

'No!' The word broke against the hard room, and I pulled back.

'It's okay. I'm not going to . . . I won't do anything. I'm just here. Do you feel? I'm here. Do you feel? That's all, I just want you to know where I am.' A pause and then a return of pressure against my shoulder, maybe two inches of pine between us.

'Thank you.'

'Fine, and now I know where you are, too. That's all. We're getting on all right. Where did you go to? It was a long time.'

It became very difficult to speak. I had to swallow and blink more than usual.

'I . . . this is not important now. I was never far. Uh. No, I never was so terribly far away. I couldn't . . . sometimes I imagined I might see you, that I had seen . . . Oh.' There was an exhalation and another movement. 'Jennifer, I have the impression very clearly to have wasted two lives. Now this is two lives gone.'

I pushed in harder. 'No. No, I'm sure – '

'Help me!'

I listened to what must have been his hand, rising to muffle the rest of his sentence.

'Just help me, I'm sorry, just help me. Please.'

'But tell me, tell me what can I do. What is it!'

'I should go. I should not have come.'

'No. You'll be okay here. You will.'

For a time we both lost all we could imagine to say. Then.

'Did you?' I could hardly hear him.

'Wha – '

'Did you?'

'I, uh . . . I, yes.' I was trying to get it right, I was trying very hard to get it right, but I didn't know what he meant.

'Did you? Think of me.'

'Yes.'

'And I thought of you.'

I listened while he said that and there was no change in me I could notice – my throat felt clear, my eyes perfectly usual. I didn't feel any different, but I was crying, fully crying. I looked out at the suddenly unfocused door and found myself weeping against my will – not, not even that – in the absence of my own will. I was just struck with it – tears, wet face, running nose and ultimately not enough breath.

'Jennifer? Jennifer?'

'Mm.'

'You are . . . how are you?'

'Fine. I'm fine.'

I pushed the side of my face against the door and we were still again, leaning against each other, with the house a big silence above and below.

Gradually I braced myself harder, slipping my feet out slightly to the side. The effort it took me to maintain my position suggested what I thought would be only a small betrayal. A necessary deception.

I increased the pressure.

I moved away.

He fell straight forward and down without a sound, one arm flying up as the door slammed past me and shut. I staggered when something clipped my ankle, but caught the sink and steadied myself. When I first saw him, I was looking in the mirror above the sink.

'Oh, God. I'm sorry.'

He lay quite still, his face turned from me.

'I'm sorry. I'm so sorry.'

Although he was wrapped round with towels, it was obvious he had lost a good deal of his weight. His arms and legs were pale, marked with old and new bruises, cuts, his feet were raw, swollen.

I did not want him to be like this. I wanted him to be as I remembered, now comfortably back home. I wanted him largely contented, with nothing out of place that a meal or two wouldn't fix.

When I saw him lying, I felt pointlessly furious, sick. But I didn't hurt. I only hurt when I saw his head. He had shaved all his head. His scalp and face were grey and bleeding. I leaned against the sink and watched the blur of my face reflected, misting the glass, partially obscuring the reflection of a fallen man. I wanted to go through the mirror and get him.

He huddled in on himself when I approached and I kneeled beside him so that I could speak softly and because he looked too much like the kind of figure there would always be somebody standing above, an average news-

paper snap of oppression. I had no intention of looking
down on him.

'Why did you do it? What's wrong? You don't look
too good, you know. You always were lousy at shaving.'
I tried a little laugh but the result felt unpredictable so I
stopped. 'Come on and we'll get you to your room. I
kept it for you. Come on, you can't stay here.'

'You tricked me.'

'I know I did, I'm very sorry. Were you hurt when you
fell?'

'You tricked me!'

'Ye –'

Remarkably quickly, he had rolled and grabbed my
feet away from under me. I landed stupidly, twisting my
shoulder. As I tried to slither to a sitting position, I found
one of Savinien's knees pressing across my throat.

'Huuah whu?'

I scrabbled uselessly with my free hand until it was
caught and held by the wrist. His grip was cold and
slippy. It was becoming very difficult to breathe. When
he shouted his mouth smelt of something low and sweet
and dying. The same sick honey scent was drifting and
building from the clothes piled on the floor.

'You tricked me! I trusted you! You cunt! Cunt! Cunt.
Oh, oh . . .'

His mouth winced and he let go my hand, slid off into
a crouch beside my head. I have to say I got to my feet
as soon as possible and got in my own share of screaming.
I was angry.

'What the fuck are you doing! I'm trying to help you!
What are you, crazy! You try that again, you're out of
the house, out of the house. I don't care who you are.
Fuck. Fuck! You idiot! Stupid, fucking idiot.'

He shivered and stared.

'Awfff . . . no, don't. I should be doing that! Don't
start. Look, I am not coming near you, you are just going

to have to sit there and be . . . I can't help you. I can't. Just stop it! Stop it!'

It was fear really, I wasn't angry at all, I was suffering from delayed fear. So I yelled and I yelled and his face pulled apart into sobs and then I stopped yelling because I was starting to just cough and it was doing no good, except that he was quietening a bit and in the end I sat down and I sort of nudged at him and he didn't do anything and then I grabbed for his hand and he flapped me away and I tried it again and he flapped me away again and that happened a few times and then we did hold hands. We held hands for quite a while. We did that.

'I'm sorry. I don't usually shout.'

'No. I must apologise.'

'Too right.'

'I should never . . . I have never done something like this to a woman. I am . . . I am terribly ashamed.'

'Yeah well, don't do it again.'

'I'll try not to.'

'That's not a very good answer.'

'I don't feel very good. I'm . . . I'm . . . I would really like to be clean. I washed and washed. I used the little brush you have and so much water, as hot as I could bear, but it has not made any difference. I can feel I am not clean.'

'I know, I know.' I didn't, but it seemed the right thing to say. 'We'll sort it out, though. But you're freezing. I'll get you something to wear.'

'No.'

'Yes. You can't stay here, you're shivering and you're – you can't sit here for ever. Right? I'll put some stuff on Peter's bed and I'll tidy up here. All right?'

'Burn my clothes.'

'Oh.'

'Burn them.'

'Yes, fine, I'll see to it all, don't worry. I'm just going

to go through to Pete's room now, okay? And then we'll talk. Okay?'

'Yes. But Jennifer?'

'Mm hm?'

'Don't be long away.'

'Fine. Fine, I won't be.'

'Eh!'

'What! What's the matter.'

'Mmm. I am about to yawn.'

I thought that he was being euphemistic and was going to throw up on my linoleum. Why not just put the cherry on the icing on the cake of unsociable behaviour, after all? He was always a very wholehearted man, why not be thoroughly committed about pissing me off. He had already been highly euphemistic about cleanliness when obviously he meant he was crawling with something or other that meant his clothes needed burning, so I would have to go to the chemist now and buy whatever it was you bought to prevent these things, while trying to smile at the shop assistant as if this was a problem I personally did not have.

Nothing is ever easy, the way you think, especially not coming home.

But when he said yawn, he meant it. He meant it very seriously. He closed his eyes while I watched the spasm of yawning climb from his feet, working through the muscle until it flowed up round his neck and kicked his mouth open in one huge gape. He began to dribble saliva. The two and a half minute yawn – I'd never seen one of them before. At the end of it he gave a watery little smile and wiped his lips with the back of his hand. I leaned forward to cast a shadow over him and caught a slight glimmer on his skin before the dampness faded. Some things hadn't changed.

'Hah. I have no idea why I have to do this now. It is very pleasant, but inconvenient when I am walking.'

'Mm, right. I'll go now. Don't do anything I couldn't while I'm away.'

'Yes.'

I went to bed that night with my head in an old knitted bobble hat and nothing to inhale but the wonderfully effective reek of delousing solution. This precaution was probably unnecessary, but after disinfecting the bathroom and kicking Savinien's abandoned clothes into a bin liner, I had felt in need of chemical reassurance.

Arthur and Liz got the benefit of a spotless bath and adjoining facilities without being burdened by any information that might have disturbed them. Well that's how I justified it, anyway. I told them 'Martin' was home and was rewarded with one mild stare (Liz) and one interested smile (Art).

As far as I know, we all got a fair night's sleep.

THE MORNING AFTER the night before and all Hell is about to break absolutely loose.

'Hey, Arthur.'

'Hey, Jennifer. Happy now?'

'What?' Art let slip a particularly gormless smile which proved to be slightly infectious. 'Well, chhhruff, it is good to know where he is. I suppose.'

'Mm hm.'

'Which leads me to your starter for ten. First question.'

'You want a favour.'

'Yes, please, Art.'

'I'm on my day off, far away from the flour and sweat and tears of the flat baked goods and you want me to do something.'

'Yes I do.'

'Even though I may be maddened with exhaustion and liable to lash out at any moment.'

'Yup.'

'Go on, then.'

'Um, you see it isn't anything really, only to keep an ear out in case, ah, Martin isn't all right.'

'Couldn't I know what his name is. If I'm going to keep an ear out. Not to mention sharing the same house. I mean, he isn't called Martin, so what do we call him – it would only be polite to get it right.'

'Savinien.' All good girls should tell the truth. Eventually.

'That's what I like, a good Scots name. Savinien?'

'Yes.'

'Sauvignon – that's a kind of wine. French. Man called

after a brand of booze – don't tell me, his mother was frightened by a bottle-opener. He doesn't have an accent.'

'He has a fucking funny way of speaking.'

'Well, who needs explanations, not me. And he does, indeed, have a fucking funny way of speaking. I'd buy it all for a dollar – satisfied as anything, me.'

'I'm telling you as much as I know.'

'No, I think you're still fibbing a bit, actually, but don't worry, I'll keep an eye on him. Where did he go?'

'Upstairs.'

'No, where did he go for all those weeks. If he'd been upstairs I would have noticed, because I go upstairs, too.'

'I don't know.'

'Ah.'

'No, I really don't know. But from the look of him it wasn't Butlin's West World.'

'Okay.'

'He hasn't told me yet – you'll find out as soon as I do.'

'Okay.'

'I'm, ah, glad, you're around, you know. You're appreciated.'

'Mm hm.'

And I went to work, leaving it at that.

At work? Nothing special. Except that I ran into Steve in a corridor. That is to say, I didn't run into him, I slowed down before I could be at all threatening. I smiled and he nodded and did not smile. I couldn't blame him. He looked peaky. That's all the feeling I got when I looked him over – that he looked a bit off colour. Funny how you won't necessarily ever know what you really saw in someone and sometimes it will go and you will be none the wiser, only bewildered when you see them without whatever gloss your will and hopefulness used to add.

I think more and more that this happened with my parents. They trapped each other into replacing their original relationship with another and another and another, all with each other, all part of a search for something they could not quite put their fingers on but would have liked to. One way or another, they certainly had each other very securely cuffed. I'd like to have asked them about it, but I'm too late to ask them now. I know how it would go anyway. I would say, 'Why?' and then they would say, 'Why what?' or 'Why not?' or 'We don't know.'

Steve finished off his nod with a sneer of good old-fashioned loathing and for the next few steps I did feel very slightly like a perversely violent worm, but the feeling didn't last. I can never sustain guilt for all that long if it has any root at all in reality.

I returned home via the Army & Navy stores with a selection of warm and suitable things for Savinien to be making do with.

Arthur opened the door to me, very angry and I didn't know why.

'You didn't tell me.'

'Tell you?'

'Oh, will you give it a fucking rest. You know perfectly well. Now what is he coming off?' I put down my carrier bag. 'What has he been taking?'

'He's been . . . on . . .' I felt immensely stupid, slow.

'He is in withdrawal, now what has he been taking?'

'Well, but there weren't any . . . I didn't see anything. No, it's just the way he can be.'

'Look I'm sure as I can be that he hasn't been injecting anything, for which we can all be extremely grateful. Did you have any idea what you were bringing in here.'

'He was my friend.'

'Oh for fucksake. Really . . . You didn't know?' He was squinting into my eyes, looking for something I didn't have.

'I didn't know. He wasn't using anything before he left. I would have known.'

'You're sure?'

'Yes, yes I am. I don't understand . . . Are you . . . This couldn't be anything else?'

'Listen.'

There was nothing to hear.

'What do you mean? I don't hear anything.'

'Exactly. It's quiet now because he's sleeping. He's been sleeping for an hour. If past experience is anything to go by, he will sleep for another hour and then wake up. Then he will shout for a bit and sweat – I mean really sweat, he's rolling with it, then he'll be burning up, dry, then he'll sweat – and then he will hide in a corner of his room before he starts to throw up. I have tried to get him to the bathroom before he gets too involved with throwing up and I have also been giving him water to drink so that he has something to throw. Now this sounds to me just a bit as if he's coming down. Even if it didn't, he isn't pretending any more – he is begging me, and I mean begging me, for something to remove the way he feels. I don't have the something.'

'He's hurting. It isn't fun watching someone hurt that much. You really don't know where he went?'

Arthur was trying to keep his voice low, evening his words out into a kind of hiss and holding my shoulders.

'You have no idea?'

'No.'

'Well, now I have a favour to ask of you.'

'We can't put him out. I mean, maybe a hospital would take him, could – '

Arthur's face began to shout before he pressed it under control and pulled me in close enough to growl next to my ear. 'Who! . . . who do you think you're talking to? Of course we can't chuck him out on the street. He's having a bad time but it's not something that needs to involve hospitals, for Christ's sake, I don't mind looking after him, he was . . . he is a nice guy. We'll do all right, we'll do all right. Probably. I mean, I don't think it'll get any worse.'

I whispered back, 'Okay,' and we stood apart again.

'All right, all right. What I wanted to ask you was if you would search Pete's room.'

'Why?'

'Because your man's got something in there. Or he thinks he does. A couple of times when I've come in, he's been looking for something and stopped himself. Then he started tearing the place up a bit. He knew I was there, but that made no difference, he didn't care. I think he brought something with him and now he can't find it. If we knew what it was . . .'

'What? If we knew . . .'

'Then we would know. I don't know. What do you think I am – I've seen this happen once before in my entire life – right? – a guy coming off booze and pills. The last place I lived. I'm not a fucking expert.'

'What happened?'

'I told you, he was looking for something.'

'With the guy before.'

'Oh, well, he started seeing things and then he went into convulsions. They took him into hospital.'

'Was he okay?'

'A psychiatric hospital. I don't know if he was okay, I left before there was any news. I don't actually enjoy this kind of thing. He was crazy anyway, he was a mad bastard, he'd been drinking for years – it was different.'

'How do you know?'

'I don't know. I just think so. If we keep doing what we're doing and stop Martin, whoever, from getting too weak, or doing anything stupid. He doesn't seem to be getting worse. He seems to be evening out.'

'Where was he looking?'

'Hm?'

'Savinien, where was he looking when you caught him?'

'Oh, the fireplace – somewhere in the fireplace. Come on, look, I need a bit of normality, all right? We'll get a cup of tea and a sandwich before it all starts up again. I promise, we'll need it. What's in the bag?'

'Nothing special.'

'Good, then we'll talk about it, what's in the bag?'

And this was how we began to be Savinien's jailers. It took a little time, but we learned to pre-empt his thinking and police his actions. He could be unpredictable, sly. Often it didn't help anyone to know we were on his side because he had stopped living in a place where that was believable. We were as patient as we could be with his lies and tried to remember the man behind them, willing us to find him out. Sometimes he would tell the truth which was much worse.

The first time Arthur burst on to the landing, half carrying Savinien, I looked away. Vomiting and then dry retching echoed in the bathroom. I could hear Arthur speaking and a thin, uneven noise answering.

Sometimes Savinien would curse in a thick flow of language I couldn't recognise. Or he might shout an obscenity in clear English, his eyes showing hurt, offended sensibility with nowhere to go.

I began my duties with a search of the fireplace – push at the tiling surround, stretch an arm up and round the chimney.

There.

Something soft and smooth was lodged between the bricks and the metal of the damper. It was a clear plastic sachet containing exactly twenty-eight parti-coloured capsules.

'Atties.'

'They're what?'

'Ativan – rose-tinted spectacles guaranteed by the milligram. Now I know what he's been asking for – his atties. I thought I was mishearing. Could've been worse. It could be a lot fucking worse. If this was all.'

'All I could find. He's addicted to happy pills?'

'It's hardly unusual.'

'Well, no . . . no, my mother was very fond of her Librium – wouldn't go on holiday without laying in an emergency supply. I suppose that was . . . unusual. But I was expecting . . . well, I don't know. How did he get a hold of these?'

'Ask him.'

'Thanks. Why don't you?'

'Because you'll do it better than me. Cool, calm and collected.'

'Every Thursday like the refuse sacks.'

'He'll listen to you. You'll be fine.'

'All right. Shall I take them with me?'

'Take one. I'll flush the others away where they belong and we'll hope he only had one stash.'

Art gave me a pat on the shoulder and I started upstairs. It had been dark outside for several hours and the intervals of peace between vomiting had elongated.

'You awake?'

He lay curled on his side, facing the doorway. I could see his eyes were open.

'Do you mind if I come in?'

The eyes gave a long blink. I moved close enough to notice the whole bed was shaking. The hands clutching the quilt to his throat were shuddering. I watched his mechanism breaking down and didn't know if there would be anything to replace it . . .

'Can you speak?'

'Yes.' Every letter of the word escaped with an involuntary stammer of air.

'Well, we need you to tell us where you got the pills.'

'No.'

'That's not very helpful.'

'Not now.'

'We found where you hid them.' His face smoothed into an innocent glow of relief. He seemed younger, stiller, in moments.

I shook my head, 'No, you don't understand.' The eyes clouded again, a dull burn behind them.

'If we gave you them you would have to be like this

all over again afterwards. This way you'll finish it and then you can get well – you'll be fine. Come on, you'll manage, you're through the worst. You know that, don't you? Me and Arthur, we'll see you right. I promise.'

He rolled over and didn't speak again.

That night Arthur and I were woken by dull, irregular thudding.

Savinien was slumped in the corner of the room, close by the window. Now and again he would turn his head and beat it off the wall behind him. The sleeves of his pyjamas were covered in soot – he must have been searching the chimney again, hoping his need would make things all right. If he wanted them enough, we couldn't have taken his pills, he must have only imagined the theft.

'I hurt.'

We walked him between us, pausing when he had to yawn or a cramp attacked him.

And in the morning I called Liz's current boyfriend/ older man friend and told him to suggest she should stay over with him for a week or so – plague in the house, better to stay away and Arthur sends his love, that kind of thing.

Which gave us seven days of working in shifts, sleeping in shifts, calling in sick and guarding our domesticated madman.

Savinien was afraid of the dark. At times the expanse of his room would terrify him and Arthur or I would have to speak to him while he cowered against a wall, his mattress closely dragged up after him.

On the Wednesday he seemed to move into a kind of calm. Arthur and I were watchful. Savinien made it across the landing alone. His chin was too high and he had the air of a tightrope walker, but we had hopes for him.

For the first time in a while, I felt like eating.

Three or four hours later, he appeared in the kitchen holding the contents of the medicine cabinet. We hadn't thought of that. There wasn't much there to harm him, but we still hadn't thought of that. Our carelessness raised a sweat on my upper lip.

He dropped the bottles and packets on to the table and stood. I thought he intended to speak, but he was brought to a halt by a long yawn that ended in a retch.

'I beg your pardon.'

'Don't worry about it.'

'Take these away from me or I will look for them. I . . . I am not my own man. I used to talk about honour, that thing we are born with. I have given mine away.'

The next day he was ill again, calling out that something was crawling under his skin, scratching himself. The gleam in his sweat was faint and sickly.

Friday was calmer. He had a poison dream, that was all.

On Saturday, he laughed about something none of us could remember later, but whatever it was, it was entirely real and funny enough to laugh about. And we all laughed with a will, made a point of it, in fact. The stubble on Savinien's head was thickening and his skin was evening its colour, no longer ashy or puce. In his surplus clothing, he looked a little like a military recruit, only fresher, more hesitant.

So, physically, Savinien got better. We lifted our voluntary quarantine and Liz came home, leaving again almost immediately in the car whose motor we heard running while she dropped one bag of clothes and filled another. She had an interesting life, very committed.

Our days patterned out much as they had before, except that Arthur brought home more unwanted pastries than we could usually face to satisfy Savinien's new, compulsively sweet tooth.

But we couldn't help feeling a weight in our air. There was another darkness coming, that was all we knew – no need to reach for it now, no need to second guess, because it was on its way.

One

Thick
Inescapable
Thought
Falling
Hard
And
Numb
And
Bitter
Slicing
Down
The Mind
Tugging
It
Under.

Having come home and fought for his health, prayed for his health, screamed in convulsion for his health, I watched Savinien regret his own survival. He left off food, slept day into night, stopped speaking. Because Arthur and I had spent so much time with him, made really quite trivial sacrifices on his behalf, we felt ourselves rejected. I was perhaps less philosophical about it than Arthur, but both of us had the impression that someone had become our child and then turned against us, grown out rather than up. I began to feel we might have been bad parents.

It was an odd time altogether. Beyond our house, in other more or less salubrious addresses, sweating armfuls of the politically incorrect were committing Moral Disarmament. Reality was running amok in a way that could only embarrass fiction. My bulletins developed a genuinely Berlin Nightclub feel while it became clear that we, the public, had become too tame a lay – Parliament had ditched the unconstitutional for the just plain unnatural acts. In many ways it made perfect sense of what we'd always really suspected they got up to behind those high, closed doors. No wonder our government's concentration often lapsed – now we could see it was cruel and arbitrary, even demented, for a reason. Screwing itself blind and rabid left it no time for us. Perversion can be quite exhausting – I should know.

For those of us unable to pursue such virulent and esoteric indoor sports, other distractions were lavishly provided. As my planet and my country spun daily further towards irredeemable dissolution, an unheard of largess was being exercised in the provision of second-hand outdoor sport. Rough-and-tumble chasing and record-breaking broadcasts were blanketing the watching and earwigging public at any and every hour.

During this particular month, Norway was filled to overflowing with men and women sliding up and down things Olympically. Their ingenuity with frozen water was depressing. But unexpected moments of terrible vulnerability flickered through the white, slithering course of it all like blood. In other words, I waited to see them fall. Especially the skaters.

I spent most of one Sunday afternoon hypnotised by skaters, sequined and sexlessly camp in a way that could only be excused by miraculous athleticism, when for the most part they were just sliding up and down some frozen water. Still it was wonderfully awful when they fell. The grace, the training, all their defences would disappear in one torn instant when they would slip and tumble like anybody else because ice is slippy, after all. I watched for their falls and their struggle to catch on a balance again, to replace the synchronised swimmer's smile and the mindlessly gesturing arms. I felt increasingly sick and nervous on their behalf, as if I was running my thumb over the line between justified bravado and utter indignity. That afternoon they looked far too much like life.

Savinien passed the doorway while a Russian duo fumbled through locomotive simulated intercourse and too much chiffon. I don't know what there was about him that made me uneasy, I only saw him for an instant, after all. Maybe I had grown accustomed to reading the tilt of moving bodies. He certainly read all wrong to me.

'Hey.'

He'd reached the kitchen, was standing in front of the sink, his face to the window's light.

'Hey, you all right? Hum, listen, I was thinking, it's all very well, you dressing like a NATO commander, forces of all nations, but maybe you'd like to pick something out for yourself. If you felt . . . maybe it would be interesting for you. Make a change.'

He absolutely didn't move. I don't think he was even breathing.

'If I'm disturbing you, I'll go.'

One drip fell from the tap and shattered.

'Am I disturbing you?'

I heard the metal clatter at the sink and saw him bend and I knew we were a little lost again, at least a little lost.

He made a ragged turn.

'Shit. Shit, oh shit. Why?'

'Oh, I don't know. I just . . .' His hands raised in defeat and bright with blood.

As it happened, he hadn't been able to cut anything vital. In anger or frustration he had closed both his fists around the carving knife. Squeezed. At the time I did not understand this and there was a great deal of blood.

'You . . . you fucking . . . God, you . . . stupid fucking man!'

I was angry. I closed in and shook him uselessly by the shoulders while he twitched his arms out of the way and began to drip blood on to my back. A warm splash on my neck called me slightly to my senses again. I stood up on my toes and pressed my forehead against his, gripping his skull with both my hands, the hot skin there under his growing hair.

I waited until he opened his eyes.

'We are going to clean you up again now and then you are going to tell me what has been going on because I have no more patience and if I don't know what has happened to you, I am afraid you will keep on being stupid like this until you get it right. This is very ridiculous and I won't have it.'

Savinien blinked.

'And don't think you're not worth all this bother. If anyone's going to think that it'll be me. Don't even consider it.'

I could feel him moving against me. When you are too close to someone like that, you are very aware of their aliveness. All the time there are pulses, tensions, readjustments of muscle, shifts of breath.

Quite together, we looked ahead, we blinked, we looked, both of us all that we could see. I loosened my grip.

'Jennifer?'

'Yes.'

'Do you know . . . I feel well.'

'How do you mean?'

'I mean that I feel perfectly well. My hands don't hurt yet. I am sure they will, but now they are only cold.'

For a moment, he shook his head as if he was settling a loose idea. 'I will be well now. Yes, I'm quite certain. I will be well.'

'Don't think I'm not pleased. I am pleased. But was all that performance really necessary. Oh, for goodness' sake, come here, you're leaking all over the place.'

His cuts were not terribly deep. The hospital casualty department seemed too much of an ordeal and my doctor's receptionist was less than sympathetic when I called, so we did the best we could ourselves. Strangely, I only felt nauseous when the cleaning and the bandaging was done, when his pain had subsided.

'I don't guarantee that I'm getting this right. Hold still, though.'

'This seems more than adequate.'

'Well I should hope so. You'll probably end up with your lifeline twice the length.'

'I would like that.'

I tried to be light and gentle, drawing away if he seemed to flinch. We co-operated well around his discomfort and smiled and smiled and smiled.

Why not? He believed he would be well now, that was good enough for us. We knew how we felt. Moment for moment we understood the slip and press of cloth over our skins, the easy temperature of our bloods, the colour of our minds. We were just as we were.

To demonstrate the advantages of having been a little dead for a long while I might tell you how I was, that I was in the position of coming upon – what – joy, happiness, gladness, as if it had never been before I was.

Once in my life, to date, I saw something very like joy. A series of little broadcasts had taken me north. I had reached almost the furthest extent of my country, a wild, odd spread of islands, afloat on the tightening bands of latitude that creep up to ice and the Pole.

I spoke for my suppers and walked as hard and as far as I could on any fair days left alone to me. The islands were good for walking. My progress finally brought me to an open bay where the high curve of the world climbed up to the depths of the Atlantic. I stepped down there to the edge of the sand and the whole hump-backed ocean lifted the sky like a blue-green impossibility.

And in my mind I was washed away. White gushed at my feet, roared at the cliffs, bleached and salted the continuous numbing breeze and took me out like a sail. I knew the right size of myself, the nothing I would be in the simple beat of miles and years of waves. Land would grow and break, gather and waste away and I would be myself beyond the movements of earth and time.

No one should go to church – take them all to the seaside, do them good.

Having exercised a touch of happiness with Savinien,

we walked up to his room and talked because it was time for us both to hear where he had gone and what he had done. Nothing he might say could harm us, we'd made ourselves invincible.

Savinien sat on the bed and I pulled up a chair to face him. He covered his mouth to cough and the movement disturbed the air near my face. I nodded.

'It's time now, really. If we wait any longer, neither of us will be able to say a thing. We'll freeze up. I'm sure you've faced far worse.'

'I am not afraid. You are very good for my courage, you know this, Jennifer? You are en-couraging.'

'Thanks. I don't have too much courage myself, I can tell you.'

'Perhaps I have borrowed more than I should.'

'I don't think it works that way.'

'I shall put it back.' He reached forward and I gave him my hand. He took it lightly. 'To keep you informed, my mother taught me this. I think possibly this is the only thing she did teach me. Espérance, that was her name – Hope – something of which she had need. My father was not the best husband and she had to spend her life with him. For my part, I spent very little time with my father and that was still more than enough. My mother, at least, made me feel like her son. She would rest a glance upon me and I would know who I was at once, if I had pleased, or disappointed. Father was the kind of man you would want to . . . to insult very badly, to steal from, you understand?'

'I think so.'

'Factually, I must say that I did insult him very badly and steal from him . . . ah . . . but he did make this as though it was his fault.'

Savinien's hand firmed in around mine. I could feel a smooth, solid pressure under the dressing.

'I know. Some people can do that. I know.'

'Eh, but we have a matter here in hand . . . I was . . . I

suppose encouraging myself. So . . . as my mother taught me . . . to give courage, some force of life, I must, with your permission . . .

'Do I have your permission?'

'Oh . . . yes. Yes, you do.'

'Good. That's good.' And he closed his eyes, bent his head, kissed my open palm. 'Now it's necessary, you close your fingers. Then it shan't escape again.'

I took back my hand. 'I remember when you did that before . . . it's very . . . I don't know . . . daft. Nice daft. You know what I mean by daft?'

Big smile, huge smile, a smile with something waiting at the back of its eyes. 'Oh, yes . . . but that makes no difference. It's the gesture, you know. The gesture stands for itself. Always. And, ah well, I have to say this has worked an effect on a number of individuals, a number of times before. I admit that I did want to know if this was still possible. This was nothing personally to do with you. I mean no offence.'

'I'm sure. I think I'll open my hand again now and we can begin.'

'Of course.'

There was a short silence.

'Yes, I shall talk to you now. But if you will excuse me – '

He swung himself slowly up on to the bed and lay back, allowed himself a small readjustment of his weight, a sigh. 'You see, I have such a tiredness. It is like an animal that waits for me, but don't worry.' He inclined his head slightly towards me. 'I will make my best effort now, to speak and not to sleep. You have been very patient through all of . . . this . . . this me. Remember that my story will be very ugly, but you are please to not mind it. The whole of this is over now, do you understand?'

'Yes.'

'I will not return to it.' He gave a small wince. 'You

know, I used to imagine from the time when was I a boy that I would make wonderful voyages and in my mind I did. I really did go away from all of those faces, all of those looks and those impacts in the street, all of myself. I broke off the earth and lifted beyond it daily, daily, daily and I saw paradise. I promise you, I ate and drank in paradise.'

He pursed his lips, flopped one hand. 'Now the journeys my body could manage to make, they were always something of a disappointment.' He shook his head softly. 'Hmm. I have had so many years to change, far more than one man (one not such a good man) could reasonably expect and so little about me is different at any point. I have made another bad journey and I did not even accompany it with good dreams. I am a fool.'

'No.'

'Of course, yes. I already have lain dying once, on my death's bed, and told anyone who would hear that I had wasted everything. Now this is two lives and no good sense between them.'

'What happened when you were away?'

Savinien stretched and edged himself up to sit. I saw the way his body moved together as one live thing, the shadow of pain around his mouth once, the way his chin tipped up and back fluidly and then fell to rest. His hands folded one above the other near his waist, they rose and fell with his breath.

SAVINIEN WAS RIGHT, the story he had to tell was ugly. Particularly, its pain surprised me. Some suffering I find intellectually dreadful but I will allow it to strangers every day. Certain words, sentences, memories, I never want my friends to have.

I don't mention this to set myself up as a great, or even an especially firm, kind of friend. I am showing you one of my ego's earliest, tenderest lines of defence – my mind is not built to support the cultivation of friends, because friendship is a source of pain. Today I know that pain is infectious, or to be more exact, contagious – it requires a certain contact, a closeness to slip in. If I feel, if I care, if I love, then life can kick me in the heart at any time it chooses. I am opened like a fish to hurt with one simple movement, one deep touch. I would rather this didn't happen, on the whole.

'But I am certain that I killed no one. Nobody died, or if they did I had no part of it. Or if I did then I regret it very much. Still, since I left you, I do not believe I took a single life.'

I closed my eyes and concentrated on the shape of the chair beneath me. Something sank away in my mind and yawned out over an unimaginable depth. 'Savinien, I don't understand what you're saying, could you explain please, to me? Could you explain. At the beginning.'

'I do not think I killed anyone. I believe I did not and I would remember killing. I know how that feels. I know the look of dying. I have told you this.' He halted himself for a moment. 'You should not have me in your home. I realise that you feel you know me, but you do not. A man of my kind, with an uncleanness inside . . . I should not be welcome in your home.'

'Well, I'm afraid it's too late for that. You're already welcome and there's nothing you can do to change that. Do you understand?'

He made a dry little laugh which I ignored.

'Look, at the beginning, you could start there and then I would know what you mean. But there is nothing you could say that would change us, your welcome here. Nothing. I do mean that.'

And then he started to speak very slowly, clearly, mainly looking ahead of him, as if the words he said were written on the air before his face, but very small so that he had to peer and concentrate.

First, he told me where he'd been which made me sad because for all those lost weeks, he'd stayed ridiculously close. For some reason, the idea of such a tiny, but total, separation suddenly set me feeling how stupidly alone we both had been. The comfort of our present state seemed very fragile.

'Yes, the entire time. I was almost still here. To be simple, I could not leave entirely. Eh . . . no, they once took me somewhere else which I would not think about now . . . on a . . . I had to do something for them there and God forgive me and also them. But above the whole of this,' he gave the twitch of a smile, 'I was truly never more than one hour of walking from here. Often much less. Believe me, there were nights when I went to sleep imagining that small walk home. I had neither hope nor faith for it, but it made a fine dream. When there was a moon . . . you know how near a moon can seem . . . I would watch it, lift my hand, étou . . . cover its light and let it shine and cover it again and it seemed then in no point proper that I could see something so beautiful as this and never touch it. I am close enough to know this thing and to desire it and yet I do not have the power to move and be with it. If I may furnish an example, I have held a man with my arms around him and my body over him to press his life back in, to hold it within his frame once a bullet has let it out and this has been all to no purpose. A moment before, he was complete with living, and next, so completely not. This is the same thing.'

He turned suddenly, open-faced, the colour in his eyes deep. 'I wrote to his wife. It's something to do, to write, isn't it? When life has baffled an author and hidden its possibilities, then he can always write.'

He put his hands to his head. 'Jennifer, I wanted to write this, in preference to being present with these words, but I can no longer write, I cannot set a mark on paper. The language . . . I am defeated . . . and I have the concentration of an angry schoolboy. And I have every right to say so, I have been one before. Then I was learning and now I am unlearning. I am nothing but forgetting. Every night God fills my mind with worlds to express and I can tell them to no one, record them for no one and be certain only that because they are mine, they are lost the moment they are born.'

I watched him scratch his ear, shrug and smile at somewhere behind my head. 'This is not precisely my ideal condition. I wish you could see me at my best, I do.' And then a long, smooth look at me. 'But now I would ask you to let me write to you.'

'I'm sorry, I don't understand again.'

'Which is my fault. I am asking that you allow me to be not here. Simple, simple, only simple, nothing complex. Close your eyes and I shall close mine, not to be away from you, but to be nearer. With your indulgence, I will make you my reader and now there can be nothing between us, nothing to check your mind from entering mine. What this is, these words, is for ever. This is our lives speaking directly, having set us aside.'

'Well, I suppose, I'm here then. I'm listening.'

'Sssh. Your eyes.'

'Are closed.'

'And now so are mine. That day when I left, yes, to start with the start . . . I stood in your park and you moved away and into your life and I stayed where I was. Very clearly I knew that I could never be a part of this world, or of your reality. You had told me that the heart of the city was to the east and I could not have borne to be in a city of yours, of your time, I was not prepared to face that, so I went west. I ran to the west.'

As he spoke this time, I could hear his throat relax. He was forgetting himself, becoming his story.

'All was very strange. Your cars, how can you allow these things? They move people but they do so much more, they make such fear. At one point I was in amongst them and I could see one driver's face, boxed up there with his wheel in the darkness, he was not making a journey, he was setting out to kill.

'And this was his choice, no affair of mine, but a suitable introduction to the customs of your country. Now I had an idea I would be safer if I climbed and I did this and found a wonderful high path that led clear between great, red stone houses and grey barracks, above the car-road and into ruined ground. I know how to live off ruined ground. This is not my preference but I do know how.'

He had found the old railway line. Some years ago, the route had been tarmacked over and turned into a cycle path which now led, albeit erratically, right to Loch Lomond. Savinien had never made it that far. Having no way of knowing that our countryside was not all one type or another of ruined ground, he had suffered no hopes of countryside if he moved on.

I think he had also chosen to stay where he could organise himself something like food. He may have scavanged a little, even stolen from the doocots by the path, although he avoided ever saying so. For part of the time he undoubtedly preyed off small game, setting traps. Or not.

'He came to my hand, I called him and he came.'

'He would have. Dogs will. You know that.'

'I know the theory. Father loved his dogs far more than I – no – far more than me. No, also far more than I. If the dog had been accompanied, of course, I would have stayed my hand, but he was just straying. A lost thing, like me.'

'You ate a dog.'

'In my time I have spit-roasted a monkey and eaten that. As I remember, its owner was the one at fault but I could hardly have eaten him. In any case, for its own part, the monkey was certainly an irritation far greater than its size might have suggested. They were very like each other, the man and the monkey. I might say they were very close in many ways . . . very sympathetic . . .'

'All right . . . I think I can guess.'

'The monkey tasted good. But the dog tasted better. And I ate it through genuine hunger, not simple ill-humour, which makes an important distinction . . . No.'

He stopped, I heard a small movement and wanted to look at him, but did not. I kept my word, stayed blinded. He coughed several times and then began again, a soft, dry note in his voice, a defeat.

'No. What happened with the dog, I know very clearly. I have just told you a large lie. Possibly I had good reason. You should know, when I met the dog I finally under-stood in my heart that I would do anything my fear and need instructed. When I swallowed the dog's flesh, I also consumed my dignity and my own proper will. I ate up all I had that made my life a life.

'This is as good a point as any to tell the truth. I think so. Eh . . . then imagine an open place which is away from lights. A path runs across it and there is a tower full of doves but it is full night and I cannot see them. The ground here is often wet, I have fallen before in the mud. I have fought here and have felt a man kick against my grip like a body dangled on a noose when I held his head in water here. Now there is the shine and the crack of ice in the dark beneath us and the deep sky above. I feel I am standing between two nights and I wish I was alone to understand this, but I am not.

'There are men with me. They found me and came for me and have kept coming for me and I do what they say. This is not because they are my masters, I have never had a master. This is because they give me what I need, they feed me my heart's ease and my sleep.

'For a time, you understand, I was very used to the peace I could find in wine until it made me slow and stupid and ill. Through my first years in Paris, in my other life, the wine was always there for me, slicing little ribbons from my soul and finding out my secrets to offer them beautiful promises and turn through the walls of my dreams. I almost dreamed myself to death. When I woke I swore I would rather drink arsenic than alcohol and I kept my word. A few of my dreams returned in life, but they lacked perfection. My writing was consistently far better and fuller than my own existence. The men from the waste ground gave me perfect dreams in little mouthfuls and I loved them.'

His words did not fumble, did not halt, they only faded very slightly sometimes at the end of a thought and there was a broken deliberation as he spoke each one of them out. Very quietly, very gently, under his breath there was the sound of his hurt. I knew this because I know how to listen and because it hurt me too.

'This night, the men and I, we have a fire. We turn and pace around it like the animals we have become. From my past experience, I know that I am here to fight. I will be engaged in another's cause, defending another's honour as I have done so many times. When I am left alone, victorious, my friend James will give me the medicine I need to cure me of the ills my last medicine left.

'And they tell me . . . James tells me with his lovely voice that the stranger who can no longer stand and so is now sitting in the mud is his enemy. The enemy of my friend is my enemy. But tonight I am not to harm the stranger because he has been harmed enough by James and his Inquisition. Tonight I am to demonstrate my skill at arms against the stranger's second. Against his dog.

'I fought the dog. They gave me my sword and I fought the dog. It was strong and brave . . . pres . . . almost the weight of a man . . . a not unworthy opponent. We were two creatures, owned creatures, kept to fight and terrify.

'But finally . . . Finally, I was angry and because I had no force to fight them and no dignity to show, I promised them I would kill the dog and eat it. I would roast it on the fire and throw them its skin. I kept my word. I have that, even at the end, my word, I had that when they laughed.

'I cannot tell you how familiar it always seemed when they laughed. I am accustomed to that ignorant ring a laughing crowd will make, standing closer than you can bear them, but still out of your reach and they look and they laugh. I would like to have a life when no one laughs at me, when my respect is with me like my shadow, something to take entirely for granted. Eh? Is this going to happen at some time? Wouldn't this be just? A just and handsome thing?

'The dog's flesh . . . the warmth . . . blood, it made me sick. The sound of it crying when I slashed its belly took away my appetite. It waited for me calmly once its strength had gone. I came to kill it and it watched me with eyes that were so puzzled. It could not understand its pain, nor why it had been so poorly rewarded for fighting with all of its heart. When I knelt by its shoulder, I gave it hope. Trusting, it tried to move towards me and whimpered and then tried to move and then I cut through its throat and into its spine.

'The men applauded me and I watched the firelight catching all about me in the blood.'

I could hear him rubbing at his scalp, steadying his breath.

'I do apologise. Believe me, I can offend no one more

than myself. Pfff . . . let me tell you how I lived before the men came. Let me purify my mind.

'When I first came to the wasted ground, I made shelters but they were broken down. Almost as soon as I left them on some occasions, they would be beaten into the earth or burned. In the night once, some of the men came to burn both me and the roof I'd made over my head. I think this was not a dream. I am sure I was woken by the rain one morning, away from any shelter. I would not have slept without covering myself, I could not have. But don't mistake me, this changeable life was no hardship. I was less than anxious to fix myself down. I believed a more permanent address would encourage unwelcome curiosity. I was trying to make an independent life. That impossible thing. Free from false complications. Still, I was never delighted to come back from hunting and find my small belongings scattered in smaller and smaller pieces, even when I had hidden my position very well. And at last the fires did make me rather despair.'

In daylight, Savinien contended with an incomprehensible stream of joggers and bicyclists. He felt they had an air of rehearsal about them, a promise of light relief, almost of fantasm, hallucination.

'I decided this little path must surely be the route for some corps of messengers, or for a huge company of acrobats to practise riding their machines. Because you hadn't told me about cyclists, Jennifer.' It was odd to hear my name suddenly, to remember myself. 'What was I to think, this is obviously not a sensible way to go anywhere, I reasoned I was observing the repetitions of a circus troupe.

'Eh, but in the meantime my appearance was slowly becoming less and less engaging, or I might have spoken to one of these supposed acrobats. I have always liked jugglers and tumblers. As a boy I taught myself to have some skill in that area. It was a question of will. Because, without any kind of unusual action, my face alone would, you might guess, gather an audience. As you might say, I am not the most beautiful of men. Nor was I a beautiful child.' He cleared his throat. 'I know this. It is the truth.

'Now, for whatever reason, the Creator of the Universe has made me another life, but not another face. Well, I am accustomed to myself, this is no hardship and it is often very difficult to hurt me, but when I was a boy I took to tumbling a little, you know, speaking all kinds of nonsense and making faces. I intended to show them, the laughers and the curious. I was telling them, 'See, I want you to stare at me. I am making you laugh and stare. This is my will over yours.' The grotesques, the actors and the street performers, I think I am close to them because of this. And what is a duellist, of whatever birth, if not a street performer, after all? Jennifer?'

'Yes?'

'Good, you're still there.'

'Of course.'

'You don't mind this? I must say it.'

'I know. I understand.' And I did, I completely did. And I wanted my friend to feel that I was with him, to reassure, so I spoke the words in the clearest way I could. Savinien began to talk faster and lighten his tone. Perhaps he thought he had upset me.

'I was organising something one might mistake for a steady hold on my own existence when the cold closed down. That true cold, the ice we had, remember? The path became almost deserted. Men would come to feed and tend their doves and I would watch and then they would take down their ladders and leave again. In the close of the evening I would move down towards the river and see our lights reflected by the farther shore. Your world is so full, there is so little space for the privacy of proper dark.

'And there would come flares and moving shadows, a roaring above the clouds, and these things had been explained to me (you had explained them – these things that are plain . . . planes) but I did not know them in my heart. I felt oppressed by the numberless inhabitants of your land, constantly in motion and screaming with noise and yet I was also utterly adrift and afraid of my own stillness.

'Far to the east, a high barn was being forged out of metal and by night a man would guard it. He would sit by his fire and watch and I would want only to be him, to hold my hands out at those flames, to drink a little and to eat and to walk around my iron building before I left in the morning to go to my own home.'

I could hear his mind falter. He swallowed several times. I made a blind reach to take his hand and missed.

'It's all right, though.'

'No. No, actually, it is not all right.'

'No.'

'But we manage our lives, even so, isn't this the case?'

'I think that's the theory.'

'God has a curious idea of free will.'

I listened to him shifting his weight on the bed. 'I apologise. I am too tired to be good company. Would you mind if I sleep? I like to show my gratitude for rest when it comes.'

'Of course, of course, sleep. Please.' I opened my eyes and found I was looking directly at his face. We both blinked a little, getting used to each other's colours and light. Since the beginning of our conversation, he had grown visibly exhausted under a pressure of words. His stare was dull, moist, slightly pink.

'I'll get out of your way, let you relax . . . you do seem . . .' And I couldn't describe how he seemed – it was other than I would have wished, or frail, or like a damaged animal, or almost frightening. There wasn't a phrase I could say out loud. 'I'll go. Thanks for, well, for telling me what you have. I didn't realise it would be so, such a thing for you. You know.'

'I think I do, yes. But, if you wouldn't mind, I would

rather you didn't go. I will only sleep a little while, perhaps you could stay. If you intend me to relax I think another person in the room would be a source of relaxation.'

'If I could be a help.' I really hadn't tried to stand, to get up and leave. I had not made the slightest genuine effort to remove myself.

'You would indeed be a help, yes. Thank you.'

'There's no reason to thank me, I would only have gone somewhere else and sat down again. I might as well do that here.'

'I can still thank you, even so. You might wake me if I detain you for too long. It is best if I sleep at night, after all, and I seem to have a less than infinite supply of rest. I shouldn't waste it.'

'No.'

'Thank you again.'

'Yes, well, you sleep now, don't mind me.'

Don't mind me sitting and watching you fall into sleep, surrendering until your face smoothes and softens and your body eases into one full movement below your thoughts. Don't mind me waiting here as you turn and steady yourself on your side while your arms fold round your shoulders, as if you might be cold, or dreaming, or dreaming of cold.

When you were sick, I often saw you unconscious, that is to say absent from yourself. Asleep you are only absent from me, I can feel you are still really very near. Then I smelt your sour, hot sheets and held your skin and this was nothing, it had no particular meaning. I was dealing with an illness which resembled you and not with you. I was never with you. Now this is different.

The sky behind the window is turning lilac and sinking into dusk and I can hear your breathing pulse, a gentle familiar private beat which I will know now always. I can feel the tick of you making up time in my lungs and listen while we turn into each other's accompaniment.

Don't mind that the room is shrinking round us, or the air between us thickening. This disturbs me, but need not ever concern you. I know I am unable to move in even the smallest way in case I disturb you. In case I touch you. I think if I move at all, I will touch you and that makes me afraid.

Quite naturally, you shouldn't mind me either. Occasionally I think too much, that's all, when thinking is really not always the best thing for me.

But at the moment, thought is unavoidable. I'm writing a book – I have to think about it from time to time. I even have to think about that lilac-coloured evening and of looking at him. If there is another way, I don't know it. This would be easier, at least different, if I was dealing in fiction, just making the whole thing up, but I'm not. I sit down here and forcibly run over the little bits of sandpaper and tin-tacks that my mind had softened, grown around, smoothed over. I'm here to make it sore again. Perhaps if I had done this before it would be a smaller strain, equally it might not. I can only report that my mind has seen fit to ambush me at several points in the course of this and I'm sure it is more than keen to do so again. Now and then, pain stops by to ream through the memory root canals with a little taste of gangrene and carbolic soap. I presume I am paying my penalty for the kind of presumption it takes to imagine anyone other than myself would be interested by the story I have to tell. Swings and roundabouts.

But my real presumption is something quite different and more serious. You see, I want to reverse or at least to arrest the passage of time. I am standing in the face of nature which is as pointless as trying to pin back a waterfall. Silly and maybe even harmful. But I want to live again in minutes and hours which are gone and to forgo my present because it is less satisfactory. In writing, I can do this, but very reasonably here is where I also discover the unavoidable price. At the end of a page, a chapter, a day of work, I have to stop. I have to come back. Just when I'm tired, when I've allowed myself a certain sensitivity to events, I have to come back and leave everything behind.

Sometimes friends will ask me what I've been up to, where I've been. Whatever I think of to tell them is nonsense. I generally lie politely, shut down with a smile. The truth is I spend all the best of my days being nowhere with no one. I sit alone in a room, surrounded by events which cannot happen now.

Before I get too morbid I can say that this is a very common problem. As far as I can understand, my entire country spent generations immersed in more and more passionate versions of its own past, balancing its preoccupations with less and less organised activity or even interest in the here and now. Far more recently the whole island of which my country forms a part was swallowed wholesale by the promise of a ravenously brilliant future. For a tiny while, in its transition from past to future, the population balanced, hundreds of thousands of opened minds all alive and possible in the given day. I have the impression that a few years may have passed during which each solitary citizen would be able to at least attempt to know and care about where and how they could be.

I may now be glorifying my own past, but it does seem that once even the really influential human beings (male and female) embraced a degree of innocence, decency, even hope. Other human beings, regarded as quite ordinary, considered themselves to be really influential and almost were. I have the impression that forty, even thirty, years ago, people worked towards what they might all do for each other. This may have been nothing more than the after-shock of two successive and horrifying wars. Or I may simply be idealising a period I never knew but which now appears in my mind as a gently coloured fact, filled with soft hats, earnest and honest voices and comfortable, dun-coloured raincoats striding unimpeded over Sunday afternoon fields of undeveloped green.

Never mind all the pictures I've seen of the same soft hats and open, sensible faces watching the tower going up to hold that first Trinity bomb. The same innocent eyes that couldn't help but watch fire and cancer blooming above the desert, boiling the sand into emerald glass. Only earnest honesty and sensible innocence could ever have invented such a thing, lies and wickedness could not have been clever enough.

I grew and felt my mind shaped by the times they left us. It may be a little harsh to say so, but I feel I came in with the dawning of the Age of Stupid Lies.

My childhood spent a moderate amount of its otherwise unoccupied time watching television when this was still slightly novel, intermittently broadcasting and brightly monochrome. Our regional station was very often unconcerned if it did no more than play 'A Hundred Pipers' over its Saltire testcard for hours at a time and, perhaps as a result, I grew to believe myself the resident of a country within but not indistinguishable from Britain. I take this for granted in a way my parents did not. This may well be good, if of dubious benefit. Between testcards, I watched 'The Man From UNCLE' where nobody who was shot ever bled and nobody made a fuss. I also watched the Vietnam War where a great many people bled unbearably and only John Pilger seemed to make a fuss. This seemed quite as reasonable as the perverse advantage my parents took of every available power cut. There were many power cuts. I remember the noises and candles in the dark, the pounce and swing of shadows. I remember knowing that the world was full of inexplicable calamities about which no one would ever make a fuss. Clearly, as children grew into adults, they also became insane.

I knew about The Bomb and The Strikes and Nuclear Waste. I knew about the student up the road who had his head amputated in a car crash and the woman who shot herself because her labrador died and I spent one complete sunny day waiting for myself to die and being curiously surprised when I did not. I had licked my fingers, having forgotten that the grass they'd just touched had been sprayed with weed killer and then, of course, I had remembered. All I got was a bitter tongue. I am sure that wonderful things also happened during my early years, but I seem unable to recall them in any detail.

For other news of reality, I went to the pictures. I think this may now be a genetically coded response to times of stress and tribulation. Certainly, nations have survived remarkable hardships, buoyed up almost single-handedly by the cinema. So I went to visit the jolly companion that stuck by us through the Depression and the Blitz.

And I learned never to travel in aeroplanes, boats, lifts, spacecraft, trains, submarines, cars or coaches. All of these would inevitably suffer ghastly incidents involving multiple casualties, deaths and mental anguish. The same could be said of any particularly peaceful or pleasant-looking towns, cities, skyscrapers, apartments, holiday resorts, gardens, woods, streets, beaches, oceans, attics, cellars and national monuments. Cars, birds, puppy dogs, fish and ventriloquist's dummies would senselessly turn on their keepers in a welter of fins, fur, feathers, Terylene, Sta-prest slacks and embarrassing cardigans.

Nothing was safe. Large assemblies of family members, friends or even perfect strangers would only ever be mustered to perish slowly at the hands of maniacs or plagues, or to vanish in one spectacular conflagration of luminous pain. The natural consequence of calm and security was Disaster – it happened everywhere all the time.

I cannot now surrender myself to any form of organised transport without considering the possibilities of escape. Could I beat out the train windows before icy water engulfed me? Could I beat out the air hostess between me and the nearest exit? Could I fight for my life?

I have exceptional breath control after many early years of regular exercises intended to elongate the amount of time I could survive under water or lost in poisoned smoke. When climbing stairs I consider whether random pyromania will reduce them to uselessly glowing rubble or a terrifying ladder of twisted, boiling metal which represents my only chance for continued, if tentative, existence.

And every one of the cinematic cataclysms found its confirmation in reality. (Except for the flying piranhas, although I had already discovered there were much nastier things lurking and killing in almost every country south of France.) Aeroplanes crashed and Jonestown swallowed poison and train doors opened amiably on fast bends and murderers murdered and public services and secret armies committed obscenities by the hour and people died and people died and people died. Even in the cinema. I was taught for two terms by an elderly unhinged physics master who had escaped as a boy from a terrible local picture house disaster. Foolish youths had raised a spurious but convincing fire alarm during a Saturday morning matinee creating a panic that crushed tens of children to death. Singing cowboys galloped over black and white sand while the fire doors jammed with bodies and with the naked sounds of injury and fear – something never accurately recreated in drama, something too large, dark and unlikely for the reality of small boys.

Sometimes we would walk, Savinien and I, for no particular reason. As the spring turned petulant, we made quite a habit of going outside just to spite it. The skies would cycle from snow to sun to rain to hail and back again within an hour and we would make ourselves stroll and talk up and down streets filled with insistently whipping air until they began to develop their own brawling kind of charm.

Savinien's instinct was to walk away any shadow of returning depression and there were periods when he would be exhaustingly intent on the study of his new time. He would ask and then usually answer a methodical catalogue of questions. He could find no reasonable explanation for the way I and my fellow pedestrians chose to dress. He looked at our reinforced workboots and our combat waterproofs, our despatch cases, flak jackets, double sewn, riveted denims and camouflaged fatigues. He considered our leather and metal and canvas and belt-buckled world. After thinking for a little while, I was able to tell him that we were not really very much at war abroad and that my city was not overly given to open combat. We were all of us simply dressing for the disasters we knew must come. We had grown up and learned our lessons. When the buildings fell and the fires started and normality splintered out beneath our feet, we would at least know we had tried to protect ourselves.

'You're seriously saying this?'

'I think so. As seriously as I say anything.'

'At times I can truly believe humanity has grown. There is a cleanliness and civilisation that can only make me glad.'

We were walking in a hard, still evening. I could look ahead and hear our footsteps shadow, cut across rhythm, then beat in close to each other and disappear in one. I could also hear his voice.

'Then I see beneath . . . I cannot recognise how satisfied you all are with despair until I remember . . . until I remember that there is nothing different here from my old wars. You still have executions and hunger and madness snapping about your streets. You are, in all simplicity, only more private, particularly in your minds.' He nodded at a man, oddly but well dressed, who was pacing on, balanced between two carrier bags, a long stain of urine, dark and new, in his faded jeans.

'His face is the drunk face. It has the shape and the shame and the colour and the eyes and the smell and the sweat of the drunk face. I know this. I have known this three hundred years ago in another country. Nothing is truly changed. Jennifer, I remember the wrong parts of my life.'

' Well, I probably do, too.'

'I think of when we moved through the villages . . . I dreamed of this last night . . . I saw myself with my army, my cadets, moving up to Arras (for the seige) and the women would run away. They would just run away, shouting in a language I could barely understand, and the children would cry, only because we were come. We were intended to be on their side. We were their countrymen and still they expected us to do terrible things always. But you can understand we were only people, young men, and we were not always terrible. We were inconstant. At times we gave people hope to face the next young men who might be less safe and do anything.'

'Did you do terrible things?'

He almost laughed. 'Me? No. I was just the Monster of Bravery. I had an agreement with God. I would kill anyone who had an intention to kill me. Other than that, I wrote poems.'

'Poems.'

'Oh yes. I have remarkable . . . I had remarkable powers of concentration, because this was in my best interest. If I thought beyond the noise, pain, hunger and being a small part of a war, then I could write. To write was to go home. No, to be, of myself, my own home.'

'It's one way to do it.'

'And this is still done. You make pictures of this, an entertainment in your homes. My Paris, my home, it loved to look at ugliness when it chose and there were many picturesque opportunities to observe. I began to think of the Devil as very well disposed towards humanity – a misunderstood gentleman – for providing so many subjects for burning and fresh-air torture. The king and his cardinal were very generous also with his subjects' flesh and blood. We rose up, for a small experiment and we tried The Revolt. And how did it end? How did we celebrate our success over Mazarin? (He was this Italian, ruined our little king, our government, everything.) Well, of course, we painted the streets in blood. Of course.'

'You're getting upset.'

'I would like to know'.

'Fine.'

'I just want to know why this way to go is the one we choose? Why are there no better ways? Think of it, I see a Gascon, a good fellow with an excellent mind trying to run into a wood. Now he is unable for this because he has only one leg. He is trying to run and he cannot properly comprehend that his leg is shot away below the knee. This man does not work properly any more and all of us that morning, we watch and watch him. He is no longer our friend, now he is something interesting.'

'I'm sure not.'

'I was there.'

He moved slightly ahead of me, rubbing at his neck, his shoulders rounding.

'Have you tried to write?' When he didn't answer, I thought he hadn't heard. 'Have you tried to write?'

'Tried? No I haven't tried. What I have done is to fail. I have failed to write.'

'It'll come back.'

'Why? Why should it? I am made the way I am made. I can't get out. I am here for no reason and I have no use. Allow me to say so, please. This is black thinking and if I speak it out this makes it, eventually, willing to go from me.'

'Whatever you say.'

The main road led us home in silence and if Savinien temporarily thought he had no use, I felt rather more permanently the same. I wanted to be of use. Savinien could step down into the kitchen in the morning and stretch and scratch his ribs and that would make me happy. This didn't involve any thought or effort on his part. Part of the way he was did nothing but make me glad that he was the way he was, making me glad that he was, ad infinitum, the way he was. I couldn't seem to be that way for him.

And that takes me back to the lilac-coloured evening. I finished watching Savinien when he woke.

'How long?'

'Almost an hour.'

'You should not have left me so long. I must have been very tedious.'

'No.'

'I should have been very tedious.'

'I was thinking. I didn't notice. Would you like to come outside?'

'It's been a while.'

'I know, but we'll take it slowly.'

As it happened, Arthur came with us. I shouldn't have minded really. Things were still at a delicate stage, this would be Savinien's first time out – anything might happen. Two of us should have been with him. It was right.

Yes, but I didn't like it. I wanted to stay listening on my own with him, stay undisturbed by anyone else. I wanted no change which was odd because our current status quo was hardly long established – only something comfortable. Rather than see this as a sign of a dangerous selfishness, or something a little closer to heart and home – which it was it was it was – I thought it reasonable not to fragment the intimacy we'd formed. This had, after all, enabled him to be well, to speak about being away and what he'd done.

But, as it happened, Arthur came with us anyway.

'How are you then? It's not too much, all this? Tell us if you want to go back.'

'Thank you, Arthur. If I have one of you here at my either side, this is good. The air is good.'

'That's grand, that's really grand. You're doing well.'

Arthur patted his back and smiled. I wanted to do that. 'You still a bit down?'

'I don't . . .'

'In your spirits.'

'Oh, I have been worse. At several times and in several places. If I could find something to do, it would probably pass.'

'I know that one. Still, now that you're getting better, who knows, eh? Look on the bright side, you could be a baker.'

'Is this a Scottish saying – that I could be a baker?'

'No, but it should be. I mean who ever sticks their head round a cake shop door and says 'My compliments to the chef' Hm? Nobody. You can begin to think that people are ungrateful.'

'Ah. I must say I had the experience a long time ago of writing plays and it was much the same. The author only hears if the play is bad. Or if the actors are bad because then, of course, the play must be at fault. I know there are human beings in the world who could reduce their own names to nonsense quite simply by saying them. But, no, this is the author's responsibility.' I could tell he was just making conversation, he wasn't really interested. 'If I could, I would have performed myself.'

'Why didn't you?'

'I beg your pardon?'

'Why didn't you?'

'I think my face is rather too much mine to be anyone else's. And my public life lay in other areas.'

'Oh. Well, I suppose. That's a shame.'

'No. I was only a little disappointed and in the end I found my place.' I felt him brush my arm, find my hand and squeeze it. 'There are so many things a person can become, I am more and more surprised that anyone is able to know what they want. And still we do know, we only have to find it.' I squeezed back and felt him withdraw softly.

'Funny you should talk about plays . . .'

'Sorry Arthur?'

He was making conversation. I could hear him making it – clatter, clatter, clatter.

'Plays. There was a guy just now on television who wrote plays.'

Clatter, clatter, clatter.

'Except it wasn't about that. He was dying.'

I didn't want to hear about dying. Not then. Not good for Savinien.

'Yes, he was dying. Cancer. Weeks to live and he . . . he sat there and, I don't know . . . well, I do know, he told the truth. I'd forgotten you could do that, out loud, on the telly. It was just him and the truth. Dying. Felt like he was giving you something. You know? I had to come out and have a cup of tea, think about it.'

'Who was he?'

'Well, I missed the beginning and then I heard you and . . . I don't know. He seemed good. Good.'

Savinien tugged at our arms. 'This man, he was a writer?'

'Yes.'

'And he told the truth?'

'Yes.'

'Then he was a good man. This is what writers are for.'

We jolted along in silence a while. Arm in arm is never as smooth as they make it look in the films. Then Arthur had an idea.

'Okay. Lighten it up. I will now escort you to the only thing I like that has anything to do with bakers. It's on the way.'

Ten minutes later we moved down across a dark car park, taking it slowly until Savinien grew very slightly nervous and I stopped.

'Arthur, where are we going?'

'We're here.'

He pointed up at the high, shining building ahead of us

while the wind carried a low mechanical rhythm through the steam of our breaths.

'This is the flour mill where they shake the flour.'

We looked at the flour mill. In the long, bright windows we could, sure enough see tall grey shapes, shaking gently. We watched the shake.

'Arthur?'

'Yes?'

'If this isn't an odd question, why are we staring at a flour mill?'

'Because I wanted to show . . .'

'Savinien.'

'Yes, well, I wanted to show Savinien the best part of my work.'

Savinien looked at the shake and shuddered slightly when Arthur took his shoulders and began shouting in white clouds that drifted between us and the light of the mill.

'You see, I never knew this was here and then I noticed it when I was going to work. It was early in the morning and winter so everything was still dark, like this, and the mill was shaking and shining away. And I hate my job Savinien. There is nothing about the bakery that I like and one day I will leave there before I go insane and I will do what I want to do. I will change.'

'I am sorry to hear this, Arthur.'

Arthur patted the shoulders he was still gripping like a steering wheel. 'Don't be sorry. It's not that bad any more. Because I found this mill. I walked down and I looked at it and I thought of all the flour inside. I imagined all the fruit and plain and treacle and potato scones, the soda bread and pancakes that much flour could make. I imagined all the meals I would have a hand in – my hands. I imagined the tiny particles of skin that would leave even scrubbed-clean hands when I kneaded the dough and that hundreds, maybe thousands of people would be eating small amounts of me for years to come. I felt depressed.'

'I can see that, Arthur.'

'Good. Because then I looked at the shake. There. The shake. And something began to be all right.'

'Why was that, Arthur?'

'Because in my head I could picture all the men and women inside the mill, working in time to the shake. I could see them shimmying out here after their shifts were over like a big samba line. Do you see?'

He was gently rocking Savinien's body, side to side, letting his feet take up a little slide, leaning in and back, in and back. DA-da-da-da, DA-da-da-da, DA-da-da-da, DA-da-da-da. I watched while Arthur lifted his arms away and let them wing out at his sides and shake. He swivelled on his heels and smiled from behind a billow of frozen laughter.

'Do you see? Now that would be a job. That would be a job. DA-da-da-da, DA-da-da-da. You'd have to be crazy, even to try. It'd be DA-da-da-da, DA-da-da-da, every bloody day.'

Savinien had subsided into stillness but he was watching, very definitely watching.

'Makes me laugh. Even when I'm up to my neck in fucking scones, it makes me laugh, have a little shake down in the flour, get it under my feet and let it slip.'

Arthur was covering a fair area of the car park now, getting fancy, negotiating pot holes in reverse and Savinien followed, very straight and slow. Finally he raised his hands as if he were holding them out to a fire, or perhaps surrendering.

'Arthur, you will have to stop now because I cannot do this.'

'You would get the hang of it. If you tried it.'

'No.'

'Yeah, come on. Sure you can.'

'No.'

And Savinien made a perfect lunge for Arthur. Precise and terribly fast he had reached and held him in a beat.

Arthur stumbled, fell back, taking both of them down in a clumsy roll.

'Whao – '

'I apologise.'

'What are you – '

'I am very deeply grateful for what you have done here and I apologise for stopping you now, but I had to. I could not watch for any longer. I'm sure you understand.'

'Let me up.'

'Of course.'

They clambered up against each other and stood. I thought Arthur looked angry, but when he faced Savinien, I could see his body suddenly relax. Moving together, they touched arms briefly, embraced with stiff little pats on the back and then broke apart, already walking back towards me. Savinien coughed and nodded in my direction, his face in darkness.

Something of practical use had been engineered. Arthur had made a contact I could not exactly understand. He had done something I could not, and in a very small way, I hated him for it.

We went home then.

THE FOLLOWING MORNING, Liz told me something nice.

'I'm moving out.'

'Hn?'

Savinien was out in the garden, standing, and I'd been watching him through the kitchen window. Liz surprised me simply by being there. Then again, she always did.

'I'm moving out.'

'Is it something we said?'

'No. I'm going to live with Sandy.'

'Ah . . . that's nice. Isn't he . . .'

'The divorce came through last week.'

'Oh.'

'Well, I'm glad you're so upset I'm going. I'll miss you, too.'

'No, no. I'm sorry. I didn't sleep very well last night. I, uh, it won't be the same without you.'

'Yeah, yeah.'

'No really. You'll have to come back and visit.'

'I will. I'll bring Sandy.'

'It would be good to meet him. Listen, we'll have to all go out and have dinner or something to . . .'

'Celebrate?'

'Yes, we should celebrate you and Sandy. What do you think?'

'All right.'

And what did I think? I thought there would be a room free now. I thought that even when Pete came back for good there would be a room free and that I knew who could have it. I thought that the time would pass and the household would settle down and maybe, who could tell, we all might get used to each other in ways I might find enjoyable. I thought of ways that would be all for me.

I went out and crossed the grass to Savinien. Simple things like this were becoming oddly uneasy. When I walked near him I became too aware of my feet which became in turn too heavy. I was suddenly anxious in case I stumbled or even fell.

'This is truly the spring here, Jennifer. I know finally this will stay. The garden knows also.'

'I think you could be right, but don't . . . I mean you can be happy even if it's raining.' His moods lately had been chained directly to the climate. I didn't want him opening himself to another disappointment.

'Come and see over here. This morning I found something.'

So that I would follow him more exactly, he took my hand. He had a hot, dry grip, a healthy pressure.

'There.'

One of last year's flowers had seeded itself back to first principles and was now producing miniature petals, thick luminous blue with an orange heart.

'I don't know what they are.'

He still hadn't let go of my hand although he was no longer leading me. I adjusted my fingers slightly but neither of us let go.

'What they are is fine. They are alive.' I felt his fingers move. 'Jennifer, I must tell you something of importance.'

'Hhum, yes?'

'Yes.'

'Well do, then.'

'You have a very horrible garden. I am going to dig at it and make it better. I no longer wish to look at it like this.'

'That's good.'

'I have to occupy myself. I can no longer make words grow.'

'I'm sure you will.'

'I cannot wait. I have come to a decision that I will be changed. I will make something new at which I am good. I am a writer who cannot write. This will be acceptable to me. I will not write. I am a fighter who will no longer fight. I have no heart for it. I cannot make a reputation here, I have no need to buy my place and no one will buy me. I am beyond this now. I will be with flowers and make them grow.'

'I am glad. I really am. I know I may not sound it convincingly, but I am happy for you.'

'Show me.'

'I am, I'm smiling. You see, I'm glad.'

'No. Show me so that I know.'

'If I can think of how to show you then I will.'

'You are very good at thinking. Why is this difficult?'

I reached out to take his free hand, but he lifted it away. To touch even his wrist I would have had to close the distance between us without his help. And I could not.

'It's difficult, that's all.'

'I understand.'

Why do people always say that precisely when they don't.

'I understand. You're very kind to me. And I am most grateful.'

'I'm not being kind.'

'Yes. You are being terribly kind and I appreciate this. You have already done more than I could expect.'

Something in his face damped and died. He retreated into courtesy, his stance slipping into formality until I was watching the man he must once have been, carefully fielding a rejection in the predetermined style. He bowed to show me the soft crown of his head, his naked neck, and I knew he would kiss my hand, felt him kiss my hand, held steady under the long, angry touch of his breath.

His eyes, lifting, let out a blink of something live then hooded themselves again.

'I believe that Arthur is watching us from the kitchen window. It would be unfortunate should he misunderstand our situation.'

I found it absurdly hard to turn and move away.

So I wrote him a letter. Not a logical thing to do – he would have been unable to read it – but then again, I was unable to send it. Our positions equalised.

I find that I can't remember how it read now, although it occupied me for almost a week. Before I went to sleep, tried to sleep, I would make letters in my head and then on paper and then I would destroy them. I never got one right.

Today my situation is quite different, but some things haven't changed. This last week I have either slept with one rather small dream fixed in my head, repeating and repeating, or I have not slept at all. And if I wrote Savinien a letter now, set words out for me to see, I think I would recognise most of what I had to say then.

Except I want to speak to him now. I want to write to him today. Still, that's my affair. Think of what follows as the letter I would have written then and it will serve you and the story perfectly well.

Indulge me for a page.

I don't have to say who I'm writing this to – we already know. We are we, Écuyer de Cyrano. We are we. I am more than myself now when I never asked to be because I am still you and I. I can remember how to be that.

The bare words are I love you.

I miss you.

I love you and I miss you. Those two verbs are so close together, I can't feel them apart. But if I must feel at all, why this?

You are the person who makes me mind the empty spaces I have and the empty rooms. You are the only human being with that much power over my life. Do you think this is something I like? I do not want to be completed, I do not want to be opened

203

up, or let free, or to live in any way more richly than I do now.
I do not, I do not, I do not and then I do. Your fault. Do you
know I miss you all the time. All of it.

I would like to see peace in the world. I would like to be
happy. I would like to touch your mouth. I would like the
universe to turn and to work in precisely the way that it must
and I would like not to lie down again without you.

Something about myself lately makes me cry quite randomly,
as if I were very old, or very young, or very stupid, and the
days are going on now – I'm afraid that I'll have to stay this
way, or that if I can change, I will simply stop living at all. I
would much rather be optimistic on this point.

'Try a piece for your Uncle Arthur.'

Arthur had made a sponge cake, which was unusual,
he didn't like to bake at home.

'I'm sorry, but I'm not really – '

'I don't care if you're not really, I'm not baking fucking
sponges for the good of my health. This is an attempt to
inject a little domestic comfort into the household.'

'Why?'

'Why? You are joking. Liz is on the verge of disappearing completely, whatshisname – '

'Savinien.'

'Is either bulldozing the garden or asleep – '

'And I'm being a depressing cow?'

'And working too hard again. You'll be ill. Have a
piece of sponge cake. It's real cream.'

'And real jam?'

'Yes, my mum made it.'

'I'm honoured.'

'You don't deserve it. Have you fallen out? Don't ask
me 'who with?' – you know perfectly well.'

'I don't know.'

'Well, could you ask each other, please? If I have to
spend another week lodging in Castle Dracula, I may
begin to enjoy going out to work.'

'All right.'

'Promise?'

'Yes. I promise. Whatever . . .'

'And how's the sponge?'

'I'm sorry, I wasn't concentrating, it's probably very nice.'

'You complete bitch.'

'It's great. I was joking. It's a wonderful sponge cake, really. Twelve on a scale of one to ten.'

'Too late. I'm climbing into the washing machine now, I may be gone some time.'

'Could you take a few blouses in there with you?'

'You'll be sorry.'

He was right, though. I had to do something. Apart from anything else, I knew that loneliness was affecting Savinien's health. He was looking far more tired than just gardening could make him.

At the front of the house we were blessed with a raw area of sandy ground where Liz's attachments sometimes parked their cars. Not being drivers, none of us had found any use for it. Savinien had spent the last two full days digging it over into something like soil, harvesting a great deal of waste paper and glass and a low mound of broken brick and concrete slabbing. We were going to get another garden from the bare ground up.

I sat on the front steps and watched him spading a pattern into the levelled earth. The sharp mineral scent of turned soil was everywhere. Now and then he would draw himself up and step away to judge the symmetry of his progress. Each time, he would carefully offer me his back, pause, sniff, and return to his work.

The pattern curled and spread within the square he'd marked while he kept his face to his work and slowly moved up closer to the house and to me. The breeze would soften and strengthen the ring of his spade and parts of the tune he was humming, something high and ornate I'd heard him singing to himself before.

I began to wonder if he was really still ignoring me, if he wasn't now simply absorbed in his work, building a poem in the ground. The line of movement rolled from his shoulders to his waist, the round snap of effort following each relaxation in his thighs. I knew how he would feel just by looking. I knew that I knew that and that I kept looking all the same.

He turned the soil and stepped and stepped and turned the soil, rubbed his face along his forearm, sighed, all of him moving for all of the time. If I could I would have stood up and gone, but that way I could only lose. I was very unfamiliar with the rules we were operating, but I still understood that if I left, that would be that, finished, no more of whatever it was we might be. And I wanted us to be what we might be.

Then again, if I continued to sit and he continued to ignore me, well, he was winning again wasn't he? And I would have to be even more defeated, if I wanted us both to win. We were in one of those tiny spaces where time thickens up and waits until what has to be done is done, but hurry in case you still miss it, all the same. No second chances, everything new every game.

I thought about clearing my throat and then didn't. I wasn't going to say anything. I was just going to stand and walk a little.

I set myself at the edge of his pattern – if he wanted to ignore me now he would have to dig through my feet. Sure enough, he eased round a curve that should have finished a foot or so behind me. Almost in a golfer's putting stance, he closed the distance down. I could see how bright and brown the outside air had made his skin, only the pale section unbuttoned at the neck of his shirt showing the way he had been.

He dipped his spade in the thin earth for one more stroke. Now there was no more room. He stopped, straightened his back, stared up at the house, offering me his ferocious profile.

We waited, we thought. Or shuffled mental probabilities in the room left by a lack of appropriate thought.

He lifted his spade and struck it down into the earth so that it could join us in standing independently. As I tried to tell if the action had been angry or simply violent, I was also aware that his arm, in falling to his side, had touched me. Whether this might have been accidental became irrelevant as his elbow raised and nudged me slowly in the ribs. It nudged again and again and again. The shoulder followed, leaning in, until the whole shape of his arm, his side, was leant against me. He let his head slip over and rest, his forehead close to my cheek. I braced one foot behind me against his weight and behind that, his mind and his will.

He felt – if it makes any sense to say so – eloquent. Breathing against me, wordless, fixed, he was clearly and precisely a tired man, a surrender, an irresistible decision, a need, a terrible patience and hurt and a body that keyed out the everlasting perfect fit to mine, hip under hip.

I had the very clear and pleasant sensation of being poured away.

'Will you excuse me please and let me work.'

I think he whispered. I remember feeling the hot, soft words that would have come from whispering.

'No.'

'Will you please move, please.'

'If I move, you'll fall over.'

'This doesn't concern me.'

'It concerns me.'

'You don't know what this means.'

'Neither do you.'

'You don't understand.'

'I know. You don't understand either.'

'I know.'

'It'll be all right, though.'

'I don't think so.'

'I don't care.'

IN THE LIVING-ROOM, I stood into him, wire-tight, and his neck bowed under my hand and let me slip in and down between his shirt and the little knuckle vertebrae and the dry, private temperature of his back.

I wanted to tell him first.

'I'm a bad person.'

'No more than I.'

'Yes, more.'

'Don't say so.'

'It's true.'

'You have "dangerous enthusiasms" – this is your point? I once had a few of my own. I could be too un-specific in my love. Henri would warn me to be more private, but we were only people, love was only love. I would always tell him that I would much rather write one original idea than repeat a very commonplace experience.'

'No, I – '

'Sssh. I didn't believe me myself. I always wanted more of the crime and less of the written evidence.'

I suppose most kisses are the same – ugly to the observer, a mystifying necessity for those involved. I won't ask you to observe.

'Don't ever let me hurt you, Savinien. Even if I ask.'

'Ah.' He smiled into me. 'No, I won't let you do that. But neither will you.'

And then for an indeterminate while we stayed in the room in the big house and were full of finding out.

ARTHUR KNEW. It's one of those things you feel obliged to lie about, even though you are equally obliged to lie very badly and be found out. Arthur knew anyway.

So now we were doing what everyone else had assumed we were doing a month or so before, maybe even earlier than that. No one was adequately pleased for us or surprised. The general reaction was merely calm.

For my part, I could feel myself smiling too much, disclosing a slight elasticity in my walk. And, of course, I felt very inclined to run a lap of honour and whoop a little bit, sort of celebrate. Almost all that stopped me placing a moderate announcement in my local paper was a sudden inconvenient tenderness and the knowledge that, just like the taste of my mouth, my privacy was no longer only my concern.

'Happy now?' Arthur carefully unloaded a box of flat apple pie pieces into the fridge. I almost thought he was talking to the pie.

'Um?'

'Are we back to normal? Or have we moved on from that? I mean, people will be eating again? Speaking? All that boring old sociable stuff. Home sweet home?'

'I suppose.'

'Good.' He closed the fridge and battered the cake box into a surprisingly small ball before throwing it away. 'That's why I brought the cakes.'

'You don't mind.'

'I always bring the cakes. If I make 'em, I can take 'em.'

'You don't mind us being sociable again?'

'Why would I mind people being sociable?'

'I don't know. It seemed possible.'

Arthur rushed water into the sink and began to bully the washing-up. I seemed to have offended him.

'Arthur?'

'Yes?'

'If you were feeling sociable yourself – '

'I'm a bit tired tonight. Sorry. If you had something in mind. Sorry.'

'Nothing special. I was going to wander up the road, have a drink maybe.'

'Go to the pictures?'

'Maybe.'

'No, I'm knackered. Ask whatshisname.'

'Well, I would, but he might not be good with crowds yet. He's never been *out* out, you know? I mean, I'm not sure, it might be fine, but I'm not sure.'

'You could find somewhere quiet – it's a week night. You shouldn't have any bother.'

'No, no, it should be fine. Maybe you'll come next time.'

Which is when I remembered the first things to go when you get that one particular kind of friend are all the friends you had instead.

As Arthur said, we shouldn't have had any bother – out on a quiet weekday night, we should have been fine.

'This is a very lucky man there.'

'Um?'

We were occupying a corner position in a coffee-serving pub with furniture constructed round an instability motif. The chairs and tables were woven out of thickish wire – not as stupidly thin as old coathanger, but only a little more supportive. The lounge was a quarter full of students, quietly sipping cappuccinos and swaying tensely. I knew how they felt.

'He may know that I'm ugly, but he doesn't know that he can't walk.'

'What are you talking about?'

'I could make him find out.'

'Listen, this is not the kind of place you've been used to. Wherever you were used to it. No one is looking at you.'

'He is.'

'Well, of course *he* is, you've been growling at him for half an hour. This isn't necessary. You're behaving like a thug, for Christ's sake. If you're a gentleman, act like one.'

'I'm sorry.' Then he said it again, as if he meant it. 'I am sorry. I haven't been anywhere like this for a long time. A very long time. As I remember, it was always unwise to relax.'

'Nobody's going to hurt you. No one is here to do anything but sit and have a drink and then go home. This is a quiet place.'

'I would feel happier with an arm.'

'An arm?'

'An arm.'

'Good God, people don't carry arms any more . . . People don't carry obvious arms. I mean, things really aren't like that here. Now and again somebody gets punched, no more than that. Quiet area. You're feeling a bit paranoid, that's all, a bit jumpy.'

'There is no one in here, I couldn't take. You know that?'

'I don't believe this.'

'No, no. I have no intentions in that direction. This is the man I am, I am showing you the man I am. I know there is no one here faster than I would be. There is no one here I could not halt. Completely. I would rather not look at my life and see only this, but I cannot unknow what I know. With every introduction, I meet a living body and all its possibilities for death, these two things come together like the water and the glass.'

'Do you know how you'd kill me?'

'You misunderstand – '

'No, I don't. You're not making a threat and I don't feel threatened. I just wanted to know. How. How would you?'

'I . . . no. I lied very slightly. There are some people for me where death doesn't come. You are one of the people.'

'That's nice.'

'I wish it was. When you walk so easily, you sit with your head back, you stare at the ceiling with your throat so opened, when you . . . there was a point where you lay on your side and your one arm covered nothing but your face and then all these times, all these times I want to give you a defence. You should have a defence.'

'Savinien, I'm choking on defence. Nobody ever touches me.'

'That's not true.'

'Yes it is. You can threaten me, shout at me, be weird at me and it won't mean a thing.'

'Why would I?'

'You plural, not you in particular.'

'This is a ridiculous part of your language – to have one word with two such important meanings. It could be so easy to cause offence.'

'No, it's easier in our language to be very offensive on purpose but hide it away. You plural need never take anything personally. That's how we are. It's not how I am. I'd much rather hit you than talk about it.'

'So you have said.'

'Seriously. I am defended, Savinien, in every way you can think. I meant it. In my final year at school – this is what I'm talking about – a note came from the office, I was called out of my class. I knew what had happened from the headmaster's face, but he sat me down and gave me tea and patted my hand and finally – once I'd had a biscuit – told me there'd been an awful accident. My parents' car had crashed. Careless driving on an easy road, they can't have been paying attention. Father was dead and Mother was in coma. And how did I feel? What did I feel?'

'I don't know.'

'Of course you don't, because you're normal. I was content. Calm. Slightly irritated that I would have to visit my mother now, until she died, but very largely calm. I made my face sad for the headmaster and went back to the class. Chemistry – the Nitrogen Cycle. Mother died that evening and my irritation faded. I remember looking at their picture a few months later – it might as well have been a drawing, an illustration from a book. I have done my best never to think of them again.'

'You were an orphan?'

'It wasn't a problem. I stayed with my grandparents for a while, turned eighteen, got the insurance money they owed me, moved away. That was that. For the whole of my life that has been that. Nothing more.'

'That's not true.'

'Well, whatever – you have been warned.'

He nodded very slightly and smiled in to himself.

'I think we are both warned and irresponsible.'

We managed another cup of tea each before the music level in the bar edged up enough to make conversation impossible. Outside a mild evening was waiting for us, bands of pink sky setting off a shine in the tenement walls.

Before we were past the red clay football pitch along the way home we noticed a small crowd, mainly waiting beside a tobacconist's. Three women stood silently by a dark bar door. It took a while before I could identify a paramedic's van and then behind it a young man lying in the road, his knees bent up in the air. Men in reflective overalls were assembling a stretcher around the man who wore a dull jacket with a bright red leather collar.

Savinien walked hard past the thin crowd, didn't move his head.

'This is a quiet quarter here? Hn?'

'Yes?'

'I admire quietness, it can be very useful. Someone, you saw, had made quiet work of that fellow's throat.'

'No, I – Oh, yes. It was blood, then.'

'Sometimes I wish I could belong here and then something will happen to make me regret that I already do.'

That night we went to sleep in our separate rooms. Although we might have joined each other tactfully during the night. Although we were free to be quite openly together, for that matter, we stayed apart. No ill feeling was involved, only a peculiar tiredness. I suppose I regret this decision now because it was a kind of waste, but it seemed then our time with each other would be so huge that we could be slow and generous inside it. I'm glad of this, I'm glad I remember us slowly, generously.

For an example.

'It's too much.'

I like to think of this part sometimes.

'It's too much.'

Savinien is standing in the completed outline of our new front garden. He is gradually gathering money for plants and household contributions by digging other people's gardens, mainly by dint of his efforts in ours which are, apart from anything, one huge and remarkably ornate advertisement for his prowess with a shovel. Thin paths of brick, evenly laid, curl symmetrically away from his feet, and the earth rests, stoneless and pacified, ready to be green.

'Too much.'

'What's the matter?'

He is holding his arms around his ribs and his eyes are over-bright. He smiles at me, peacefully.

'The bird.'

'Where?'

'Exactly here with us, listen.'

A little concentration lets in a bright, baroque warble. Something is practising the best of its evening songs.

Savinien pinches at his eyes and then holds one hand out from his side. I find it completely unoffensive that he assumes I will step forward in order to hold this hand and do nothing to disappoint his expectation.

'It's very nice, but birds are meant to sing, that's how you get birdsong.'

'I know. It's all too good.'

'Hm?'

'That there is this song in the world and all the other songs. They are far more than should be required for their purpose, there is too much delight in them.' He spins round to me very seriously. 'I would like to plant my garden now. To begin it.'

'Well, why don't you? Do you have enough for flowers and all that?'

'If you and Arthur persist in taking nothing else from me –'

'Yes we do refuse, that isn't an issue any more. Bear in mind we aren't paying you anything as our official gardener.'

'Then I have enough, at least for a very promising beginning.'

'Well, the place to go is up over the back of the hill.'

'I've seen it. I have looked at everything I would choose.'

'And?'

'I can't.'

'Why not?'

'It would be too beautiful.'

'You big daft bugger.'

'I beg your pardon?'

'Plant us a garden. A Paradise Garden for little old us – go on. Except you can miss out the fountains, the Arabs would have too, if they'd lived in sodden bloody Lanarkshire. Plant it.'

'Then I will.'

Soon the long dusk will begin, roaring from either edge

of our horizon with a harder and harder blue. Because Arthur is upstairs recording the folk music programme from the radio we are going to go inside soon to the living-room. There we will forget that we have to be wary and listen for Arthur's movements, for one of Liz's final, final returns. We will stop having to be anything but us.

With the curtains drawn back and the door unlocked we will court each other patiently, straight in to the skin. We will cling and slip together like fish on the sofa we can no longer pass at other times without sneaking a look. We will be here again, at that first time in again, at that starting of being home and rolling home and finding home again. There is nothing like us, no thing better, not even close. And someone is lifting a cold chisel up to my heart and I do not mind.

BUT WHAT ABOUT the world, what about my work?

Well, they continued very much the same. Or rather, they both got much worse and I cared much less. I began to wonder if contented people were, in fact, any kind of useful addition to society. It seemed that, having become contented on one front, I was quite likely to remain contented on many others. Equally, I never had actually done anything with all my prior discontent. Perhaps this was the still moment fixed at the top of my ascending arc and, in only a little while, my course of action would change completely.

I had begun to read out romantic novels on to tape for the visually impaired. This proved to be as great a disturbance as it was a comfort. On the one hand I was constantly up to the waist in a lukewarm sump of thin, over-scented emotions, constantly reminded of my sentimental shortcomings and constantly distracted by roaring little episodes from my own very recent past which made me want nothing more than to go home and roll through them all over again. On the opposite hand, time turned beautifully clear and soothing when it was locked up with me in a baffled room with nothing but syllables. I was free to be a living bellows drawing and shaping air into fiction, to be a mouth without a brain.

My news-reading treadmill was a kettle of an altogether different type. My scripts became more and more like the products of a demonic Ealing comedy while Steven had decided to take actively against me. This wasn't a problem, only an inconvenience. During my late-evening stints he would slip into the box and look out at me,

217

accompanied by someone whose name was, I believe, Sonja.

They would fumble and ogle each other in a rather dull and theatrical way, possibly even fuck. I had no urge to discover if actual penetration was taking place. That would have meant paying them both far too much attention. I simply wondered what it was about me that made other people want to have sex with each other. I was unable to decide if I had first drawn out this behaviour in my parents, or if something they once did caused a change in me. It didn't really matter.

Which I find wonderful, even now. It didn't really matter. I would do my work and finish and go home to love. My love made many other questions unimportant. I would open the door at home and walk into love. Before I was half way down the hall it would be in my hair like smoke.

So Steven was not a problem at the Station. No. My problem was one of tone.

That was how they put it.

'You seem to be developing a tone, Jennifer.'

A tone.

The way they said it, a tone was something midway between slight catarrh and a Polish accent. An unnecessary colour in the voice, an air of negative comment.

Negative comment. I don't know where I could have got that from.

Help me out here. Try it for yourself, our late May and early June menu of events. Selected highlights.

Our prime minister wishes to fine the penniless and homeless for being homeless – not to mention shabby and down at heel. Unforthcoming fines will be used to build prisons in which to store those homeless persons unable to pay fines.

Can't see a thing wrong in that.

A bill to legally defend the rights of those with special needs is talked out of parliament while many of its supporters are attending the funeral of the leader of Her Majesty's opposition.

Public testimonials prove that the only good leader of Her Majesty's opposition is a dead one.

I could read that without flinching – flat as a billiard table, smoother than all of the balls.

Then of course we could go on to the broader points. For example, my government continues to smile upon the manufacture and export of manacles and anti-personnel – that is to say anti-people – explosive devices. My government continues to smile upon the manufacture and export of many further types of sophisticated armament to forces engaged in campaigns of systematic genocide. My government continues to smile upon the manufacture and export of ball squeezers, houses of electric fun and other instruments of torture not presently legal in my country.

Sounds good doesn't it?

A serial killer and torturer of little girls is finally captured and imprisoned. He looks very much like many other human beings. Lack of funding in police information technology delayed his capture by decades.

The Nazi League of gentlemen is happily shafting history all over those parts of Europe not currently at war.

Another in a series of prominent MPs is shown to have been happily shafting in very many of those parts of Europe not currently at war.

And coffee-coloured parachutes bloom in the skies over Normandy. And politicians step – thank God this is only radio and we cannot see – from cars and helicopters to wave and smile along lines of appropriated heroes, knowing we see nothing but their own personal smiles and waves, knowing there will be no sign of any inappropriate response, no memory of what was fought for, no memory of that naughty, naughty post-war election result, no memory of what we needed the peace to win.

Say it loud, say it proud, this is when I finally become certain that only my time, the one I am used to and where

I feel at home, has the power to make belief irrelevant, sentimental, banal. For a month I see and hear nothing but women and men willing to die because they thought it would help towards something good, because it was a sad necessity, and I cannot find it in myself to be anything but bored. I am told nothing about these people that might allow me to find them admirable, loving, human, beyond my scope.

And I know that we won the war, we have not been invaded, we have not been shot in our streets, blockaded, bombed. No one seems ever to have made us give up those fought-for things, those odd little old-fashioned things, now sewn close to the born-again Nazis' hearts and otherwise not heard of at all. The freedom, the decency, the fairness, the public safety, equality, opportunity, peace – they have left us so slowly that even now we cannot see clearly when they first started leaching away.

And don't forget the whole wild, peaceable world is dying, that innocence is born every day, very literally poisoned in the womb. I used to be secretly happy because my relative youth meant I would most likely outlive all but the most lunatic regime. Now I know I will have to survive in what carelessness, plans and theories I never agreed with have done to my air, my water, my soil, my food.

Sorry to go on, but I found that I cared about these things. Someone I loved was living here and I cared about them. People who cared about each other were out there, beyond the studio, up to their necks in crap. I had to say.

I couldn't help it.

I had to say. Sit me in front of an open mike often enough. Put me loose in a studio often enough. Give me pages and typed out pages of misery and crap often enough. And probability must be fulfilled and I must, one day, simply say what's on my mind. Fuck everything and say it.

No.

Only joking.

I never said a word. I only thought. My tone was the only protest I could make. I went into the studio with my mouth tasting of ash and when I stood up to leave it, the taste was worse. That was the only change. When the European election came by in June, I couldn't even bring myself to vote.

NOW HERE IS the fourth day of June. Not bad weather and up and down the street below our house the people who mended bits and pieces of cars were outside with the people who mended bits and pieces of motorbikes. The pavement was happily shining with weak sun and metal. It should have been possible to be there and contented indefinitely. Apart from all the bad things in the world and all the bad things in my head, we were all right.

We. That's Savinien and I.

Us.

Goodbye me and welcome to we – please remember you now have two front lines to defend from the world of enemy actions and conduct yourself accordingly at all times, this constitutes a friendly warning.

Our dreams even became simultaneous. Or one of our dreams, at any rate and although the idea of this might have been endearing, the reality was not. I woke very early on the morning of the fourth of June and knew I was afraid.

Because we still had not slept together in that house I had to walk across the landing to Savinien. He was already sitting up, slightly bright in the dim room, something stunned under his smile.

'Uhn . . . pardon . . .'

'What's wrong?'

'Eh, I . . . forgot how to speak, that's all. I am not fast at waking myself. Did you . . . why are you here?'

'Well, this will seem silly, but I had. I had an odd dream.'

'Of what kind?' And now that I think, he said this with a sort of care, a wariness.

'Of the odd kind.' I sat on the edge of his bed, he moved away a little and then back a little. 'I saw the sky, a sky . . . total blue and high and hot. I don't know how I knew it was hot, but there you are, it was.'

'What else.' He knew what I was going to say. I guessed that then, but I think now he'd known for weeks, perhaps months.

'Nothing, really.'

'You didn't see trees?'

'That was it, yes, the other thing. I must have been lying on the ground and looking up because I could see the tops of these thin, long trees, three or four of them. Would they be poplars? It was almost like looking at a picture, a hot picture.'

'Ah.'

'The stupid thing is, it felt like you. Not like you being there, but you dreaming.'

'This is only natural if I was dreaming also. I have seen this place.'

'You've been there?'

'Only asleep, this is where I was waking from, a sky with trees. I didn't see you there.'

'Maybe we should go again.'

'You mean what?'

'I mean that I'm here and it's still very early and I could do with a little more sleep. How about moving over. Perhaps this way we can go there together.'

'Should we?'

'If we're tired we should sleep, yes. That's just nature.'

And he only shook his head and opened the bed for me and I slipped into his temperature and his tiredness and his hold.

After a while, I felt him settle, sigh.

'Jennifer?' I couldn't tell if I heard him or only imagined his voice, I couldn't make any answer. 'Jennifer?' I dropped a degree or two further from understanding, began to lose myself. 'Tell me, when you saw the trees, did this feel like death?'

He woke and left without my noticing it.

Some little time later I was drinking my breakfast coffee when Savinien ran past the kitchen window and clattered open the door.

'Come and look.'

It wasn't too bad. Shock made the reality seem incurable at first and then it only took logic to shrink it back again. Still, it was a mess.

'I know who has done this.'

Someone had tramped over the new front garden, torn up plants, thrown bricks out of position, into the street. I could see they had been hurried, not too thorough, but their harm was undeniable.

'I know.' Savinien picked up a brick and threw it into the street, kicked out another. 'I have been very stupid. I purely had assumed that because I felt like someone else now, I would look like someone else.'

'What do you mean?'

'One of the days when I walked home with my plants, I was very happy and slow. To keep in my humour, indeed to strengthen it, I turned for a tour through the park and came a long way home. This is when I thought I saw a man, I think his name is Charlie and if he is Charlie then he is a friend of James. He is one of the men I knew before. I have brought them here.'

'When did you think you saw him?'

'A few weeks.'

'Well, that doesn't make sense. They would have done something before now.'

'James is similar to me, he likes to wait and move in his own time.'

'This could have been anyone, kids, jealous neighbours,

somebody falling down drunk. I mean, if they'd wanted to do damage, they could have done more.'

He began to laugh in a small way and then dipped forward so that I had to step up and let him fall in to me. I hadn't fully thought how much this must have hurt him.

'It'll be all right.' He shook his head against my shoulder.

'We'll sort it all out.'

'No.'

'It isn't that bad.'

'This is something I do for you. I do for the house. I do.'

'You'll do it again. Please.'

As he lifted his face, he pulled a hand away to rub it, rearrange the grief. 'This is ridiculous. A few plants. This is nothing.'

'Yeah. Why should we worry for nothing.'

'It needn't be them. It needn't be James.'

'If it is, we'll do what we have to do. There are laws.'

'I should not bring you trouble. You have never been anything but good to me. I should bring you good. This is my intention.'

The street that unrolled below us continued to empty and fill with innocent activity, but when I walked along it to work I wondered if any of them had heard our garden being broken up, had seen something they were keeping to themselves. I looked at the little girls squatting at the corner with their plastic cart, building out their states of mind in tiny stones and tried thinking they might have done it, or their older brothers. I wanted our street to be free from blame, but I did not want to imagine how we might be threatened by a stranger. I hoped we had only been touched by an arbitrary movement of the city, as if it had struck out in its sleep. Nothing personal.

There was hardly any moon when I came back home, no more than a sliver of light, flowering and splitting through cloud, then shrinking to a hard line in the black.

I was tired. Steve had been needling me and a woman in a suit had come into the studio at the end of my shift and suggested I might take a break for a week or two, after all it had been a very long while since I took any kind of holiday. She seemed quite solicitous in a power-dressed kind of way and wondered if I might have anything I wanted to share with her. She mumbled soothingly about life being what happened when we were making other plans, that I should explore my child within and engage in healing play. I got the impression Steve might have told about my excursions into naval fantasy, but maybe it was all about that problem I was having with my tone.

The funny thing was, the woman had enunciation so poor that I felt I should recommend an emergency speech therapist. After all, if you're going to occupy your time in passing on witless psychobabble to helpless souls you should at least be sure they can pick out, say, one word in three. I said I would certainly bear her suggestions in mind and she warned of the dangers of unexpressed rage. Presumably she was unaware of how personally danger-ous she would have found my expressed rage.

Climbing the path to our door I could smell the earth beginning to rest in the garden again and dimly see the order Savinien must have restored while I was away. I was glad he'd had the heart to do it. Perhaps if he was still awake I could look in on him, or perhaps I could have a cup of tea and go to bed. That would have been nice. I had no major demands to make on the remainder of the day – just a need for something small and nice. Nice word, nice.

'He's a bastard.'
   'Well – '
   'A complete fucking bastard. I believed him.'
   'You couldn't help . . . I mean, when I met him – '
   Liz started crying again while Arthur floundered and Savinien paced behind them tugging at his hair which was

now quite long enough to tug, but noticeably greyer than when he'd first arrived. They filled the sitting-room with visible distress. I could guess what had happened.

Liz stared up at me when I came in, as if she'd been expecting someone else.

'It's Sandy.'

'Hhnu. I'm, I'm sorry.' I looked sorry.

'No, you don't understand.'

I looked less sorry. 'Well, it's . . . these things . . .'

Arthur gave Liz a forcible hug and explained over her head. 'He wasn't divorced. Actually I think he wasn't ever married.' Liz sobbed. 'It's all a fuck up.

'I'm a fuck up.'

'No, you're not.'

I could only repeat Arthur. 'No, you're not. He was a bastard, a very convincing bastard.'

'I just, I came back and I looked for my cardigan, the blue one and he's still got it. He's even got my fucking cardigan.'

'Then I shall get it back.' Savinien had stopped pacing.

'What?'

'I shall get it back. I shall get back whatever you wish. I shall bring you his sincere regrets.'

'Savinien.'

'I thought he was called – '

'It's a long story, Liz. Savinien, you can't just go about extracting regret from people you don't know.'

'I can.'

'All right, you can, but you also can't. I mean, it won't help. That isn't how we do things.'

'Listen, he can go round and fucking kill him for all I care.'

'I can do this, if you truly wish it.'

'Seriously?'

'No, he isn't being serious. Arthur, explain how men behave with each other now. Civilised men.'

'Jennifer, I am a civilised man. I am offering my help

to the household. Some points of honour have a natural justice with them and must be attended to. Did you think I would do anything less?'

'No, well, I didn't mean you weren't civilised. I mean, I'm not getting at you. I just . . .' faltered off into complete silence. Which is something I should really have stuck to for the rest of the evening.

Arthur finally woke his ideas up and tried to help me out. 'No, look, we could both go round to his place and do him over or something – '

'Arthur!'

'We could, I'm saying, we could, but there would be no point because the damage is done and we would both end up arrested. He would win.'

'We would be arrested for doing this?'

'Yes.'

'Yes, you would.'

'Even under these circumstances?'

'Yes.'

'Then how is one to prevent anyone doing precisely what they wish?'

'We just have to hope that they won't.'

Savinien sat opposite us and talked to the room while he looked at me. 'You are defenceless and your world is breaking in half. In all honesty, I believe your world has broken, it has split itself apart. There is such savagery and darkness and then such ridiculous openness.' He was trying his best to be reasonable and calm in his own way, to understand me, and I wanted to answer him well, but then I heard my voice snap out and patronise before I could do anything about it.

'No, Savinien. We're not open, not defenceless, just apathetic – we really don't care very much.'

'Speak for your fucking self.' Liz plunged out past me and Arthur made to follow her.

'Sorry, Art.'

'This really isn't the time for one of your bloody

debates, you know? That little shite's taken her money, pulled her in completely and now he's fucked off. She doesn't even know where to, so going and cutting his head off or whatever is completely academic.'

'I'm sorry.'

'I should think so.'

'I had a funny day.'

'Didn't we all.'

'I don't know – did you have some kind of trick cyclist pedalling by to suggest you should take a holiday if you want to keep your job? Does that happen in the high pressure world of baking fucking technology?'

'Congratulations, you have just offended everyone in the room.' Arthur turned away and stared past Savinien.

I decided I'd better get out. 'I'm going to speak to Liz.'

'Don't upset her.'

'I'm not going to upset her, Arthur, why would I upset her? I don't normally upset anyone.'

Savinien called from beside the window. 'Perhaps, Arthur, you would like to be here and look at the garden with me. I would like to ask you a question about it.'

I left before Arthur had time to answer.

Liz was across in her room.

'I'm sorry.'

'Uh hu.'

'I am.'

'Uh hu.'

I took a seat where she could look up and see me if she wanted to. 'I'm a prat. You know that. It's not my intention. It doesn't mean I don't want to help.' She rested as she was, sitting on the empty floor with her back against the stripped bed. The anger had stopped and she was starting down into something more like despair, I could taste it. 'I don't know if Arthur said, we'd never even got round to advertising your room.

'Thought I'd need it again, did you?'

'No. We wanted you to be happy with Sandy.' Wrong

thing to say, wrong thing to say, wrong thing to say. I edged myself on to the floor beside her while she sobbed.

'Oh, God it's a fuckup. I'll have to move my stuff back from there and he never paid the rent so that's got to be done and I . . . I don't want to do it.'

'You don't have to.'

'Yes I do.'

'You don't now. We'll help out. It'll be all right.' She breathed out in a way that disagreed. 'Don't be sad. I hate it when people are sad.'

'Of course I'm fucking sad.'

'I know, but, it'll go and . . . everything gets different, that's what happens . . . it's only logical. It'll go.'

She rolled round suddenly and cried into my chest, clinging across my arms ferociously. I didn't want to move in case I gave some kind of signal that it was not fine for her to do this if she wanted, but after a while I was also becoming quite claustrophobic. One of my hands had gone to sleep.

I tried to think of other things. Of how I might apologise to Arthur, of how I might apologise to Savinien, of how much more time there would be in my life if I did not very often have to apologise. From time to time I wondered if all of that formerly naval brutality hadn't really been a little distraction from a more consistent cruelty – the kind you will always trawl behind you if you're used to being permanently calm.

'Thank you.' She disengaged, sending a violent rush of blood back into my arm.

'Hm?'

'Thank you. For being there.'

And I couldn't deny that I had been there. Thoughts and feelings all inappropriate, but the body had been there and wearing a suitable face. 'That's fine. Sorry I upset you.'

'You didn't, not really. He did that.'

'Well, fuck him.'

'Yes. Fuck him. Not that I would.'

'Absolutely. Would you like to have one of Arthur's cakes or something?'

'No.'

'A cup of tea?'

'No, really. But go on and have something yourself. Go on. I'll be fine. Go on.'

I was trying to go, my legs were simply too stiff to allow me to rush away, but she looked across for me gently, appreciating my concern. So I appeared unwilling to leave her alone, I appeared concerned in the proper way. That was fine. I am always capable of doing the right thing by accident.

AND THEY ALL forgave me.

Liz, Arthur, Savinien, they all agreed to have been only a little offended by my social inadequacies and to have then entirely forgotten that offence. What offence? They didn't know, they'd forgotten.

For my part, I agreed to be very favourably impressed by the people I shared a house with. Arthur prodded me cheerfully in the arm before he went up to bed and left me with a significant nod towards the living-room door which I then opened.

'Hi.'

Savinien was sitting on the sofa – our sofa – bathing in the silent underwater glow of the television. He always preferred to watch like that if he was on his own, enjoying a source of moving light and excluding all possible sound.

'I said, Hi.'

I continued to stand, watching the shadows rise and then recede across his shoulders and hair.

'If you're not speaking to me, it's okay. I knew I would upset you eventually – I do most people if they hang around long enough.'

I felt cold. I wanted not to.

'Come here.' He didn't sound upset, only slightly dry.

'Oh. Okay.' I sat just out of touching distance and watched the faded colours of the late-night news chase each other over my hands.

'How else might you offend me?'

'I don't kno – '

'How else would you hurt me, with words, what would you say?'

'I can't . . . how can I?'

'You can do me the courtesy of permitting me to ready my defence.'

'You don't need a defence against me. I promise.'

'What would you say?'

I found that when I reached across he allowed me to take his hand.

'What would you say?'

'That you were short.'

'I am short. This used not to be the case, but now I am, yes, a short man in comparison with others. You're telling the truth, you're not hurting me.'

I wanted to ask him how many times he thought I'd told the truth and managed to get out and away with no harm done.

'I am short. And?'

'Well, you're crazy sometimes.'

'Yes. And?'

'Your chin is perhaps small.'

'Yes.'

'Your nose isn't.'

'Yes.'

'You're very beautiful. Say yes.'

'Yes.'

'And I love you. Say yes.'

'Yes.'

'I love you.'

'Yes.'

'I love you.'

'I love you.'

I'd been alive for more than thirty years to reach that evening, that room, that hand which was always so solid and taut and clever about the things I liked to feel. Thirty-five years of sleeping, waiting, shuttered months before I could make and feel and mean a sentence about present love. Worth the wait, I think.

He tucked himself against me and I whispered something – that we shouldn't be apart again – something like that, while my thought went missing in touching the heat of him through his shirt, in the dusty smell of the day's sunlight still on his skin, in the taste of his throat.

I remember that we sat together until we were grazing the edge of sleep and all the time we promised and promised each other impossible things with all our hearts. We used words like forever and never as if they were locks, the secrets we only needed to believe in before we could handcuff the world.

'Today, I wrote you a thing.'

'Hm.' I turned my head in closer beside his chin and then realised what he'd said. 'You wrote?'

'Sssh. Yes. It came back.'

'That's wonderful.'

'Maybe it is, I don't know. Might I give it to you?'

'Of course, of course.' I had never been written to by a writer, certainly not by my writer. I had never been a part of someone's work, that very politely closed part of their mind.

He reached down to his side and brought up a folded sheet of paper. He was writing again, in his old ways again, back to his old self and perhaps more. I was happy for him in a way that I might not have been if he had not been, at least for a little while, writing about me. I had no cause to feel lonely when he drew back into his words because I would be there, too.

'Here.'

'Thank you. Really. For thinking of me.'

'Thank you for reading me.'

I still have the paper I held then, leaning it into the cool, broadcast light so that I could see.

Jennifer,

Y a-t'il sur toy un atome de chair, qui ne soit coupable de ma mort? Parce que je t'aime trop. Je me meurs depuis que je vous ay veuë, je brusle, je tremble, mon poux est déréglé; c'est donc la fièvre? Hélas! c'est ne l'est point. C'est la Mort. C'est l'amour. Brusler d'amour, cette flame si douce, personne n'en est jamais mort.

And that was as far as I even attempted to read, my focus slipping from line to line to find some understanding of either his words or his intention. I could feel him shift his weight beside me, hopeful, apprehensive.

'I can't . . . could you . . . this is.'

'What's wrong, Jennifer? I have offended you?'

'Of course not. Of course not, you couldn't. I'm sorry, I just . . . this isn't in a language I can understand.'

'Oh, but – ' He pressed in neat against my shoulder and scanned his own lines. 'This is . . . this is very clear . . . I know my meaning absolutely . . . So. I am in all simplicity now writing in my proper tongue. Why? Why now?'

'I don't know, love. Tell me what you say. So I know.'

'Eh, well. I say that I love you.'

'With all those words, that's all you say.'

'You know this is more difficult to speak than to write.'

'Not if you mean it.'

He breathed a small laugh and turned himself so that he lay across the sofa with the weight of his head and shoulders across my stomach and my legs. 'So now I am here, like the letter. I ask if there is an atom of your flesh I couldn't die of because I love you so. I have been dying since I saw you first, burning, trembling, my . . . um, perhaps I might say flesh is beyond my government. Fever? Not at all. This is love. This is love. To burn by love, the flame so sweet none ever dies of it.

'I say you boil in my veins and distil a perfect image of your soul inside my heart. I say all kinds of things. I . . . when I speak of love in my language, I also speak of death because the words sound so much the same – La Mort, L'amour – I mean nothing by it. Except love.'

He was a rotten liar. I knew the love he meant, the one that included darkness and loving on alone.

I won't tell you the rest of his letter because it's here and it's mine. If I do not touch the paper often I hope that when I lift it out and warm it there will always be something about it like the scent of him.

That evening we comforted each other without especially having to say that we needed to. Our minds and selves knew what to do and we looked out from inside them and were brave and sleepy together as hard and as much and as softly as we could.

In the morning, our garden was broken again. Arthur walked me out of the front door to see Savinien standing in a ragged, Saturday crowd of neighbours who shook their heads, or shouted, or stared back at the shattered stems, the missing bricks, torn earth to see if it really was as bad as they'd remembered.

I left for work with Arthur still stationed earnestly out on the pavement and talking with a small group of casually familiar faces. Liz was sitting with Savinien in the kitchen. I thought it was nice of her to stay with him, particularly when she was still upset herself, but I also wanted her to leave him the fuck alone. Nothing but jealousy, I knew, so I smiled extremely broadly, patted her, kissed him on the cheek and went away.

The house I returned to was, even in the late, long summer dusk, still opened to a remarkable stream of volunteers. A succession of ladies Savinien had gardened for bought him plants, scones, advice. Arthur's bakery boys had been summoned and two of them were still sitting out on the steps and drinking beer. The gentlemen Hell's Angels from half way down the street were walking inside, just ahead of me, with carrier bags of privet and super lager and not inexpensive white wine. The garden looked raw, but restored, now very obviously the product of several imaginations within one plan.

'Where's Savinien?' Liz was in the kitchen, hatcheting four loaves of bread.

'I don't know. Haven't seen him for a while. Would you like a mug of wine?'

I wondered for a moment if she or Arthur had attempted some kind of mulling experiment and then noticed her own tea-cup of cold red wine and realised we'd run out of glasses. We weren't a household used to impromptu entertaining on any kind of scale.

'No thanks.'

'You needn't worry, he's fine. We're all fine. We've all had a wonderful day. I've never seen so many people be so nice. Mrs Jenkins or whatever her name is gave us three different loads of scones.'

'Mrs Jenkins next door? She's not even speaking to us.'

'She wasn't speaking to you.'

'Whatever.'

'Well, she's speaking to everyone now. I think we're reminding her of the war.'

'As long as she's happy.'

Upstairs Arthur had obviously moved his stereo near the window. Elvis Costello began to plead and swagger out above our heads and into the old garden at the back. An uneven cheer went up from both sides of the house.

'I can't get over it. Everyone's been so good. They've spent all day putting things right.'

'So now you're all having a party.'

'And then watching the match.'

'Match?'

'World Cup – you remember, that big ugly gold thing they all kiss at the end of the match.'

'Oh, right, of course, I'd forgotten.'

'Any objections?'

'Oh, no. No. I, ah, it's great to see you looking so happy.'

'I am happy.'

'Me too.'

237

Which was true. I'd just told my line manager that I would indeed go on holiday, thank you for suggesting it, and the garden was fine and it seemed we had more friends than we'd imagined. I didn't know many of them too well myself, but that was only to be expected. For me, it was more than enough that the house had friends and that I was in the house.

If our position seemed vulnerable to me, if the growing dark concerned me while I wondered if whoever had attacked our garden – Savinien's garden – intended to do something more, then I didn't need to mention my thoughts right then and damage the atmosphere.

'He's here.' Savinien was near the window in the dark front room. 'He's here.'

'Who?'

'The man who did this or who had this done.'

'Well, he can't do anything now. The house has never been so full. Have you seen him? He's really here?'

'You think this is imagination?'

'No. I wasn't sure if you were guessing or if you'd actually seen him.'

'He has shown himself of course. I have also.'

He spoke as if he were describing the figures of a dance, an old performance reviving again. 'He understands me and I him. I had thought we might leave each other be. Although this is almost always not possible.'

'It's this man James?'

'Yes. Naturally.'

He answered from a deep calm I didn't recognise while his mind's attention quartered the window, quickened his movements and breath.

'Why don't we call the police.'

'This is not for your police.'

'I'll call them.'

'You will not.' He had stepped to face me before I could realise. There was a strange charge about him, a hard open distance in his eyes. His cunning was creeping ahead of his intelligence while his thought and will and feeling became muscle. In a few minutes he would be nothing but dangerous. 'You would have nothing to tell them and the matter between us would be unsettled, it would go on.' He gave a sudden, empty smile. 'Let me protect you.'

'I can't stop you.'

'No, you can't.'

'What are you going to do?'

'Oh, I don't know. Be your champion and die for you.'

'Don't you dare.'

'I am going to take what action I must and then this will all be done. We will be alone together.' He nuzzled my face and I let our lips meet, so that we finished by tasting each other too deeply for me not to need more. When I did what I must and drew away there was no part of me or my thinking that did not feel pain.

'Come back.'

'I promise.'

'You'd better.'

'I'll come back.'

Someone had brought us candles and while the dark swung in with a fine cloud to keep us warm, small flames began to pipe up outside from beside walls and paving stones and all round the borders of our grass. From inside the house our television leapt alive and opera raced out. Soon millions of people would simultaneously stare at Italy's team of footballers and Brazil's team of footballers playing a decidedly uninspiring game of – conveniently enough – football. But first, there would be opera.

I watched Savinien walk smoothly across the lawn and back inside. I hadn't seen him come out. I no longer knew about him, except that he would do something soon. Something bad would happen soon. The bad something would step into my life, right past me, and I wouldn't see.

In the living-room huddles and couples and solitary shapes found what space they could to watch Pavarotti singing in French with his usual bewildered eyes, as if he were always astonished by the sounds leaping out of his mouth.

'How long this?'

'I don't know. Half an hour maybe. An hour.'

'Fuck. And they're all fucking Italian. Biased.'

'He's Spanish.'

'Yeah, but who's heard of him? Is that Richard Attenborough?'

'What?'

'There, with a beard, playing the oboe.'

'Looks like it.'

Arthur was dismembering a pizza in the hall.

'Art, did you see Savinien?'

'Sorry.'

'But he came in here.'

'No, he went out for some air.'

'He just came back.'

'Then you know more than me. Sorry. Isn't that a wonderful noise? The singing.'

'Yeah.'

'That's all over the world. The entire planet is waiting and listening to one man sing.'

'Yeah, great.'

Savinien wasn't upstairs. I had the very clear feeling that I had been constantly one or two minutes behind him.

'Hey, Jen! Come in and see what's left of Gene Kelly.'

'In a while.'

I sat on the stairs while somewhere in America brittle celebrities were hoisted up by careful young women in good suits to wave and face sympathetic ovations whenever their signature tunes were roared out. Never mind that the voices singing could rip through any melody lighter than Offenbach and reduce it to nothing but passion and insanity. 'We like to be in America' fountained up like a direct proclamation from a lunatic God.

Ahead of me, the partly opened front door let in a dark breeze. I went out.

BEYOND OUR HOUSE, the night was wholly still, a regular pattern of windows was blue with television light and something achingly choral hooped and bounced and multiplied down and down until the deep end of our street was cut by another and went out. I could smell cooling stone and a sweet breeze from the park. Of Savinien there was no sight, no trace, no sound.

I made an effort not to move without thinking. They would need privacy. If they were together now, Savinien and his man, they would be looking for a place to find each other undisturbed, like lovers. A free place, a dim place, somewhere not overlooked.

No one would be outside to disturb them, not now. They could hide in the plain sight of the dark. Free. I was more and more certain I would find them in the park. Unless something had happened to check his instinct, Savinien would have chosen his ground in the park. I began to make a run uphill for the back gates, the blood already high in my head, prepared to beat away thought.

Better to walk, though. I shouldn't become a distraction. I shouldn't be seen. I shouldn't be noisy. I should be calm. Even if I understood that to be safe my lover would have to win absolutely. Even if I was certain I wanted all of that absolute, to see that playing out. Even if I felt and felt and felt until emotions were peeling and furling away my brain. I was to hold calm.

In the air about me, images were transmitted, arias were released in relay, their singers embracing and running, perspiring and praying between simulated pillars, palms and rainbow-shaded waterfalls. Lunging for the lectern, they caught the peace before the next assault.

The tiny lane that ended in the park was black with dense hedging and trees, I found it hard to judge my distance to the fence. I listened. I stood. I stepped closer, closer, closer. I listened again.

Steps muffled in grass. Swung motion, light, gentle night sounds. I knew what they meant. It had begun.

But in the park, the two men were all that there was. Like the tenors scalding with music, standing on tiptoe, sweating and braced, barely keeping their balance in the rush of roles and words that raged up about them like flame, the two men became what they wished to become. So Domingo sang 'Vesti la Giubba' and wept as honestly and irreconcilably as if he were quite unobserved. So Savinien and his opponent made their own wet metal heat between them to extinguish everything but will and death and life. They were not noble or redeeming or anything I ever should have seen.

Moving in and out of deep shadow, all points shifted round the lock of their attention. In the grey light between the trees, both wore anticipation in the mindless half smile I must have seen in a thousand photographs, paintings, news bulletins. They smiled the 'I know a secret you don't know' smile of liars everywhere. Because they were liars. Their secret is only death and everybody knows that.

Real duelling is theatrical but not in the way the theatre might make us believe. In the place where drama is indistinguishable from mystery and religion, living bodies tear against each other. They are faster and more terrible than understanding, every instant cuts itself free of sense, but in the sum of completed actions there is a kind of spectacle. A fight follows its course from beginning to end like a fatal disease or a funeral service, there is no stopping it.

And I write all of that so I won't have to tell you how good Savinien was. Oh, the other man – James – he knew what he was doing, but he didn't know enough. After a while, I realised he was left-handed, that the wink of metal always showed from an unexpected place. His right hand was wrapped in something – I couldn't tell what. He covered the ground well, long-boned, lean, whipping hands, armed with what looked like a cavalry sabre, light ringing palely down a home-sharpened blade. But I knew he wouldn't make it. A sour, thick joy started to burn at the back of my throat. I knew he wouldn't make it.

Savinien had taken off his shirt and was swaying it from his left hand, his right held something dull and solid like a length of pipe. He was hardly well defended; he had, effectively, no weapon, but as soon as he slipped forward I could see he was thinking only of death and how to make it. He was fast and economical, not entirely without grace and he knew precisely what to do.

He knew when to feint with his shirt so it shone out a distraction.

He knew when to catch a stroke before it fell and when to slide by one and aim his pipe end for the joint of the striking arm.

He knew to keep his head because the only useful anger is cold as clay.

He knew how to jab at the ribs while the opposing blade was rising.

He knew the sabre was made to kill but tricky to manipulate on foot.

He knew how to slash for the eyes and open the forehead in a blind of blood.

He knew how to break for the forearm and fingers.

He knew to be unaware of the pattern of sweat and saliva, a little blood moving and shining on his skin.

He knew how to tangle the legs with his shirt and catch his opponent's throat as he folded.

He knew how to elbow and kick a body flat to the ground.

He knew how to bend piping by striking it over legs and head and back.

He seemed frustrated by the inability of his weapon to win him an outright kill. I noticed my voice calling out, when he stamped down again on the hand that still held the sabre and reached for the one thing he might use to finish his job.

His head snapped round and the body beneath him lurched up. There was a surge of movement before Savinien fell back and his man struggled to stand. Savinien seemed confused, even dazed, while the other figure stumbled towards the perimeter railings. He looked back through the dark at where he guessed the voice had come from and I was almost afraid that he would come now for me. Instead, his head ground slowly back to fix on the black shape, still trying to run away.

Savinien stood and waited. His opponent slithered against the railings, buckled, tried to brace himself, fell. Savinien stood and waited. Another attempted climb slewed away and down, leaving an ankle jammed clumsily in ironwork. Savinien began his stroll downhill to the fence.

I couldn't say anything. My legs had cramped underneath me and were numb and clumsy when I straightened myself and moved to stand at the back gate. Perhaps I wanted Savinien to see that I was there, to realise he couldn't kill this man if I was watching. Still he kept walking, arms loose, head level, slowly dipping down the slope and away from me. I came to believe that I would see a murder soon and I did not know what I should do.

And something in me wanted to see that man finished. Something wanted to see our victory made complete.

Savinien stopped by the railings and I heard the man make a thin little noise and then a kind of squeal before he was lifted and pushed and finally tipped over the fence. For a while when the body landed, it didn't move, but then it began the struggle to rise again, managed a few steps.

Apparently checking its progress, Savinien walked

alongside it for a little while with only the thin metal bars to keep them apart. In time he turned away up into the thick of the trees where I could no longer see.

I rested my forehead against the wrought iron of the gate and liked that it was hard and cool. I suddenly felt the need to be sick and to go, to go home.

As I WENT UP to bed, the house was being snuffed out around me. I remember it was maybe one or two in the morning and the last of the visitors had taken themselves off. Doors and windows were closing.

'Did you find him?' Arthur stopped me on the stairs.

'Hm?'

'Savinien.' He tipped his head, frowned faintly. 'Are you all right?'

'Yes, don't I look it?'

'Not really.'

'Well, maybe I'm not then, I don't know.'

'I don't think he was avoiding you – when you were looking – it's just this garden business upset him, that's all. You know.'

'I know.'

'He was out the back for a while, but he's upstairs now.'

'Upstairs.'

I looked at Arthur; his soft-collared shirt, his sensible eyes; and I wondered if I could have walked from the park and what had been there into this good house where I usually lived with this reasonable, ordinary man. I thought it sensible to expect that more than a short walk would be necessary to make such a change.

'Upstairs, yes. I don't suppose he's asleep yet. I don't know. None of my business. 'Night. Oh, Brazil won, by the way. Penalties.'

'Mm? Yes, sorry Arthur. It's just kind of too late to think, isn't it?'

'Ach, there's a candle that isn't out. Have to deal with that. Night night.'

'Okay.'

I knew without looking up that Savinien's door would be open by the time I reached the head of the stairs. He was waiting for me, his hair still spiked and dark from washing and his skin visibly fresh. Dressed in a clean sweatshirt and German Army moleskins, he seemed the man he always had been, the one that I loved and remembered, intelligent, gentle, humane.

In the heart of his eye there was light again and no emptiness and I wanted to ask if he was hurt in any way, to be glad that he was there, to be angry that he risked himself, to be repelled by what he had done, appalled, revolted, happy, afraid and anxious for the skin beneath his clothes.

'I am the man I always have been.'

I think I was a little too confused to listen. I think he had to repeat himself before I understood.

'I am the man I always have been.'

'You would have killed him.'

'I cannot unknow what I know. But if I had meant to kill him, I would have.' He ran his hand through the hair at the crown of his head and winced very slightly. When he lowered his hand one finger was oiled with blood. 'Hah. What must I . . . I feel I did right. Jennifer. Please. Come in here.'

'I don't think I can.'

'We can't talk this way. I have nothing I intend to shout in a corridor.'

I am very unsure of all these matters, even now, what goes on between people, but I was certain that if I went into his room we would make our situation seem all right and I really didn't know if it should be all right. Still, I knew what frightened me in him was only what I recognised of me, we both needed to catch up the edge and then throw it away. There were times when we couldn't help ourselves.

'You said you weren't ever going to do those things again.'

'Come in.'

'No.'

'Then I will not tell you. Then I shall not speak. These are words I will not whisper and I will not say where we are not alone, do you understand? Jennifer, do you understand?'

And I did understand, I understood more than I could say, more than I can tell you.

'Come here.'

'No, you come here.'

We stood together lightly, cradling, trying to catch our breath. I heard Arthur pass us quietly, going to bed, perhaps relieved to see us so clearly together, perhaps not, it didn't matter at the time.

'Now.' I sat on the edge of his bed and tried my voice, it was steady and comfortable and low. Savinien lowered himself into his chair, his muscles were starting to stiffen.

'Now tell me. What do you want to say?'

'You need not have, should not have seen.'

'Why, because you said you wouldn't do it again?'

'This was not again, this was . . . something no person I love should see. Do you imagine I have never seen men killing and wished death here and life there . . . out of love? Death should never come out of love. I do not believe it must. Not any more.'

'Why did you do it?'

'He would not have let me be. You and the household would have been always in danger.' He said this too quickly, too easily, and I waited for the truth. 'Yes, well then I was angry. How can . . . if you've never known – in the presence of this man I had no power. Like being a child, like being nothing inside a child. He did things to me that no one has ever done. I would go on my knees for what he could give me, for the Atties, the Eggs, for the crying and the flying. I gave him my soul. A man cannot be without a soul.

'Tonight I did nothing I have ever done before because I have never had to fight for my soul, only sometimes for my dignity. This is my life begun – free to be yours. So that you will understand me I will say that my heart is clean and that now I can give you access to my soul. *My* soul. I can be private with you here for our first time because I have my privacy.'

What else we chose to say, I won't write here – small measures of comfort, confirmations of content. I charted his bruises and cuts, the fresh dressing on his arm. We had already left aside any scales and regulations I found familiar and I felt it was only reasonable and natural for me to unfasten, unbutton, uncover what Savinien was and borrow his privacy.

Between the closed door and the curtained window I stood in thin air and waited for the tiny impacts of meeting skin. Before we had kept to the light and the half light and now we were safe with the dark.

And he shone, you know. He really shone. We had the brightest bed in the world. I remember how quickly I caught his fire and the two of us burning and gleaming between electric sheets. We were enough to read and write by. We were altogether enough.

No need to say how effortlessly we subsided into sleep, nothing left of us but animal laziness. It was lovely.

Until we both dreamed a dream together of green leaves and narrow treetops, moored in a sky of impeccable, screaming blue.

FOR THE NEXT few days I scanned the newspapers and my broadcasts carefully. A handful of men had been admitted to accident and emergency departments around the city, none of them named as Jim or James. I waited for justice to fall on us, but it didn't make a move.

Savinien assured me that he'd thrown both of the weapons into what I gathered must have been the skip at the back of the bingo hall. He had walked through the candlelit garden with his coat buttoned over the blood-stained shirt I later machine-washed and then hid for him in the last bag of rubbish left after the party. These meas-ures should not have protected us, but they did. In fact, they were probably quite unnecessary. No one who'd been at the park had any intention of being found out. It was quite possible for us to get away with this.

Only a week or two later I found myself discussing the assassination of a Colombian footballer. He had been shot twelve times not long after returning home, having scored the own goal that finished his country's hopes of victory in the World Cup. His murderer was alleged to have drawn his attention to this fact.

A rather close friend of Steven's, I can't remember her name, announced that this was all we could expect of a third world country with a ruined economy dominated by foreign powers and undermined by high-ranking cor-ruption and drug abuse. They had nothing left to hope for but their football team, no wonder it became a matter of life and death.

In other words, just like home. None of our island's teams were playing in the Cup and this may well have been a very good thing. Even my one small city took its games more than seriously and beyond the games we had everything to let a duellist feel at home.

My duellist padded in the garden, slept out the after-noons, wrote occasionally in what I later learned was antiquated rather than eccentric French. Any possible fight seemed to have gone from him. The reticence in his walk which I'd thought showed nothing more than the after-effects of the park became almost permanent. Still, no matter when my shift ended, he was always awake and live for me. I became quite unused to spending a night in my own bed.

'You don't have to wait up for me, you know. Not when I'm so late.'

He stroked his hand on my stomach. 'I would rather not miss anything.'

'But then you get tired.' The hand stopped. 'Don't you?'

He lay apart on his back. 'No.'

'What is it, then?'

'Eh, I cannot exactly say. Do you see the trees?'

'What do you mean?'

'When you sleep, do you see the trees?'

'I suppose I do. Yes. I do.'

'How often?'

'It doesn't matter.'

'How often?'

'Every night now. You?'

'Every night. I think this is making me ill.'

I told him, 'No one gets ill from a dream. It doesn't happen, not even to you,' but I was not in the least convincing, not even to me.

We held each other clumsily, too hard, as if there were a storm outside our window. So that we need not sleep he talked to me about his father, his brother's house, his brother, the morning when he sat on his nurse's lap in the courtyard and a cloud pressed all of the sunlight away.

He had cried because he couldn't understand the sudden cold.

Of course, in the end we slept, we could not pull ourselves free. I can recall that I wished he might be there with me, if we were to share in identical dreams. I think half the fear of it came from the fact we saw what we saw and went where we went completely alone.

So my mind lifted me away from his close arms, our knees tucked in together, and left me standing on ashy clay above the slope of a little town. Across the valley a windmill turned on a wooded hill. The air shivered and baked, reduced to the flows and whorls of liquid. I clung to the fear of falling while my thinking drove and spun down between narrow roofs, past a dark house, over a garden and a small, squat church and biting the air up again into white nowhere. The white bled into blue and sunlit treetops; the corner of an ugly terracotta-coloured wall.

There was no point in speaking about it when we woke. Both of us still felt the shock of snapping back into our bones, the feverish chill of our journey.

July had just opened with thin, hot rain when Savinien shuffled into the kitchen and told me what I'd guessed he would.

'I know where it is.' He pushed a handful of tiny weeds into the bin and rinsed the wet earth from his hands. 'I know where it is.'

'That's good. Isn't it?'

'Please excuse this, but I must ask – '

'What?'

He turned, leaned over the sink again and ran the tap. When I pushed back my chair to come near him he waved me away. 'No.' The water ran, clean and hard, and I waited. He cupped his hands under the flow and then doused his face.

'I'm still here.'

'Oh, I know this. I am', he stopped the water and tried

a smile for me, 'simply wasting time until I say what I must.'

'It's all right.'

'I do hope so. You see, I have now to go and meet my dream.'

I didn't want to be angry with him, but I was. 'Well. If you have to.' He had survived everything and now he was being crushed by his imagination. Or my imagination. I just didn't want him to go. I had a cold, sliding feeling. I didn't want him to go.

But make an effort, look at his face and see how you are hurting him already when he is not well and you don't even understand what's going on. Look at him. He wanted something from you which you did not give. Get it right. Tell him.

'I'm sorry, I'm afraid. I don't know what to do.'

'To do – what to do is to not leave me.'

'I wouldn't.'

'Here you did, your heart did.'

'But you're leaving me, what am I supposed to – '

'Come with me. I can't go there without you. I would not.'

'I wouldn't want you to. God, I'm an idiot. I don't say what I mean – I can't, I never have – I don't feel right. Whatever wiring I'm supposed to have, it doesn't work, or it isn't there. Sometimes, I want to be somebody else. You make me want to be somebody else.'

'Will you come with me?'

'Yes, I couldn't not. Yes. Yes. You see, I don't say the right things.'

'You say them. You say them at peculiar times and in the wrong order and in odd ways, but you say them. I like this. You're always a surprise.'

'I'm the best I've got.'

'Yes. The best I've got also.'

'Tell me where we have to go.'

'Home.'

FLIGHT, IT'S A curious thing. In fatter days I shuttled almost weekly between Glasgow and London to voice-over ads for a Caledonian brand of fizzy tap water. At a pinch I could sound just their kind of Caledonian. Damp and carbonated, too – that is, I suppose, what they wanted.

Whatever they were after, I must have delivered because for quite a while I strapped myself obediently aboard to ride the hour or so's hoop between cities. These trips were consistently very slightly outside my imagination, our optimum heights and speed, little more than surreal, but I could not deny that I climbed aboard in one place and set down firmly in another.

'When I was a kid we had wonderful clouds at home. In the autumn I would watch at the top of the bus coming home from school and they made a whole other country. It was like this, but from below – wide bays and open plains and mountains – everything clean and still and better than going home. You know?'

Because I wanted to make it all good for him, I asked if, as far as London, he would want to fly. Not the direct route, but if he wanted to fly at all, it would have to be then. He was so happy I had to kiss him, happy like a boy. I bought him a children's book on aircraft, because I had no real idea of how they worked or what to tell him. The night before we left we read his book together and were too excited to do anything much more than doze.

The morning we left the house I had never seen him look so well. He said goodbye to Liz and Arthur, kissing them both, and then walked out to the street beside his garden without a glance back. I followed him. He was in better form than ever and going home, going to fly.

'This is closer to God than a church.'

'I try not to think that way, but I do. I tend to wonder if He gets us up here so it won't take Him so long to call us back.'

'And you have done this how many times?'

'I can't remember.'

'Ha.' He gripped my hand and squeezed it, I noticed both were sweating slightly. 'You cannot remember how many times. Dear Lord, this is proof of Creation. This is not a sketch at the edge of man's vision, a piece of scenery. This is detail, this is a craftsman working though we never see it, for nothing but the joy of making. Dear Lord.'

He stared out of his window for the duration of the flight, even when they doled us out our invalid's portions of moulded food and moulded knives and forks. Between mouthfuls he told me how he had looked up as a boy and imagined riding in high galleons of cloud, perhaps sounding my bays, naming the plains and the mountains I'd never reached. We flipped over the journey's back and into our descent while my sinuses stung and thumped. I think this was my least nervous flight, because I was being unnervous for him.

As we cut in towards London the sky outperformed our thinking and became like nothing but itself. Towers of boiling white stood off impossibly from our wings, motionless, feathering into nothing, opening on to searing canyons, closing in a glacier of silence, air and light. It was just the kind of show I might have asked for – an exercise in awe.

Savinien talked, in fact yelled, his way across the city as we rattled underground to South Kensington and Victoria. Above us, the piping-hot sun blazed through our depleted high-altitude ozone to cook up low-altitude ozone and other photochemical delights. Children, the invalid and elderly were warned to keep indoors and, I suppose, to avoid breathing wherever possible. My final broadcasting day before coming away had included segueing in a hopeless plea for better public transport and fewer motor vehicles from a hesitant environmentalist with little or no breath control. Maybe she was asthmatic.

The coach part of the journey passed off quite easily. We were, of course, too hot and slightly delayed, but we made it. All we had to do was get on and off one hovercraft and we would be in France. That was all I had to get right.

There are ways of getting round this I have heard of or read about and we're all Europeans now so it shouldn't be an issue, but it is – you need a passport to leave the country and Savinien didn't have one. I wish I could say that I worked out a way to get round this which would have held water under any circumstance, but I didn't. I had three things to rely on and I hoped to make the best of them.

My own passport was in order.

I had stolen another in-order passport from Arthur in whose name I had bought Savinien's ticket. This put Arthur, although he didn't know it, at great risk which was why I thought it best he shouldn't know it.

The last point in my favour was that I live in an intensely arrogant and racist island. Those leaving are scrutinised far less than those unfortunate foreign souls arriving on our blessed shores, those who have white skins may be almost ignored while this is not at all the case with who do not, and those who have British passports of the old, blue variety are generally regarded as the happiest, whitest, most innocent voyagers on earth.

That was all. I was hoping and wishing and praying that passport examination would be as cursory as I'd found it at ports before. Dear God, say I hadn't imagined that sometimes a glance at the outside of the document was enough, or a flick at the first page. If they reached the photograph we didn't have a chance.

I watched as he pressed forward with the bulk of the passengers. We reasoned a little rush of custom could do no harm. He did well, didn't seem nervous or out of place, only lonely and much shorter than the cloud of families around him. I had no plan for what I might say if it all went wrong. Nothing to do if they took him away.

He kept his head quite high, at the angle which would most foreshorten his profile. I wondered how much of a lifetime of comments and stares it took before a man knew how to do that so perfectly.

Smile.

Ticket.

Boarding pass.

Passport outside.

Passport inside.

One tiny glimmer of a further page. They have the same haircut, similar shapes of face.

Smile.

Yes, God. Yes, God. Yes, God. Yes. I will do anything you want, give up anything you want, I don't mind, I love you and the baby Jesus, too.

The hovercraft bounced horribly between swarms of permanent rainbows and we didn't give a fuck. The train from Calais was two hours late and we didn't give a fuck. I enjoyed – eventually – the novelty of a clean and spacious railway carriage and Savinien – mainly, he breathed. He inhaled and exhaled France, looked up through French air, held his arms out in French sunshine and listened and listened and listened to French birdsong, footfalls, words. When we stepped out of the Gare du Nord into the dusty, musky scent of Paris and a hot evening pavement, he dropped his borrowed holdall and embraced me.

'Thank you.'

'It's going to be different, maybe disappointing. Three hundred years.'

'But it tastes the same. And I can hear, I can really hear. I had not the smallest idea I was so deaf. Now I have the beginning of hearing – yes, it has changed, yes, it is strange, but already these are so close to the words my heart would use. I am arrived home. Thank you.'

Pedestrians bumped gently round us as he gripped me by the shoulders and tried not to shout. 'I do thank you. God, I do.'

'There's no need, it was your idea.'

'But how could I have forgotten so much of myself? How could I have done that, do you suppose? I had no knowledge that I should be here.'

'You have had a rather eventful few months. Maybe that's what the dream was for. Do you feel better, though? Really?'

'Do I appear cured?'

'You appear practically luminous with being cured. But how do you feel?'

'New. Like an infant is new. I feel – with no disrespect to your own country – as if I have come into Paradise.'

Several vélo engines brayed past in an entirely unangelic din. 'Well, it does make a nice change. I think almost anything would. It's good to get out for a while.'

'Bringing me here, you have given me what I could not know, but always felt the lack of. I had a space in my mind, or my soul perhaps, which is no longer the case. If I hadn't met you . . . Eh, but this is good. So good it hurts in my bones.'

'Well, take it easy. We've got days to be enthusiastic and we're not all the way there, yet – still the hotel to find. Do you think you could tell a cab driver where we're going? I'm relying on you, you know – you're the nearest to a local I've got.'

'In this case I am, I believe, the oldest living Parisien possible and I welcome you to my city. Absolutely. Absolutely. Where do we find this driver?'

I was happy that he was happy, naturally. Rocking in a purple fur-upholstered cab, while Savinien yelled delightedly at the elderly Algerian driver, I could only be glad. I presume that if I had discovered he could play the piano miraculously well, or sculpt, I should have felt much the same. Another part of him was opened now, so there must be all the more for me.

Except that I was discovering he talked in French – odd French, but French. He *was* French, more than anything else. Already he was speaking and thinking and hearing in melodies and sentences I could not understand. I wondered if I would become someone foreign to him. Clearly a few hours in France had proved more therapeutic than anything I could do and who knew what would happen next.

The cabbie swung us along insanely beautiful prospects and the sun lowered to burst against a variety of high golden statues and Savinien asked questions and questions and questions and squeezed my hand and pointed and shouted and really did rub his eyes in disbelief and I realised that I was jealous. I was experiencing a highly spontaneous and actually rather extensive spasm of thorough jealousy, directed against an entire nation, its language and its past. If it hadn't been so painful, I would have laughed.

No HOLIDAY SNAPS, I promise. Not too many, anyway. I did keep a diary, because it seemed important that I should, but I will try not to quote from it here. Many of the entries would be nonsensical to any reader other than myself. I think what I most want to say is that when I open that little book now, I remember my life falling into an easy, humid pace under a curiously merciful sun. With Savinien, I walked in a double city, listening to the past shimmer under the present and now and again blink through. I think at this time most of all, we were both very close to the sheer miracle of Savinien's existence.

To use a simple example, I stood one morning, watching the light clear over the river beyond what is today called the Square René Viviani behind the church of Saint-Julien-le-Pauvre. Two men were clipping the lavender bushes and unleashing their scent in clouds all around us while pigeons wandered and women washed fruit under the fountain. To my left was Savinien, hands comfortably in his pockets and face raised to the sun, one huge smile. To my right was a tree, a Robinier, named for and planted by the botanist Robin – a thick almost petrified stump, slumped over wooden supports and fortified with concrete. The Robinier was planted in 1601, eighteen years before Savinien was born.

Eighteen. We thought about that while water scattered over the lawns, soaking into the light, making form and shadow in the air.

Some days we would touch each other very often, making sure we were still there, firmly in our own skins. Savinien also developed a habit of sidling into the compo-

261

sition of any potential photograph. He was already familiar with the theory of cameras and film and had developed another theory of his own.

'Look, what are you doing?'

'Moy? Eh. I am working in the service of history and art.'

'Toi. You're sidling about.'

'No, no. They wish to make a picture of this building which is a hideous construction and is named in honour of a bourgeois oaf who was most certainly conceived by the hindmost passage because as a man he was no more than a piece of ordure with a mouth.'

'Speak your mind next time, won't you?'

'I am being scrupulously polite.'

'Good, good. Look, the chances are, they know nothing about that.'

'Naturally, they have never endured his company. And rather than disappoint them by explaining these details, I am very happy to appear within their photograph and to represent an honourable part of the Paris of history.'

At the time, I found this new hobby slightly embarrassing, but I do like to think now of the slides and videos and snapshots in the homes of all nations, each containing a small impossible addition, beaming selflessly in the background.

To tell the truth and shame the devil, I wish I had all of the pictures here. I never did take any myself and without them I have almost nothing left. You know, you must know, that when I finish writing this there will be so little of him here with me I can't think what to do. For almost a year I've had my own doubled life within the present. I can tell you exactly how it feels to be this way, all the sensations are natural, focused, strong, entirely normal and I want no part of them. If this is normality I would rather have something else. How can it be that a tick or two of electricity in the meat that fills my skull can be worse than a blow, worse than disease, worse than any fear I can imagine. The movements of my own body, the rooms of my own house, the loveliest of my memories are only pain. I want amnesia.

But of course I don't. In only weeks, I found that I could not hold the image of his face in my mind with any clarity – apparently a common problem, very normal among the bereaved. My will has no power to bring him back, even in thought. And against my will, in moments with no logic, no kindness to them, the whole sense of him – the touch, the scent, the taste – will slice in sharper than fire. He walks through me, atom by atom, but he never stays.

I won't go on about it – that would make no sense. When we first came to Paris, I had only as much knowledge of our future together as made it possible for me to be unreasonably happy, that is to say, without feeling the need for any particular fixed or permanent reason. Perhaps I had at the back of my thinking the dark idea that Savinien might want to stay in France – that it might, indeed, be extremely difficult for him to leave it, but I was filled with the sense that we would conquer whatever difficulties arose, just as we had before.

Our first night, the 20th of July, we lay uncovered together, under the pressing, lapping half light of our little room. Our opened window let in hot air and din. Savinien had been initially disappointed to find that his idea of an hotel and its modern translation involved a considerable step down in accommodation, but was equally, if not perversely pleased to find we were staying in a narrow, raucous alley off the rue Saint-Jacques. The tiny street was lined with lurid food stalls and shops selling amulets or alchemical books. The glistening cobbles underfoot drained into a central open gutter full of dark water and cabbage leaves.

'This is better. This is so good. Paris in the summer, it always stank like a rotting dog and howled like a dying one. I could take you to my house from here. I will not because I would much prefer to be unaware if it has gone missing.'

He was brave about that – all the missing landmarks. For hours at a time he could follow a thread between sidestreets only to find – for example – that his parents' house had vanished somewhere in the vicinity of an underground shopping mall and the greasy hulk of the Pompidou Centre.

'Eh! Probably they did not expect I would come back to check.'

I don't think he minded about buildings – his return offered him compensations. I heard about them on the morning of the 21st. He had let me sleep on after our first night ever in a double bed and, never mind the heat, we were so glad to see each other there we barely needed to touch, although naturally we did. Naturally we did.

'I am still here.' He was out of breath, fully dressed, kissing me in a room it took me seconds to recognise. 'I'm still here.'

'Mm? That's good.'

'Good? This is worth anything . . . I could never have expected . . . this is. Oh, I can show you how this is good.'

I remember the silly discomfort of his buttons against my skin and that his hair smelt of morning.

'You're still feeling better, then.'

'And here.'

'I'd swear to it – you're definitely here.'

'But so you will see how much . . .'

I think it was a writer kind of thing, maybe a macho kind of thing, too – it doesn't matter now – which meant that I woke under a giggling, insistent, triumphant author.

He'd woken without me, you see, and visited the bookshop at the corner of the street. It must have been barely open. Savinien explained that he was looking for any trace of Savinien de Cyrano de Bergerac.

'The real man? Not the play? We don't sell plays.'

'The real man.'

And there he was, apparently, referred to respectfully in alchemical reference books and volumes of the work available if he wished to order them. He'd known le Bret would see to it, he'd known he would be published, but now to be alive and see it. After all these years. Still here.

'That's nice.'

'Nice! This is a word with completely no meaning. This is almost as large a miracle as I am.'

'I suppose it is. I always thought you would have been a good writer.'

'Thank you.'

'It's no bother to say so.'

'I wish they were here to see this, also.'

'Who?'

'My friends – Henri le Bret, his brother, Roy de Prades, even d'Assoucy, the bastard. They were the best. And Pierre, Pierre Gassendi, the finest teacher and wisest philosopher in France – never mind Descartes locking himself up in his own intestines and reinventing the universe like one enormous fart – Pierre's dead like all the rest of them. If he were here I could have told him he was right 'There are Spaces, immense, without borne, without end in which God has created and placed this world'. I've seen the spaces, I've been in them for centuries and now I have proved there is something beyond matter. No, he would correct me there. I have not myself proved – I am, in myself, proof that there is something beyond matter. There is a soul. He was sure there was a soul. And here, he must have convinced me so much that I had to have one for myself. I have an immortal soul.

'God, I miss them all.'

'It's only to be expected, coming back to where you knew them. So they still have your books, that's wonderful. I'm proud of you.'

'I am quite proud of myself.'

We cooried in so as not to let any more sadness creep

in about us and I thought of an addition for the morning's good news. 'Savinien?'

'Yes.'

'Did you have the dream last night?'

'Ah well, no I did not. You?'

'No sign of it.'

'We were right to come here. This will make me well. I can live for the rest of my hundred years.'

'I hope so.'

'But you have to live the hundred with me. I wouldn't wish to do it alone. They were the best friends, but you are my best love.'

He had a way with compliments – the best phrase to offer at the right, snug time.

And the dream stayed gone. For three days we ate and drank and walked as if we had both come home. If I was, at first, tired quickly by the strangeness of the city and apt to be sunstruck, this only meant that we could make our way in the afternoons to the tip of the Ile Saint-Louis where Savinien had mastered the trick of looking above automobile height and fooling time. I would slip up on a bench and lean against him to sleep a little while the hotels he knew as hotels waited behind their summer shutters for their owners and their new or the old money to return from their country homes. Just the way it had always been. He would rest his arms against me and the Seine would roll to meet itself beyond the prow of the whole narrow island and the trees and the shade would slowly push round the sun.

Sleep was our friend, we could dip into it anywhere, knowing we would each be there when we surfaced again, still running with the impossible, shaking it out of our heads like tepid water.

I have tried to discover if we did something wrong, if I missed a sign. But all that really changed was the moon – it began that commonplace monthly journey from a fat, bright eye to a shadowed space. It waned. I never had cause before to consider the meaning of that word – to wane, to dwindle, to black out.

'I watch. I was a legionnaire and we are taught. Watch, never be seen.'

The hotelier, M. Sablons, had taken to greeting us with little speeches on themes from his former life.

'I see the enemy but they never see me.'

'Good, that's the idea I suppose.'

Savinien smiled benignly and nodded to our key, but there was no way we were going to get it yet.

'She thinks I am not knowing what she does, but without a doubt I do.'

In her absence M. Sablons constantly maligned Mme Sablons, a small grey lady who seemed, to be honest, far too bad-tempered to be easily embroiled in torrid liaisons. Although she did seem constantly tired. One never knew, of course.

'Well, one never knows, of course.'

'I do know. It is categorical.'

'Might we have our key.'

'Yes, do you think we could have our key. We'd like to go upstairs.'

M. Sablons nodded. 'So would I, so would I.'

We didn't quite understand what he meant by this, but it directly preceded his rising, adjusting his stomach and belt and then hooking down our key. He smiled at us badly. Whatever we were going to do, he knew it would pall.

'God, I could do without this performance every night.' We started the dim climb to the second floor – brown flock wallpaper and then blue.

'Mm.'

'Do you think there's any way we could distract him. Maybe if we set fire to one of his legs.'

'Mm.'

'What do you think?'

Savinien, a few steps ahead of me, stumbled back and leaned against the wall.

'Hey, careful. I don't want anything of that broken.' He continued to lean. 'Are you all right? That bloody idiot kept us standing too long.'

'Yes. I would rather not stand.'

'Well, do you want to rest here, or we're almost at the room.'

'The room.'

He revived quickly – a bottle of minibar Coke, a shower, a chance to lie out on the bed and the colour pulled back in his face.

'How are you now?'

'Perfect.'

'I can see that. How do you feel?'

'Perfect – perfectly fine and brave.'

'You had me scared for a while.'

'It may be a greater drain on my forces, aligning myself to this city, than I supposed. Tomorrow, we might be slower.'

'Of course. We could be slow now, too.'

'Oh, good. I like slow.'

'I like slow, too.'

And maybe that was it – maybe we were simply too slow and the end of our story caught us up. The instant before I turned fully away into sleep, I could taste our future, I could smell its nondescript streets, every one of them leading to the sharp, hanging shadows under the memorial trees. Trees and sky, trees and sky, trees and sky. By the time we could escape into morning, we had dreamed every moment of cloudless blue and every leaf.

'BASTARD. Oh the bastard.'

'Sssh.'

'Henri, you do this to me, after everything we were to each other. This. Hnah, hnah.' Savinien was searching his vocabulary for anything adequate. I persuaded him to move away with me while he wrung and unwrung invisible necks ahead of him. Once we were downstairs among the cool and relatively soundproof book stacks, I could risk calming him.

'What is the matter?'

'Ouff, nothing much at all. A tiny point of nothing. Only my best friend has, yes, published my work. I thank him for it, but he has . . . his fear of what is correct, what is not correct, who I will offend. He changed it. He changed it.'

'I'm sorry, I thought it would be good to come here.'

Because it had seemed a sensible idea. If we could get ourselves into the Bibliothèque Nationale – his very own national library – and find his work there, this could only please him. I could think of nothing better to rally his spirits. Half an hour's queueing and bargaining, explanations and queueing finally won us two readers' tickets and we'd then loitered in a corridor like petitioners to the court – his metaphor – before we could get into the Grande Salle.

We were both a little nervous, sitting in what appeared to be a mammoth gilded ballroom with added shelves and waiting for our requested volumes to appear. I also worried that this might conceivably be the one place in

France where Savinien would be recognised. I couldn't have explained him to anyone.

Savinien muttered the minutes away darkly – he hadn't liked the edge of amusement that greeted any mention of his work.

'Must we stay here. It's like a writers' mass grave. Gold and marble and busts of the deceased.'

'It won't be long, I'm sure.'

'Like a tomb.'

A tall, bronzed body wearing a very unacademic cut of dress swayed past.

'She's not exactly in mourning.'

'Black dress.'

'But not exactly funereal.'

'Black, black is funereal. And her legs are in mourning, one can tell.' His smile drained suddenly. 'God, I don't want to find out, I don't want to see. Can't we just go?'

'After all this?'

And then the little, battered volumes came. For several moments, neither of us could touch them.

'Go on, then.'

'I can't.'

'They're yours.'

'Dear God, I know. Dear, dear God I know. My words, my books.' Every opened page sent up the harsh, cold scent of pure time. 'My books.'

But it didn't take long for him to find the first alteration. His joy sank without trace into one constant hiss.

'Listen. I am here in this story, falling hundreds of miles to earth, or rather to the earth of the moon, and all that saves me is a lucky collision with the Tree of Life. I have fallen into Paradise, my soul leaves my body and is then almost instantly recalled. That lunatic has me say . . . what, what . . . I can't even think of it. Ah yes, that the next thing I remember I am under a tree. Any tree, nothing especial, no explanation of why I am not utterly dead, no imagination . . . not even a good sentence. What was he thinking of?'

'I'm sure he did it for the best.'

'If they have my manuscripts. They said they did, didn't they say that?'

'I don't know. I can understand one word in twenty.'

'They would read my manuscripts, they would know this wasn't me.'

'Yes.'

'They would know.'

'That's right. Come on, now.'

'No, I can't face it.'

'Come on. Even if we're only leaving, we have to go out that way.'

'Bastard. Bastards. Who made him? Who made him do that?'

But he did go back and did eventually settle on another piece of le Bret's writing.

'My God.'

'Please, we'll be put out.'

'He has written my life, almost all of it. He . . .'

And he read the short account of his own life and death. I held his hand while he smiled and nodded and closed his eyes and in the end sat very gently, staring at something which I could not see. 'God keep him, God keep him. He was a gentleman of excellent spirit. A very loving friend. May we go now, I think I must.'

He walked round and round the small courtyard at the back of the library while I sat. There was nothing I could do. We should never have gone there, should never have crossed into France, and yet we could do nothing else. I stared at the sparrows and the yellow gravel and the yellow dust and I may have attempted to pray, but I know I could think of nothing to ask for. He came to sit by me and touched my arm.

'Hello. How do you feel?'

'I don't know, Jennifer, I don't know. Today Henri reminded me I am dead and last night I saw what you saw and I understand it. You also understand.'

I lied. 'No.'

'I have to go there.'

He said 'I', not 'we'. 'I want to come with you.'

'I would love you to. I'm sure we'll go there together and all of this will be finished, we'll be able to go on.'

He was lying, too.

We held each other under the afternoon sun and we lied. I smiled at him and he smiled at me and we tried to discuss a future we didn't have and then held on in even tighter so we wouldn't have to see our faces when we cried. We sobbed and were nothing but hopeless and hurt.

I think that we felt what we felt as deeply as we could and yet it had no effect. When the worst of the spasm was past, we were both still there, still alive, as though we had simply subjected ourselves to a senseless joke. The truth was that we would have to go on until we were finished and no short cuts.

The next days were peaceful, we spoke a great deal, oddly enough a great deal about childhood. Savinien couldn't walk far in the end, the slightest incline made him breathless and dizzy, so we enjoyed the small sections of the city we could still reach in some depth – we had time to really see them. His weakness did not cloud his mind in any way, although his voice became faint and his articulation careful.

I want now to tell you everything ever we did, in Scotland or in France, everything about everything, right to the start again, to hold it all back. He wouldn't want that, though. He was much braver than me.

I only hope that if I've managed nothing else properly, I put this down right.

In the night of the 27th, Savinien woke me and we made love simply and quietly, with a terrible gentleness I didn't recognise.

'Jennifer.' He said my name more carefully than anyone else did – I loved that.

'Yes.'

'Tomorrow – '

'No.'

'Do please listen, tomorrow I have to go somewhere. I hope you could come with me because I think I will be afraid.'

'But we still have time, there are five more days before we have to – '

'It has to be tomorrow. Will you come with me?'

'I can't not. But let me come back with you, too.'

'Don't make me say a promise I can't keep. You know I have to do what you ask.'

'Let me ask you not to go.'

'Jennifer, Jennifer, Jennifer.' More carefully than anyone else, ever.

On Thursday the 28th July, 1994, Savinien de Cyrano enquired at the railway station and then caught the train to a town near Argenteuil called Sannois.

THE JOURNEY TOOK half an hour passing comfortable sub-
urbs and little villas, a cats' and dogs' home. The humidity
plastered our clothes against us unpleasantly and left us
mopping our faces every few minutes. Although for much
of the time we had a carriage to ourselves, we could think
of little to say. Words slipped out in nervous rushes,
stopped for no reason.

'You know here in my time they had a priest, a Mr Pig.
An atheist attacked him once during the monstrance of the
host – wanted to be struck down by God, that way he'd
have no doubt. Instead the King struck him down very
slowly in Paris and Cochon the priest continued his masses,
but behind an iron grill. Cochon – Pig, he was very kind.
Such a bad atheist, me, but he was only kind . . .'

When Savinien reached into his pocket for his handker-
chief, he noticed his hands had begun to shake and gave
a small laugh.

The station was clearly signposted, pale and neat. Just
before the carriage doors opened I panicked and reached
for him. He squeezed my shoulder and whispered, 'I
know.'

'I love you.'

'I know it.' The doors slipped apart and let in a raw
burst of heat. 'I do love you, also.' Another shuttered
laugh, 'God, I would rather not be here,' and we stepped
down.

He knew the way. But he walked like a man who
expected a tripwire at every step.

The main street was quiet, not unattractive. We turned
north, working through a series of pleasant lanes until

we reached an area of blank modern apartment blocks. Savinien began to run.

He came to a halt in front of a low, grey slab of flats and began to giggle between uneven breaths. He heard me rushing to close the distance and turned to shout.

'It's all right, it's not here. It's all right. Jennifer, we are safe.'

'What do you mean. I mean, that's wonderful. What do you mean, though?'

'The house, number five. Oh, I love this ugly building, this is the most wonderful piece of grotesquery in the world.'

'Tell me.'

'I died here. Number five, rue du Puits Mi-ville, but I didn't die here because there is nothing of here left. I dreamed Sannois as it was and it is different and I am different. I am safe. I can breathe again, listen, I can breathe again. See? Do you see? You are a beautiful woman. Did I ever tell you this?'

'I don't, I can't remember. You're sure?'

'This is the road. Where is the building? It's not here. Where is any of it? Not here. Paouff! It's gone.'

'Oh, God. Oh, God, thank you. Thank you, God. Come here.'

'I'm very hot and moist.'

'Come here.'

'I'm here.'

We crossed over to the shady side of the road and wondered if there might be a shop nearby. The sun was so bright and we were so thirsty, if we could just buy a bottle of water we would be fine.

'Maybe we could go back to the station, they might have something.'

'No.'

'Or there could be somewhere closer, I suppose.'

'No.'

When I breathed out I was looking at parked cars and

garages, a few shrubs. When I breathed in I had followed his eyes up.

Narrow green treetops. Burning blue sky.

'No.' He was already stepping across a planted border, stumbling. A simple kerbstone tripped him and he dropped, his arms fending away a threat I could not see. When he tried to stand I was there to hold him, to feel him gripping desperately at my arms.

'What is it? You don't have to go there. Nothing can make you. What's the matter? Please tell me what's the matter.' His breath was light and fast, nauseous, his weight shifting wildly.

I watched his struggle for words he was losing. 'Afinque . . . je . . . dear God, I'm afraid. I am in the garden.'

'No.'

'I see it . . . I see now and you, but I see the garden planted here. You're not strong, you're leaving.'

'Feel me.'

When I touched his hands they were cold.

'I don't feel. Hold me hard.' His head shied up as I pressed against him. 'Lead me.'

'Then come away.'

'Lead me there.'

'I can't!'

He started forward, dragging me with him. 'Please.'

'I can't; you'll die.'

'I am dead. Please, please. Sweet Jesus, I have such a hurt.'

I did go with him then, guiding him on a way he could no longer understand. His feet struck the ground flat, anticipating another height, while I kept my arm round his waist and did not look at him because I was frightened. I did not want to know what he was becoming. I did not want my last memory to be a death mask.

And I did not wish to die with him, to go with him. I

could not, I tried, but I could not want that and so he frightened me.

The trees were waiting for us over a small empty street. We crossed on to an open stretch of brick, bending and aching with sun.

Savinien slowed a little, tugged back, and without thinking I turned to his face, it was pale and emptying. He had to lift his hand and keep it pressed under his jaw to support it while he spoke. His breath was over-sweet.

'Thank. You.'

'Please don't.'

'This is right. God. Is always right. In the end. Goodbye.'

'Goodbye. Love.'

'Yes, yes.'

He brushed my cheek with cold, hard lips and I turned away.

When he pushed me I didn't understand immediately what was happening. I fell to one side, jarring my neck, rolled and saw.

I saw him rock on his heels, stagger and then tumble softly forward. Like parting water, the bricks took him in and there was no more.

And I think I heard a sound like a little breath pushed out, but I may be quite wrong.

I stood up.

Between two blocks of flats, the high trees shivered in a tiny breeze. Flats, trees, a shabby public pissoir, a fat grey church and a scatter of clothes on brick paving. His clothes, warm now, full of the smell of him alive. I folded them, wrapped them around his shoes and followed the signs back down to the railway station. It seemed most comfortable to hold my bundle tight to my stomach and chest as I walked. I crossed the concrete piazza in front of the complicated and ugly civic building which Sannois has chosen to name the Centre Cyrano de Bergerac.

They still remember him there, where he died. I liked them for that.

'He had to go ahead without me.'

'This is usual.'

'No, he had to go ahead without me.'

The hotelier didn't understand and, after a while, I felt I didn't need to make him.

In the next few days I became used to incomprehension, even my English stuttered. But I never got lost. I found I could follow the routes I had taken with my dear friend, my love. I only very slightly expected that he might come back and would need to know where to meet me.

Until the morning came for me to leave Paris, I believed I was as sad as I could bear to be. I relied on a touch of calm I could return to and then the train doors shut and movement began and I broke.

I travelled home with two bags, one of them not mine.

'JESUS loves the medium,
Loves them for their tedium,
Loves the boring and the sad,
Including me so I am glad.
Yes, Jesus loves me,
Oh yes, Jesus loves me,
Yes, Jesus loves me,
And that is all I know.'

Arthur was very good – sound, reliable Arthur. He sang
and battered round the house and was living and cheerful.
I knew I was not alone in missing Savinien. A door shifting upstairs, a creak in the boards and we would all have
to pause before we could fully remember that we were
no longer expecting anyone else.

Upstairs in my room I had Savinien's bag. There was
nothing – is nothing – I could do but keep it. It took
perhaps a month before I could open it and before I found
what he had written in Paris.

One of Liz's friends made me a translation. I won't bore
you with all of it, but I do still quite often read this which
is not the last entry, but towards the end.

*I have seen the great sky over my city shed itself of rain and
lighten to rose and young blue. All quietly, calmly, it forms and
closes above like the one vast shore of an invented sea. Now, as
we lose the sun, our cover parts and fades. Were I to walk out
I would tremble under the colour of my death, the infernal blue
of an infinite ascent.*

Jennifer, believe me, I would rest here with you this day and never go forward. So that you will know, even if I am gone and you cannot see me, even if I have been returned to the dark and the frozen existence and forgetfulness of death I will keep you with me. If I stay in God's shadow for ever and never touch his light, I will keep your light with me. No torment will harm me, no demon will come near because I will have the extent of Hell's eternity to need you with all the force of my soul.

You were my Paradise on earth and that was enough, I hope for no more Heaven. Love me and live without me, for the sake of the man who loved you best.

Savinien de Cyrano, écuyer, sieur de Bergerac.

You'll have read, I suppose, the opening of this book, about all of that calmness I no longer have. Sometimes the best beginning is a lie. But I hope you'll accept my apology for it now.

What do I have instead of the calm. A voice. I remember everything of one man's voice, not a part of it fades.

Arthur came to me today and asked me how this was going. I told him it was almost over.

'Really? What'll you do?'

'What, afterwards?'

'Mn hm. It'll be odd, not having you disappear at all hours.'

'I suppose I'll get a life. I don't know.'

'Will you miss it, do you think? Or be glad it's over?'

'Both.'

'Well, if you need any company, I might be about later on.'

I can see Arthur now, through my bedroom window. He's hopping alongside his bicycle, then over and away. So now there's no one here but me and you and this.

I will miss this and I will miss Savinien and I will be glad.